REPEAT

NEW YORK TIMES BESTSELLING AUTHOR

KYLIE SCOTT

Repeat

Cover Design: By Hang Le
Cover Photograph: Brian Kaminksi
Interior Book Design: JT Formatting

Repeat / Kylie Scott – 1st ed.
Library of Congress Cataloging-in-Publication Data
ISBN-13: 978-0-6484572-0-6

REPEAT

CHAPTER ONE

The shop sits on a busy street in the cool downtown neighborhood of Portland, Maine. *Larsen and Sons Tattoo Parlor* is written on the window in elegant script. Inside, music plays, two guys lounge on a green velvet chaise flicking through books. It's all very clean and neat and awesome looking. And there's a sound like an electric drill in the air.

The girl behind the counter stops, mouth gaping when she sees me. She's pretty and petite with a shaved head.

"Hi," I say, attempting a smile. "Can I speak to—"

"Are you fucking kidding me," a deep voice booms.

I meet the eyes of a tall man covered in tattoos. Shortish, light brown hair, lean but muscular. He wears jeans and designer sneakers, a T-shirt advertising some band. For sure, he'd be handsome if he wasn't scowling at me. Actually, strike that. He's handsome period, irrespective of his glare. His angular jaw is covered in stubble and it frames perfect lips. Straight nose, high cheekbones. Unlike me, this man is a work of art.

"No, not happening," he says, striding over. His large hand wraps around my upper arm, grip firm though not cruel. "You don't get to come back."

"Don't touch me." My words are ignored as he marches me back toward the door. Panic bubbles up inside and I slap his chest hard. "Hey, buddy. Do. Not. Touch. Me."

At that, he blinks, a little startled. "Buddy?"

I don't know what he was expecting, but he lets go. It takes me a full minute to get my breathing back under control. Dammit. Meanwhile, everyone is watching. The girl behind the counter and the two guys waiting on the chaise. The woman with brown skin and big beautiful hair holding a tattoo gun and the older woman she's working on. We have quite the audience assembled. The man screaming about being back in black over the sound system is the only noise.

"You need to leave," he says, voice quieter this time, though no less harsh.

"I have a few questions I need to ask you first."

"No."

"Did you do this?" I ask, pulling up the sleeve on my T-shirt to display my shoulder. It's a beautiful piece. A cluster of violets with olive-green stems and leaves. It's almost like a scientific drawing, but missing the root structure.

His gaze narrows. "Of course I did it."

"I was your client. Okay." That's now a definite. Good. Definites give my world structure and help things make sense. Unknowns just piss me off. "Did I not pay you or something?"

"'the hell are you talking about?"

"You're angry."

And it's obvious the moment he sees my brow. The hostility and confusion in his eyes changes to surprise.

I immediately smooth down my bangs, trying to hide. Stupid to get self-conscious, but I can't help it.

He gently brushes my hand aside, parting my hair to see. An intimate gesture that sets me on edge. As hands-on as tattooing must be, the way he's touching me and getting in my space is . . . more. I try to step back, but there's nowhere to go. Besides, he's not actually hurting me, just making me nervous. And as much as I abhor being crowded, some part of me doesn't mind him touching me.

Weird. Maybe I need sex or something. Maybe he's my type. I don't know.

Deep lines are embedded in his forehead as he studies me. This is exactly the reason I cut my hair in the first place. The scar starts an inch into my hairline, ending below my right eyebrow. It's wide and jagged, dark pink.

That's enough. I put a hand to his chest, pushing him back. Happily, he goes. A small step, at least.

"So you *know* me?" I ask, trying to clarify things. "Like, as more than a customer."

The man just stares. I don't know what his expression means. A mix of unhappy and perplexed, maybe? He really is quite handsome. A new song starts, this time it's a woman singing.

"Well?"

Finally, he speaks. "What the fuck happened to you?"

A week earlier . . .

"Are you ready?"

I stop kicking my feet and hop down off the hospital bed. "Yeah."

"Good. The car's waiting in the drop-off zone and we'll go straight home. Everything's organized," says my sister, a confident smile on her face. "There's nothing to worry about."

"I'm not worried," I lie.

"Did you want to see the photos of my house again?"

"No. It's fine."

My sister's name is Frances (not Fran or Frannie), and she's a police officer who lives in North Deering. She blames herself for what happened. It probably comes with the job.

At thirty, Frances is five years older than me. We have the same strawberry-blond hair and blue eyes, small breasts and child-birthing hips. Her words, not mine, and I told her it was a shitty descriptor. But given my current condition, there's something to be said for relying on others' descriptions.

Anyway, my sister and I look alike. I've seen this in

various photos and in the mirror, so it's a definite.

"Hey, Clem." Nurse Mike sticks his head around the doorway. "Everything's sorted; you're good to go. Any last-minute questions or anything?"

I shake my head.

"Call Doctor Patel's office if you have any problems, okay?"

"Yes."

"Keep in touch, kid. Let me know how things go."

"Okay."

Mike disappears.

"Did you want to bring the flowers?" asks my sister.

I shake my head. This is it. Time to go. Frances just stands by the door, waiting.

My first memory is of waking up in this hospital, but really, I was born late at night on an inner-city street. A couple found me unconscious and bleeding on the sidewalk. No identification. Handbag and wallet missing. And the weapon, a blood-splattered empty bottle of scotch, lay abandoned nearby. Walter, half of the pair who found me, gets teary every time he describes that night. But Jack, his partner, did two tours in 'Nam and has seen far worse. They're the first ones who brought me flowers. Not that I got many. My friends are few.

Previous me had, apparently, gone out to dinner alone. Her last meal consisted of cheese and spinach ravioli in a pumpkin sauce with a bottle of Peroni. (Detective Chen said it's a yeasty Italian beer that goes well with pasta. It sounds nice. I might try it sometime.) From there, security cameras have her withdrawing a hundred and fifty dollars before walking off into the night. There were no cameras on the quiet side street where she'd parked the car. No one around apart from the attacker.

That's how Clementine Johns died.

Out in the hallway, there's a mix of patients, visitors, and medical staff. Same as always for midmorning. I wipe my sweaty palms on the sides of my pants. It's nice to be wearing actual clothes. Black sandals, blue jeans, and a white T-shirt. Nothing too exciting; nothing that would make me stand out. I want to blend in, watch and learn. Because if we're the sum of our experiences, then I'm nothing and no one.

Frances watches me out of the corner of her eye, but doesn't say anything. Something she does a lot. I'd say her silence makes me paranoid, but I'm already paranoid.

"Sure you're all right?" she asks while we wait for the elevator.

"Yes."

The elevator arrives and we step inside. When it starts to move, my nervous stomach swoops and drops. Through the crowded lobby we go, then out into the sunshine. Blue summer sky, a couple of green trees, and lots of gray concrete. Nearby traffic, people, and lots of movement. A light breeze ruffles my hair.

The lights on a nearby white sedan flash once and Frances opens the trunk for me to deposit my small suitcase. Anxiety turns into excitement, and I can't keep the smile off my face. I've seen them on TV, but I've never actually been in a car since that night.

Now . . .

"Amnesia," he mutters for about the hundredth time. Usually, 'fuck', 'shit', or some blasphemy follows that statement. This time, however, there's nothing. Maybe he's finally getting used to the idea.

I sit on the opposite side of the booth, inspecting the cocktail menu. It's as gross and sticky as the table.

"Can I get you guys something else?" asks the waiter with a practiced smile.

"I'll have a piña colada."

"You hate coconut," Ed Larsen informs me, slumped back in his seat.

"Oh."

"Try a margarita."

"What he said," I tell the waiter, who presumably thinks we have some kinky dom-sub thing going on.

Ed orders another lite beer, watching me the entire time. I don't know if his blatant examination is better or worse than my sister's furtive looks. He'd suggested going back to his place to talk. I declined. I don't know the guy, and it didn't feel safe. So instead we came here. The bar is dark and mostly empty, given it's the middle of the afternoon, but at least it's public.

"How old are you?" I ask.

In response, he pulls his wallet out of his back pocket and passes me his driver's license.

"Thank you." Information is good. More definites. "You're seven years older than me."

"Yeah."

"How serious were we? Did we stay together for long?"

He licks his lips, turns away. "Don't you have someone else you can ask about all this? Your sister?"

I just look at him.

He frowns, but then sighs. "We saw each other for about half a year before moving in together. That lasted eight months."

"Pretty serious."

"If you say so." His face isn't happy. But I need to know.

"Did I cheat on you?"

Now the frown comes with a glare.

Despite his don't-fuck-with-me vibes, it's hard not to smile. The man is blessed in the DNA department. He's so pretty. Masculine pretty. I'm not used to being attracted to people, and he's giving me a heart-beating-harder, tingles-in-the-pants kind of sensation, which is a lot new and a little overwhelming. Makes me want to giggle and flip my hair at him like some vapid idiot.

But I don't. "It's just that I'm getting some distinct vibes that somehow I'm the bad guy in all this."

"No, you didn't cheat on me," he growls. "And I didn't cheat on you either, no matter what you might have thought."

My brows jump. "Huh. So that's why we broke up?"

"This is fucked. Actually, it was fucked the first time."

He turns away and finishes the last of his beer. "Jesus."

I just keep quiet, waiting.

"You have no memories, no feelings about me whatsoever?"

"No, nothing."

A muscle jumps in his jaw, his hands sitting fisted on the table.

"It's called traumatic retrograde amnesia," I say, trying to explain. "What they call my 'episodic memory' is gone—all my memories of events and people and history. Personal facts. But I can still make a cup of coffee, read a book, or drive a car. Stuff like that. Things that were done repetitively, you know? Not that I'm allowed to drive at the moment. My car's sitting outside my sister's house gathering dust. They said to give it some time before I got behind the wheel again, make sure I'm okay. Also, apparently the part of my brain in charge of inhibitions and social restrictors, et cetera, is a bit messed up, so I don't always react right, or at least not necessarily how you'd expect me to behave based on previous me."

"Previous you?"

I shrug. "It's as good a label for her as any."

"She's you. You're her."

"Maybe. But she's still a complete stranger to me."

"Christ," he mutters.

This is awkward. "I'm upsetting you. I'm sorry. But there are things I need to know, and I'm hoping you can help me out with some of them."

Our drinks arrive, the glass of the margarita lined with salt and smelling of lemon. I take a sip and smile. "I like it."

He reaches grimly for his beer, the ink on his forearm shifting with the muscle beneath. His tattoos cover a variety of topics. A bottle marked "poison" with skull and crossbones set amongst roses. An anatomical heart. A tattoo gun (very meta). A lighthouse with waves crashing below. I wonder if it's the Portland Headlight, the famous one at Cape Elizabeth. There was something on TV about it the other day. His tattoos are hypnotic in a way. As if, combined, they tell a story, if only you could understand.

Ed pushes his beer aside. "So, because you don't remember, I should just forget all the shit you pulled and help you? Because that was all the 'previous you' and not the girl sitting in front of me?"

"That's your decision to make, of course."

"Thanks, Clem." His voice is bitter, full of a kind of controlled rage. "That's real fucking big of you."

I flinch, unused to people swearing at me. Not that he hasn't been swearing in my general vicinity since the moment we met, but for some reason, this time it has an effect on me. Can't help but wonder how angry does he get, exactly? The man is taller than me, his shoulders broader than mine. And I've already had a small taste of the strength he holds in his hands.

"Shit." He sighs at my reaction. "Clem, don't . . . don't do that. I would never hurt you."

Unsure of what to say, I down more of my drink.

"You don't know me; I get it," he says, voice softer, gentler. "Look at me, Clementine."

When I do, his eyes are full of remorse and he's sad

now. Not angry.

"I would never hurt you, I swear it. You're safe with me."

"Okay." Slowly, I nod. "It's a stupid name, don't you think?"

"Yours? I don't know. I always liked it."

I almost smile.

"You're staying with your sister?"

"Yes."

"How's that going?"

"It's all right."

The side of his mouth lifts briefly. "You and Frances were always fighting about something."

"Actually, that makes sense." I laugh. "Did she approve of you?"

"You'd have to ask her that."

"Oh, I have lots of questions for her."

This time, when he looks at me, it's more of a thoughtful kind of thing. Like he's processing. I've given him a lot of information, and I know it takes a while to sort things out in your head. So I drink my margarita and watch the woman behind the bar, the two men sitting on stools, chatting. Even though their hygiene standards are lacking, I like the place. It's relaxed.

Maybe it's my kind of place.

"I don't seem to have many friends," I say, a question popping into my head. "Was I always like that, a bit of a loner?"

He shakes his head. "You had friends. But apparently you cut them all off when you left me."

"Why?"

"I don't know," he says, shoulders dropping slightly. "Maybe you wanted a fresh start. Maybe you just didn't want to talk about the breakup and shit. Maybe you just wanted to be left alone."

Huh.

"Give me your phone; I'll put my details in." He holds out a hand. "You would have deleted me from your contacts."

"Oh, I don't have one. My bag and everything was taken in the attack."

His brows rise. "You're walking around without a cell? Clem, that's not safe."

"Pretty sure having a phone didn't make much of a difference last time."

"Finish up your drink." He tips his chin at the glass. "I'll give you a lift back to Frances's place. We'll stop by a shop on the way and get you some things."

It's an interesting idea. And he seems like a nice man, one who used to care about me. But from what little he said about the breakup, it sounds as if it was a special level of hell. Despite his assurances, he might very well have cheated on me. Crushed my heart. Torn apart my life. Shit like that.

After all, what would a cheater say?

"You should have a can of mace on you too, given they haven't caught the bastard who did this to you. One of those keyring ones." He pulls some money out of his wallet, setting it on the table. Then he stops. "What?"

"Just thinking."

"Yeah?" He cocks his head, a lock of brown hair falling over one of his eyes. "What about?"

"Lots of things," I say. "You're being very helpful all of a sudden. It makes me suspicious. I mean, why would you even want to be friends with me, given our past?"

"I have no interest in being your friend."

"Oh?"

"Trust me, that's definitely not going to happen." He settles back, watching me with a faint smile. Holy crap, his smile . . . it's just a bit mean yet still wholly affecting.

I squirm in my seat. "I see."

"No, you don't," he says. "Clem, you fucked me up. You fucked *us* up. And I'm not going to forgive you for that whether you remember doing it or not. But nobody deserves to be assaulted and have their mind messed with. So I'll answer your questions, make sure you've got a cell and something to protect yourself with. Then you're on your own."

"You're only helping me today?"

"No, that's why I'm giving you my number. Like I said, you think of a question you need answered, you can text me and I'll answer it for you if I can."

"I can text you with any questions." If he wants to define any future interactions, I can work with that. "But that's all."

"That's right."

"Okay. That makes sense." I nod. "Ah, thanks. Thank you."

"One or the other is fine. You don't need to say both."

I smile, nervous again for some reason. "Yeah, I just

. . . never mind."

"Whenever you're ready," he says, sliding out of the booth. Which means he wants to go now. I don't know why people don't just say what they mean.

I finish off the margarita, then wipe the salt off my lips. When I catch Ed watching, he turns away with a sharp sort of motion. Odd. For a big man, his movements have been mostly fluid, almost graceful. Guess he really wants to get rid of me. Can't say I blame him.

"Hey, how was your day?" Frances flops down onto the other end of the couch with a bottle of water in her hand. "You got a phone?"

"Yeah. I was careful when I went out," I say, heading off the next inevitable question before it can be asked.

"Good."

My sister would probably be happiest if I'd hide at home for the rest of my life, staying safe and sound. Bubble-wrapping me isn't out of the question. But it's never going to happen. I need my freedom, the space to figure out my life for myself.

She picks up the TV remote and starts flicking through the channels. Some drama about people on a spaceship, the evening news, a woman singing about a dude named Heathcliff, and a tennis match. Finally, she settles on a wildlife documentary.

"Poor gazelle," she mumbles, taking a sip of water.

"What did you want to do for dinner?"

"Pizza."

"Again?" she asks with a smile.

I'm working my way through the local pizza place's menu, figuring out my favorite. It's taken a week, but I've got it narrowed down to either the pumpkin, spinach, and feta, or the tomato, basil, and mozzarella. For some reason, the vegetarian options appeal to me more. Sometimes I get a bit fixated on things. Happily, pizza has been one of those things.

"I met Ed today," I say.

Her whole body tenses. "You did?"

"Why didn't you tell me about him?"

"Because he broke your heart." She sets down the water bottle, turning sideways to face me. "Clem, you were a mess, absolutely miserable, crying all the time. It was almost worse than right after Mom died. With everything that's happened, the last thing you need is him back in your life. The one silver lining of this whole disaster has been that you've been able to stop tearing yourself up about it."

"He says he didn't cheat on me."

She sighs. "I honestly have no idea about that. In the month leading up to the attack, you refused to talk about him or what went down between you two. So basically, I was just following your wishes."

"Hmm."

"You were crazy about the man. Can't imagine you'd have left him without a damn good reason."

Was Ed the type to cheat? Thing is, he didn't appear

to be lying, and watching people is kind of my thing these days. The things they try to hide. The things they're not saying. What comes out of people's mouths versus what they do is often way off. With Ed though, I hadn't gotten that feeling. In fact, I'm not even sure he cares enough about what I think of him these days to lie. Not like the man would have too much trouble finding someone to take previous me's place, if that's what he's after.

"How did you find out about him?" she asks, voice low.

"What? Oh. I went down the street for coffee and someone in line there recognized his work. Apparently his style is quite distinctive." I nod in the direction of my tattoo. "So I went to his shop. He was not happy to see me. But we talked, and he answered some questions. Doubt I'll see him ever again."

"I actually used to like the guy," she says. "Always seemed like a straight shooter, but I guess I read him wrong. Still, I would have taken you to see him if I knew you wanted to go."

"I'm a big girl, Frances. I can get a cab."

She rests her head back against the couch, staring at the ceiling. "He wasn't involved in what happened to you. I checked him out. Photos of him at a tattoo convention in Chicago were all over social media."

"Why would you even think he was involved?"

"Just being careful."

"Another woman was attacked and robbed in the same area as me the week before. The police officer who interviewed me at the hospital said there's a good chance the attacks are linked." The words come faster and faster, until they start to run into each other. "It was random. Not directed at me personally."

"Don't get worked up. Like I said, just being careful." She shrugs. "It's part of the job description. As a cop. As your sister. No harm in that."

"Was he ever . . ." I swallow. "Was he violent with me? Or anyone?"

"Tattoo parlors are not the most peaceful places in the world, in my experience." She frowns. "But no, violence was not one of Ed's faults."

"From what I've seen on daytime TV, people screw around on each other all the time. It's not that uncommon and it rarely leads to trying to kill the other person."

Frances squeezes her eyes shut for a moment. "I realize your knowledge is limited, but trust me when I tell you that life is not accurately reflected by daytime TV. And I've seen enough victims of domestic violence to be wary of situations involving a recent breakup. Though, as I said, he never gave me those kind of vibes."

She has a point. Two, actually.

The pained look on her face is familiar. Same goes for her favorite wide-eyed and mouth slightly open expression. That one is used for shock or surprise. My sister is a pretty dominant-personality type. And I'm guessing previous me was quieter, less prone to speaking her thoughts regardless of consequences. Doctor Patel warned me it could be a problem.

On the screen, a crocodile drags a zebra into the water. Lots of thrashing and blood. At least it's not pointless violence, since the crocodile needs to eat. I like to think whoever assaulted me was desperate, starving, and alone. Out of their mind on drugs, maybe. It's still no excuse for the ferocity of the attack, but it helps a little. I can't spend the rest of my life in hiding, afraid of everything, and hating on civilization.

"He bought me a small can of mace," I say.

"How romantic." My sister grabs a pillow, stuffing it behind her head. "Actually, that's a pretty good idea, now that you're going out again. Same with getting you a phone. Things have just been so hectic, I hadn't gotten around to it yet."

"You've done enough already. I need to figure out how to look after myself."

She doesn't speak for a moment. "Did he pay for the cell too?"

"No, I did."

"Hmm." She sighs. "You would have had to find out about him eventually. Your name is still on the mortgage for the condo you two shared. He owes you half the down payment back."

"Really? He didn't mention anything about that to me."

"It can be hard for people to remember that you don't remember."

"True."

She says nothing for a moment. "So far as I know, he was in the process of getting the paperwork sorted to take your name off the deed, and I think you were giving him time to pay you back the money. But you'd have to ask him what the actual agreement was. It's what you sank your half of Mom's life insurance into."

"So, I'm a homeowner . . . sort of. Not that I'd be welcome there." I stare at the TV, letting all of the new information settle inside my head. "I've never had anyone look at me with such animosity before. He really doesn't like me."

"And how do you feel about that?"

It always makes me smile when she tries to play therapist. Like I haven't spent a good chunk of my second life around the real thing. "I feel very little regarding him, Frances. Why would I? The guy's a stranger. And before you ask, no, nothing looked familiar."

She just nods.

"You should have told me about him."

"I would have gotten around to it eventually."

No apology is offered for her lie of omission. For not telling me about Ed. This is why I need new sources of information. My sister can't be allowed to pick and choose what I know. To try to dictate who I was, or the person I might become.

Whatever her reasons for keeping things from me, it can't be allowed. We're family, but sometimes I'm not exactly sure we're friends.

CHAPTER TWO

Clem: *Hey. Question: How would you describe my personality?*

Ed: *Used to be a bit of a worrier. Uptight sometimes. Detail-orientated.*

Clem: *Sounds awful.*

Ed: *Maybe I'm not the right person to ask.*

Ed: *Once upon a time it seemed cute.*

Ed: *No idea what you are now.*

Clem: *Me either.*

Clem: *What did I used to do with my time?*

Ed: *Read, watch TV, we'd go out most weekends or have friends over.*

Detail-orientated made sense. Previous me worked at a bank. Given my current situation, the chances of me going through retraining and returning are slim. Doctor Patel warned me the first two years would be the worst. Brain injuries are tricky. "Possible cognitive and behavioral issues. A long list of side effects." So I need to figure out what to do with my life. I have some savings, but they'll run out eventually. After the breakup with Ed, I'd temporarily moved in with Frances. And despite how good she's been about letting me stay here, I get the feeling she likes her space.

Ed thought previous me was cute. I'm almost jealous of my former self. Which makes no sense at all.

The cell goes into sleep mode. My sister lives about twenty minutes from the city, out in the suburbs. Sometimes, the quiet gets to me. But right now, it's peaceful.

Clem: *Where did we live?*

Ed: *Condo near the shop.*

Ed: *I'm still there. The memories suck, but it's convenient.*

Clem: *Frances said we bought the place together.*

Ed: *Yeah. You gave me six months to pay you back your share of the down payment. That changed? I'd rather not sell the place if I can avoid it.*

Clem: *Let's stick to the original agreement.*

Ed: *Good.*

Clem: *What was my favorite color?*

Ed: *Shouldn't you make your own mind up about this sort of thing?*

Ed: *Go outside. Look at some flowers. Find a rainbow. Take a position.*

Clem: *Was just wondering. Will go out later when this headache is gone.*

Ed: *You have a headache? Is that normal? Headaches?*

Clem: *It's not a big deal.*

Ed: *Violet was your favorite color. Hence your tattoo.*

This makes sense too. There's a fair amount of the color in the wardrobe she left behind. It's not a definite for me yet, however. Maybe I'll pick another color. I don't know.

Clem: *What about food?*

Ed: *Italian.*

Ed: *Try Vito's in Old Port.*

This information makes me feel a bit better about previous me's last meal. It still sucked what happened to her. But she truly had eaten what she enjoyed. And if the attack hadn't occurred, I would never have come into existence. Complicated situation. Let's be honest. Any and all possible wrong ways of dealing with amnesia? That'll most likely be where I'm at.

> **Clem:** *What's your favorite food?*
>
> **Ed:** *You don't need to know about me. Anything else?*
>
> **Clem:** *No. Thank you.*

So much for making conversation. It's not as if I even care what he eats. Not really. I'd just been trying to picture our life together. Us out at a restaurant, a happy couple talking and laughing. Him sitting across a table from me without the anger and distance in his eyes.

What I'd most like to ask is if he loved me, if we were in love. But if he won't even tell me his favorite food, chances are emotional statuses are a real no-go area. He might even get mad and block me. It's too much of a risk.

I slide my cell onto the bedside table, close my eyes, and try to nap.

I don't know where the pornographic dream about Ed comes from. But it's very pleasant. The one of being lost in the dark with warm sticky blood in my hair, far less so.

It's been three days since I'd texted Ed.

Meanwhile, I've done a thorough inspection of belongings. Clothes-wise in the bedroom closet, we have the uniforms from the bank and a mix of summer and winter stuff in mostly light, happy colors with some floral prints. Some of it is okay, but a lot of it just doesn't feel like me. There are a couple of pairs of sensible heels, some wedges, sandals, a couple pairs of ankle and knee-high boots, and sneakers.

In the garage, there are eight boxes. One is full of old assorted paperwork and family photos I've already seen. When I was in the hospital, Frances brought them in to see if I might recognize anything. I never did. The other seven are full of books. Lots of books. Apparently Ed was right about the reading.

I bring the most worn and beloved-looking of them upstairs. *Anne of Green Gables* by L. M. Montgomery, *Beauty* by Robin McKinley, *The Stand* by Stephen King, and *Pride and Prejudice* by Jane Austen. A reasonably eclectic mix judging by the blurbs.

I finally regained access to my email and other digital things. Nothing interesting in any of the emails or text messages. And any mention of or photos taken during the period of dating Ed are gone. Whatever happened, previous me sure seemed determined to erase all trace of the man and anything related to him.

There aren't many people in her contacts list. No close family to speak of and few friends. The exceptions being a co-worker at the bank, a nice-sounding woman from high school, and a guy she used to share an apartment with (platonically, so far as I can tell). There are no others. According to her phone log and text messages, she hadn't contacted any of these people in months. She was a bit of a shit friend, and I kind of resent the fact she hasn't bequeathed me a few more sources of information about my past life.

Though maybe I'm being too hard on her, given the breakup, et cetera. Three friends/acquaintances isn't a bad amount. Enough that you could catch a movie sometime or grab a cup of coffee with someone if you wanted.

It's not like the new me is rushing to bond with anyone.

Speaking of coffee, I'm waiting in line at the local café. A small, popular place with yellow walls and bright aluminum furniture. It's about fifteen minutes' walk from Frances's place and I go there every morning. This way, the exercise box gets ticked while I receive my recommended daily dose of caffeine and exposure to people in the outside world. My sister would rather I wait until she's home to go out. But I'm not big on having my hand held. I mean, it's just not feasible. You can't live your life that—

The only warning I get is an odd taste in my mouth, then my left arm suddenly stiffens. Everything goes black.

I hear Ed before I see him. The heavy thud of his footsteps and raised voice demanding, "Where is she?"

"Sir, just—"

The curtain around my bed is thrown back and the man himself appears. Eyes wild and a sheen of sweat on his skin. He looks like he ran all the whole way here. Of course, sweaty and worked-up look good on him. The man has presence. Meanwhile, I probably look like hell.

"I didn't know they called you," I say.

"Your face . . . holy shit. What the hell happened?"

"I had a small seizure. It's fine. They happen sometimes after a brain injury."

"A *seizure*?"

"You're good to go." Doctor Patel calmly rises to his feet. Luckily, he was here visiting another patient. Even Nurse Mike stopped by to see me earlier. It's just like old times. "See you at our next appointment, Clementine. Don't forget."

"Good one." I attempt a smile. It's kind of our inside joke, not that it's particularly funny. But I've found I have a certain appreciation for gallows humor these days. Meanwhile, I feel like utter shit in all the ways.

Ed sits on the side of my hospital bed, staring down at me. Then he takes my chin in hand, gently turning it this way and that to inspect the damage. It's weird, being touched by him. How he feels he has certain rights to my body. I can't deny I'm pleased to see him, but this is not okay. Apart from a couple of awkward hugs from Frances, the only physical contact I've ever had is from disinterested medical staff going about their business.

"Ed." I push his hand away, slowly sitting up. "Don't."

"Sorry. Can I help? Are you all right? Should you be moving?"

"I'm fine, really."

"Clem, half of your face is black and blue," he says, disbelief heavy in his voice. "Not my definition of fine."

"It could have been worse. At least I didn't hit the damaged side when I blacked out and fell."

"What, so you're Jessica Jones now and nothing can touch you?"

I start to frown, then stop. It hurts. "I don't know who that is."

He hangs his head, rubbing at the back of his neck. Pretty sure it means I'm pissing him off. They shouldn't have dragged him all the way over here. God knows what he was busy doing. He's wearing jeans and sneakers, a button-down shirt with the sleeves rolled back. A pair of black sunglasses sit on top of his head. Maybe he was at work. Maybe he was prepping for a lunch date. I don't know if that would bother me or not. Not that I have any claim on him. But best not to think about it just the same.

At least I feel too crappy for any of the worrisome pants-tingling thing this time.

"Why didn't they call Frances?" I ask.

"They did. She couldn't leave work, so she called me," he not so patiently explains. "Guess she didn't have any other options. Plus, I was also probably closest. The doctor said you could go?"

"Yes. If you want to get out of the way?"

He stands and I swing my legs over the side of the bed. Everything mostly feels okay. All of my parts in working order.

"Do you need any meds?" he asks, hand hovering by my elbow just in case.

"Just Tylenol, which we have at home."

"Okay." A heavy sigh. "All right. You better come to

my place."

"What? No." The bottom of my T-shirt had ridden up a little and I tug it back down. "She shouldn't have called you. Sorry about that. But I'm all good, and I'll be fine getting back on my own."

"Are you serious?"

"Yes."

"You get a concussion when you hit your head?"

"A mild one." I shrug. "At least nobody tried to kill me this time. I'll catch a cab back and rest up, put another ice pack on."

"Doctor told you not to be on your own, didn't he? That's why Frances called me in here," he says, leaning closer. "But instead of being reasonable, you've got to be a pain in the ass about it."

"Ed, why are you being like this? You don't want me in your life."

"You know what I want even less? To have to talk you into letting me look after you for an afternoon, as if it's something I want and you'd be doing me this great favor," he says, jaw clenched. "Honestly, it's like nails scratching down the chalkboard of my soul."

"Well, that's dramatic. Here's your chance to walk away. Take it."

"Not going to happen. Not when you look like you've been running around Nakatomi Plaza fighting Hans."

"Again, no idea what you're talking about."

He just blinked. "It's one of your favorite movies."

"Just assume all cultural references mean nothing to me."

"Really? Huh," he says, taking a step back. Thank God. "You get to watch *Die Hard* again for the first time. I'm almost jealous of you."

For a moment, neither of us talks.

"So, Clem, you want to stand here and fight some more?"

"No."

"Good. You can lie on the couch with your ice pack at my place. If you feel like it, I'll put on a movie for you to watch."

"Shouldn't you be at work?"

"Shop's closed on Monday. Stop looking for excuses."

Damn. "You're not going to let this go, are you?"

"If there was literally any other option presenting itself, we wouldn't even be having this conversation."

I sigh, feeling a bit guilty that I was so bereft of friends and he was all I had. "All right. Lead on. And sorry."

We don't talk in the car, letting the silence grow nice and long and awkward instead. As previously texted, Ed lives in a big old red/brown brick building in the same cool urban neighborhood as the tattoo parlor. Five blocks away from his work at the most. The condo is on the ground floor.

"This is where we lived?" I ask, following him down the white hallway.

"Yes."

"I appreciate you doing this."

"Oh, I can tell. You're positively overflowing with appreciation."

And I deserve that. "I don't want to be indebted to someone who hates me."

"That why you stopped sending questions?"

"One of the reasons."

"Yeah? What are the others?" He puts his key in the lock and from within comes barking and the sound of nails scratching. Whatever is on the other side of the door seriously wants out. "Shit, stand back a sec."

He doesn't have to tell me twice. Cautiously, Ed opens the door, just enough to stick a hand through and grab the collar of the dog. The dog, on the other hand, wriggles and struggles and fights to get free.

"Gordon," he says. "Yes, it's Clem. But that's enough. Calm down."

The dog does not calm down. If anything, at the sight of me, his enthusiasm goes up a notch. Gordon is a silver Staffordshire terrier with pale blue eyes and a white stripe down his chest. Step by step, Ed hustles him back into the house. And all the while, his tail whips back and forth in unrestrained joy.

"Close the door behind you," he instructs me. Then, to Gordon, he says, "Come on, boy. Sit. I know you're excited, but you got to sit."

Gordon whines softly, keeping his gaze on me all the while.

"Clem, come over here and let him sniff your hand."

I do as told, carefully extending my fingers to within range of his nose. But Gordon inches forward, licking my palm and as much of my arm as he can reach. His whole body shakes with happiness and I swear he smiles. I rub beneath his chin, coming closer.

"I'll let him go in a minute," says Ed, patting him on the back. "Just want to make sure he doesn't get carried away and you get knocked over again."

And while his words seem polite, his voice sounds strained, bitter even. Maybe he thinks Gordon is giving me a welcome I don't deserve. It might be true, but with the day I've had, the dog's sheer happiness is welcome.

I go down on one knee, all the better to scratch behind his ears. But Gordon decides to go one better and roll onto his back, asking for belly rubs instead. No one has ever been this happy to see me. Frances was relieved when I woke up from the induced coma. However, this is something entirely different.

All of the stress of the day catches up with me. Waking up on the hard-tiled café floor with people surrounding me. The pain and fear. I'm grinning at the dog, but my throat tightens and a tear falls down my cheek. "What a good boy, yes you are, and so handsome too."

"In the place for less than a minute and you're already babying him again."

"I like dogs," I say with wonder.

"You haven't pet any others?"

I shake my head. "No."

It must sound weird, but for a moment the hostility is gone from his face, and Ed just smiles. The curve of his lips there and gone in an instant. No surprise that he too is a very handsome boy. My stomach does some weird swooping thing in response to his nearness. Maybe it's just muscle memory, the way I react to him. It's not real, just leftovers from another life. Not that knowing it helps me or the situation any.

"Are you all right?" he asks.

With the back of my hand, I wipe away the inconvenient tears while doing my best to ignore my reaction to him entirely. Talk about overload. "Yes. Just . . . not a great day. It's better now though."

I rise and Gordon rolls back onto his feet, content to rub himself against my legs and sniff my shoes. Beneath my fingers, his short fur feels like velvet, his still-wriggling body warm and solid. The devotion in his eyes is stunning. I think I'm in love. When Ed gives him a stern warning, he doesn't jump, taking the opportunity to learn farther into me. And he's strong. I have to brace myself, so I don't stumble back a step.

"You should get that shirt off," says Ed.

"Why?"

"There's some blood from when your cheek split." He points at the front. "It needs to go in the wash. I'll grab you something of mine to put on."

I ease it up off over my bruised face, holding it out.

Mouth a tight line, he turns away, ripping the item of clothing out of my hand. "Clem, I didn't mean . . ."

"What? You told me to give it to you."

"Do me a favor and keep your clothes on in front of me, okay?"

I scrunch up my face. Which hurts on both sides now, courtesy of this morning's injury. "Ow. It's nothing you apparently haven't seen many times before."

"Yeah, and I don't need to see it again. Ever."

Huh. I give myself a quick look over. My breasts might be on the smaller side, but they look quite nice in the pale-green lace bra. It's pretty. Previous me was into pretty. And while my stomach is far from flat, everything seems reasonably in proportion.

"Fuck's sake, would you stop that," he growls. "There's nothing wrong with your body."

"No, I didn't think there was. So it's a problem with you, not me. Okay."

"No, it's not a problem with me. Or you. It's a problem with *us*." He glares at me, his amber-colored eyes growing darker. They're very expressive. How the light in them tells of his mood, reflecting some of his thoughts. Right now, he's angry. Again.

People in general fascinate me. Yet Ed takes it to a whole new level. I don't know if it's the knowledge that we have history or just his hotness. Truth is, I could watch him for hours. No, days. With the bonus that attempting to read him distracts me from feeling how every bit of me from the neck up is hurting.

"Were you always this moody?" I ask, genuinely curious.

In lieu of responding, he walks off into the back hallway, shaking his head. I do my best not to stare at his ass, despite it seeming to be particularly spectacular. Tight. A nice handful, but not too much. It's a definite, I approve of his ass.

Meanwhile, Gordon looks between us before deciding to stick with me. Good dog.

The place has high ceilings and an open living area.

Living room followed by a kitchen and dining area. It looks recently renovated. White rectangular tiles in the kitchen with black grout between. White cupboards, a shiny black counter, and aluminum appliances and pendant lights.

He doesn't have a lot of furniture, but what he has is nice. Two dark gray sofas, chunky wooden coffee table, and matching dining table and chairs. Paintings and drawings hang on the walls. All done by the same artist, which is undoubtedly him. No tattoo designs, maybe he keeps those at the shop. Instead, these are portraits and landscapes or cityscapes. A picture of the front of his shop with people wandering by on the sidewalk. Gordon sitting outside on the grass rendered in exquisite detail. The man is talented.

Next in the house comes a small hallway with rooms opening off to each side. A similarly renovated bathroom, an office, art studio, or small spare-bedroom type space, and the main bedroom. I reach the doorway of the last just in time to have a T-shirt flung at me.

"Thanks."

A grunt. "Lie down; I'll get the icepack."

His bed is huge with dark blue sheets and comforter. Through the open closet door, I can see half of the space is still unoccupied. Like a line has been drawn down the middle. We only lived together for a bit over half a year, but I guess previous me just moved out what was actually a short time ago. It'd be better if he'd shifted his stuff and taken up all of the space. Because if he's still processing (a Doctor Patel word) the breakup, then I really shouldn't be here. This isn't even remotely fair to him. Then again, it's not like I'm having the best time either.

I pull the T-shirt over my head and take a seat. Gordon stands by the side of the bed, resting his chin on the mattress. Guess he's not allowed on. After a moment, he sinks to the floor with a heavy sigh and closes his eyes.

Ed enters with a bag of frozen vegetables in one hand, a glass of water and Tylenol bottle in the other. The water and painkillers he sets on the small bedside table, while the mix of peas, corn, and beans is gently applied to the side of my face. After this, he sits down at the bottom of the bed, well away from me. I think we both appreciate the space.

"Thanks," I say, lying back.

He gives a nod.

My fingers twist and turn in the hem of his black T-shirt. "I like the darker colors, but all I seem to own is light, happy shit. Why is that?"

"It's what you liked at the time."

On the wall is a framed drawing of a woman's back, the line of her spine, the flare of her hips, and curve of her ass done in simple lines.

"Who's that?" I ask, nodding at the picture.

"Just a girl."

"Wasn't I jealous, having a picture of another woman hanging in your bedroom?"

He turns away, brows raised. "If you were, you never said anything. Then again, getting you to say what you were thinking used to be fucking impossible. Now it all just comes out."

"I don't mean to upset you."

"I know. There's no filter, huh?"

"Pretty much. Or at least, it's at a reduced working capacity. Sorry about taking my top off before." I stare at the ceiling with the eye that isn't covered in frozen goods. "I heard a story about a woman who was a mediator, really good at dealing with people, getting them to find common ground. She had a bad car crash. Total personality change. She just became this nasty person who said horrible things all the time. Couldn't help herself. Isn't that sad?"

"Yeah."

"I mean, forgetting your life is bad enough. But not being able to rebuild . . ."

He sets his ankle on the opposite knee, getting comfortable. "You were going to tell me the other reasons why you stopped texting me questions."

"No, I wasn't. But since you're asking, why not." I half smile. "The information I get from Frances doesn't feel totally reliable. I feel like it's influenced by her personal beliefs and biases."

"Like her not telling you about me?"

"Exactly," I say. "We were almost constantly together for the last year or so and she never even mentioned your name. She says she was protecting me and would have told me eventually."

He thinks it over. "Are you worried about my biases?"

I shuffle around a little, getting comfortable. Trying not to think about how this is the bed where our bodies used to meet in all the ways. Or at least I assume so. "Who

I am, the person I become, that's on me. But I don't need anyone messing around with what's left of my head. You said you're still angry at me. I mean, you obviously are, and that has to affect how you see things, what you tell me."

"I guess so, yeah." He nods. "But it's not new."

"What's not new?"

"You being suspicious of me. It might even be said that it turned out to be something of a defining feature of our relationship."

I wonder if maybe I am a suspicious person. Suspicious of him. Of Frances. Of everyone. There was a moment when I was walking to the café the other day when I could have sworn someone was following me. But it was nothing. "Is this something we can talk about?"

"Why don't you just start from scratch?" he asks. "I don't think anyone can completely keep their own feelings and experiences out of what they tell you. People just don't work that way. But do you really need all of the history to start moving forward?"

"I don't know."

On the floor, Gordon farts, and we both wrinkle our noses. Dog farts are gross. Another definite.

"If you want, I'll still answer your questions," says Ed.

"But only some questions . . ."

He frowns, taking his time to respond. "I don't hate you, all right? It just hasn't been that long, and some of the stuff you're asking about is still a little raw."

"Understandable."

Outside, a bird calls and a car drives past. Life goes

on for billions of people regardless of what's happening here and now for me. It's a lot to get my head around. Especially with the lingering headache.

The ceiling in Ed's bedroom is as high as the one out in the living area. I like the feeling of space, the scent of him on the sheets. Laundry detergent, a trace of cologne, and him. For some reason, it's comforting.

"Who do you think I am?" I ask, still holding the thawing bag to my face. My fingers have long since gone numb from the cold. "How would you describe me?"

"You're Clementine Johns. Twenty-five years old. Work in a bank. You're kind, nervous sometimes, tend to overthink shit and worry about people's opinions. Meaning you don't always let others know what's on your mind." He sets his foot back on the floor, leaning his elbows on his thighs. "You're good with figures and you like reading, Italian food, and hanging out with friends. Not that you had a lot."

"Why is that, exactly?"

"The thing was, you dropped out of college to look after your mother for two years when she was sick. Watching her die in so much pain . . . well, it'd be hard on anyone," he explains. "Anyway, you leaving college to take care of your mom meant you lost touch with most of your initial college friends. Then you didn't necessarily have a lot in common with the younger college kids when you went back, or even people your own age. Or that's how you explained it to me. I think in the year or two after your mom died you were pretty reserved. Doesn't make it easy to meet people. After we started seeing each other, you grew close to some of my friends, but after the breakup . . ."

"Right." This makes more sense now, the lack of people in my life.

"Ah, what else?" He makes a small humming sound. A thinking noise. "Things have to be tidy; you were always picking stuff up and making sure the dishes were done. Guess you're kind of restless like that. Let's see, you snore after you've had a few drinks and even though you like violets, you're useless at keeping the plant alive. Absolutely hopeless. Every time you'd bring another one home, I'd honestly just feel bad for the poor thing."

"Ha," I said, closing my eyes against the glare of daylight. "Some of that sounds like me, but not all of it."

"So you're saltier now and you like different things. People change."

"Guess so," I say. "Can I ask something about you?"

His lips thinned.

"Not about us," I assure him. "Just about you."

"All right."

"When did you start drawing?"

"Can't remember a time when I wasn't," he says with a smile. It takes him from attractive to rocketing into outer space. It's just as well I'm lying down or I might actually go weak in the knees. The man is heavenly. "I always had pencils and paper. Didn't matter, I'd put my art on anything. Eventually, Mom and Dad gave up on trying to stop me from drawing on walls, just restricted me to the ones in my bedroom. Once a year I'd repaint and start all over again."

"Your parents sound nice."

"They are." His smile fades and he stands. "They liked you a lot. You should rest."

And he's gone.

". . . after what you did, you're probably the last person she needs anything to do with."

Slowly, I sit up, woken by the noise.

"You don't know what you're talking about," says Ed, voice low and angry. "And it doesn't matter. She can make her own decisions."

"She's not herself."

"So who's going to make all the decisions for her? You, Frances?" Even from a distance, Ed's sarcasm is palpable.

"I'm grateful you could help out today, but surely you can see that staying in contact would be emotionally confusing for her."

He doesn't answer.

"Whatever happened between you two, whoever was at fault . . . it doesn't even matter anymore. Right now, she's vulnerable. I have to protect her."

Gordon stands in the hallway, watching the showdown in the front room. When he sees I'm awake, he starts wagging his tail. It's gray outside now, dusk leading into night. The streetlights are on. I must have slept for hours. Long enough for the pain meds to wear off because my face and brain are not happy. Other parts of my body are lodging similar complaints. Carefully, I climb off the bed and gather my cell and the meds off the bedside table before wandering out into the living room.

"She just doesn't know what's best for her." That's my sister, and she sounds all worked up. Not so surprising.

"She's awake," I say, shielding my eyes from the light.

"God, Clem, are you okay? You look like hell."

"Thanks."

At this, Frances makes a noise in the back of her throat. "You know what I mean."

"I'm fine. Doctor Patel isn't overly worried." It's only a little lie, but it'll save me much hovering and sibling concern in the long term. "Seizures are apparently not unheard of after an injury like this and it was only a small one. Once I rest up for a few days I'll be as good as new."

She doesn't look convinced.

"Everything okay at work?" I ask.

"Same old, same old."

Frances either can't or won't talk about her job. At least, nothing specific. Maybe she thinks talking about violence will give me flashbacks or something. Or maybe at the end of her shifts, she'd rather just forget all about it.

I wander toward the kitchen, bottle of painkillers in hand. Before I can start opening cupboards, Ed is there, grabbing a glass and filling it with water. Guess I should have asked first. Though I'm pretty sure he doesn't care. He doesn't seem the type to worry too much over niceties.

"Thank you." I down the two pills and then finish off the water, my throat as dry as something seriously lacking in moisture. I don't know. My brain isn't working well enough for similes. "He came to my rescue today."

Frances makes a pained face. "I know. I'm sorry I couldn't get away."

"It was fine," says Ed. "Take the Tylenol with you, just in case."

Nails click against the hardwood floor, Gordon pacing back and forth over by the front door.

"He's past due for his walk." Ed gives me a grim smile. "How you feeling?"

"I'll live. We'll get out of your way. Thanks again."

"Sure."

Frances continues to say nothing. Might be for the best.

A leash is attached to Gordon's collar and his excitement levels soar. It's the whole-body-wriggling thing again. When there's too much anticipation for it to be expressed via tail wagging alone, the delight spreads. I crouch down, giving him a hug and receiving a doggy kiss in return. Ed just watches. Frances, meanwhile, is already gone.

"Thank you again," I say, and he nods.

When we drive away, they're walking in the opposite direction. I resist the temptation to turn and watch. Twilight in this neighborhood is nice. Cafés, restaurants, and bars are open for business, a good amount of people filling the sidewalks. There's a studied air of casual cool to the whole scene. I bet it's not cheap to live here.

"Is that his shirt?" she asks.

"Mine had blood on it. You really need to give him a

break."

Her lips press tight together.

"We're not getting back together. There's nothing to worry about."

Car lights cast shadows on her face. "I don't want to see you get hurt again."

"I know."

Her scowl deepens and she sighs.

"What?"

"I didn't tell you, but . . . I was married a few years ago." Her gaze stays fixed to the road. "He cheated on me, so I guess it's a hot-button topic."

"Shit. I'm sorry."

"It's not something I like to talk about. My own stupid fault really, I knew better than to marry a cop," she says. "The job can mess with you, leave its mark on you in different ways."

"Well, I'm glad you told me. What an asshole."

"You know, you didn't used to swear so much."

I snort. "No? I wore pastels and spoke nicely, huh?"

At this, she laughs.

"I enjoy swearing. I find the words to be eloquent and expressive."

"Great. Whatever makes you happy." She smiles, but it soon fades. "But you were never a doormat. Don't think that. You just used to be more polite about how you told people to go fuck themselves. And I *am* glad he was there for you today, that he's being helpful. Just be careful. There are different degrees of assholishness, and Ed might not be as bad as some. But, Clem, you were gaga about him. You wouldn't have left unless you were a hundred percent certain that he'd screwed you over."

"Understood."

For a moment, she's silent. "Guess I'm mad at myself for thinking he was a good guy. My radar is usually better than that."

"Hmm."

"Like I said, it was great that he could help out in an emergency," she says. "But hopefully that won't happen again. Pizza and TV?"

"You read my mind."

We turn onto the highway, heading toward the suburbs. Bit by bit, the painkillers kick in, easing the tension inside my head. The aching in my face. It might not have been the best of days. I definitely wouldn't recommend having a seizure as a good time. But with Frances getting a little more real with me, talking some more to Ed . . . things were achieved. I feel like I might be getting somewhere. Not that I have any real idea where that somewhere might be.

As for staying away from the man, I just don't see that happening. There are bound to be questions about me only he can answer. And after all, it's not as if he can hurt me when I have no real feelings for him. A little lust doesn't mean anything.

CHAPTER THREE

Swelling from the bruises alters the shape of my face. I study it in the bathroom mirror, taking in all of the differences. The scar looks to be about the same, a heavy red line cutting across my forehead. Best hidden away beneath my bangs. Most people have a lifetime of seeing their own reflection. Of knowing what they look like and making peace with themselves. Not me. If not for the way the pain of my bruises matched up with the marks on my reflection, I could be staring into the face of a stranger. Mostly, I think I'm about average looking. I'm okay.

I pick up the scissors and start hacking into my ponytail. Warmer weather is coming and I hate the feeling of all the hair sitting heavy against the back of my neck. Giving myself bangs wasn't so hard, but this is trickier. No way will I be able to get it straight. I settle instead for cutting out some layers. An edgy look, maybe. Or maybe it will just look like I stuck my head in a blender. Oh well.

It's cathartic, changing my appearance.

One of the things I admire about Ed is how at ease he seems with himself. How comfortable he seems in his own skin. Then again, I like a lot of things about the man. His scent and his voice and his strong, solid presence. And why wouldn't I? I'd fallen for him once already. Frances has a point about me needing to be careful. Given everything, the last thing my mess of a life requires would be a love interest. I have to sort things out on my own.

Time to put down the scissors before I make things worse. Actually, the result isn't that bad. Similar to a short, sort-of-fucked-up bob. It certainly feels better. I grab a garbage bag and broom and clean up the bathroom. First job done.

Next, with more bags in tow, I start cleaning out my closet. Gone are the pastels. Blue jeans are fine, along with a couple of pairs of black slacks and shorts. But the happy-happy joy-joy colors have to go. A therapist would probably say something along the lines of me feeling the need to reinvent my wardrobe in an attempt to distinguish myself from my former identity. To control my outside appearance since I can't control the inside of my head. At least, that's what the internet tells me. And it's right on both counts. Clear as can be, I draw a line between now and then. Me and her.

Out go the floral dresses and pretty vintage-style tops with shiny buttons. Gone are the baby pink, violet, and soft sunshine yellow. One thing I have learned in the last few weeks of life, I can only do what I feel to be right. And asserting my own identity, starting over from scratch, feels good.

"What are you doing?" asks Frances, appearing at the bedroom door. Her gaze takes in my new hairdo, but nothing is said. Same goes for Ed's T-shirt, which I'm still wearing for some reason. I haven't even washed it because that would get rid of his smell.

"Get off work early?"

"I don't like leaving you on your own."

I frown. "You've already had to use up some of your vacation time because of me."

"Not a big deal," she says. "Want to answer the first question?"

"I'm having a clean out."

"Yeah, I can see that." Arms crossed, she leans against the doorframe. "Why don't I put it all in storage for now? In case you change your mind . . ."

I just shrug.

"You're not throwing out the books, are you?" Her voice sounds vaguely horrified. The colored clothes lay in a heap beside the boxes from the basement. "They were your favorites."

"No. Not without reading them, at least."

"Good." Her shoulders slump in relief. Can't blame her for being worried. From a distance, self-destruction and reinvention probably look a lot alike. "Clem, how's your head?"

"Still there. A little sore, but nothing too bad."

"Did you take the pain meds?"

"Yeah, earlier." And it's not a lie. I'm a few hours

overdue for the latest dose of Tylenol, but she doesn't need to know. The idea of popping pills all the time doesn't sit well with me. Life is full of so many crutches. Props to hold us up and help define who we are. Shit to lean on to get us through the day. My attempt at growth, or at least understanding, has me stripping all of the detritus away in a bid to get to the heart of matters. To gain some understanding of myself. It might not be possible, but I'm going to try.

"Since you're here, feel like going on a shopping trip?" I ask.

A line appears between her brows for a moment. Then she smiles. "After a purge like that, you're probably going to need it."

I smile back at her.

"Are you sure you're up to going out?"

"Absolutely."

Ed: *How you doing?*

Clem: *Fine. It's Friday night. Shouldn't you be busy with friends?*

Ed: *I'm out. Just waiting on someone. Thought I'd check on you. No more seizures? Falls?*

Clem: *Someone—not plural? Are you on a date?*

Clem: *Sorry. None of my business. Thank you for checking on me. Bruising is pretty spectacular but* *head is otherwise intact.*

Clem: *Would I be able to visit Gordon sometime? Take him for a walk, maybe?*

Ed: *He'd like that. Sunday afternoon? Say around five?*

Clem: *See you then.*

"I didn't bring your shirt," I say, climbing out of the Uber outside his building. And it's not a lie. If I'd said I'd forgotten to bring his shirt, then my immortal soul would be in trouble.

"Another time."

"Sorry." Okay. Maybe that one's a lie.

Ed stands on the sidewalk, one hand stuffed in his jeans pocket and the other holding Gordon's leash. At the sight of me, the dog just kind of vibrates with excitement. I'm happy to see him too. Ed's in his usual T-shirt, jeans, and sneakers. All of it looks good. Too good. Because it's like my hands have some phantom itch. The urge to touch his skin, trace my fingers over the muscles in his arms, the line of his jaw. My body's attraction to him is distracting, to say the least.

Meanwhile, I'm trying out one of my new navy V-neck distressed T-shirts, boyfriend jeans, and sandals. Simpler and less girly than my previous style. I place my copy of *Pride and Prejudice* in the cotton sack I found in

Frances's kitchen cupboard. It contains my bank card, thirty dollars in bills, my cell, mace spray, and lip balm. All of the basics.

Now for the important stuff. I go down on one knee, giving Gordon lots of scratches and pats. "Hello, beautiful boy. How are you? Did you have a good week?"

"He can't actually speak," says Ed.

"Ha-ha."

"You cut your hair."

I shove my hand through the shorter threads self-consciously. "Yes, I did it myself. What do you think?"

"Very punk rock."

"Is that code for crap?"

"No. It's just different."

"I can live with that."

The dour expression seems embedded on his face. Gaze slightly pained and/or uncomfortable, forehead a little lined. Still handsome as fuck. Being around him would be easier if my heart didn't beat faster at the sight of him. Perhaps my body really does still remember the feel of his hands, what it was like to have his mouth on me.

Being someone's ex is strange, all of the history such a title involves. It's hard to be the villain of the story when I don't even remember why I left him and apparently broke both our hearts. If he did mess around on me, his behavior now makes no sense. At least, not to me.

"Not sure green and yellow really suit you, though," he says, inspecting my face.

"Me neither. I'll be glad when the bruising fades and

the weird looks stop. Pretty sure the Uber driver wanted to stage an intervention, bless her."

"Here you go." He hands me the leash, nodding in a northwesterly direction. "Park is a couple of blocks that way. Do you know where you're going?"

"No. Guess I'll figure it out."

"Are you even supposed to be wandering around on your own?"

I frown. "Now you sound like Frances."

"That's just harsh." He almost smiles. It's a close thing. "Mind some company?"

"It's fine, but don't feel that you have to. I'm not a child."

"Aware of that." He slips sunglasses over his eyes and starts walking. "Still worried about being indebted to me?"

"Mostly I think I'm waiting for you to decide I'm too much trouble and you're better off dropping back out of my life."

He lifts his chin, saying nothing for a moment. "This about me not responding when you gave me shit for going on a date?"

"It's about everything, really." So he *was* on a date after all. Not sure how I feel about that. Nothing good, I don't think. On the other hand, the man might have been on a date, but he'd been thinking about me. How interesting. "And I wasn't giving you shit. I was just . . ."

"You were just, what?"

I sigh. "Honestly, it's hard to think of an answer that won't piss you off."

His lips roll in, pressed together as if he's holding in

laughter. With the sunglasses on, I can't see his eyes to confirm this, however.

"Why were you texting me when you were out with someone else anyway?" I ask. "Shouldn't I be the last person you'd be thinking about under the circumstances?"

The man just grunts. Any mirth is now long gone.

"Not that I was surprised you were out with someone. I mean, you're *very* attractive. Like, jaw-droppingly so. I've never even remotely seen anyone as . . ." I just shrug. There are no sufficient words to describe his innate hotness. His raw masculine appeal. Where is a thesaurus when you need one?

"Clem," he grits out.

"Yes?"

Apparently complimenting him is a bad idea, since he's turned his face away. His body once again radiates pissed off. The seemingly go-to setting when I'm around.

Shit. "Oh, okay. I'm going to stop talking now."

"Good idea," he says.

All right, so maybe I shouldn't have pressed the question. Or mentioned anyone's attractiveness. In a rare display of wisdom, I keep my mouth shut and give Gordon some pats. At least *he's* still happy I'm here.

We move aside for a couple pushing a stroller, the baby fast asleep. The two women don't look much older than me. I can't imagine having a child yet. One with Ed's smile and my eyes, maybe. God, what am I doing? The situation is complicated enough without imaginary infants intruding.

"Did you ever get around to choosing a favorite color?" he asks eventually.

"Undecided. I mean, I like blue in general. But royal blue is a hard no."

He snorts. "Yeah. You were the same about purple. Violet was fine, but the hate was strong for burgundy and maroon."

Gordon doesn't tug on the leash. Instead, he trots alongside me, sniffing trees and fences, pausing occasionally to mark his territory. The sun hangs low, the world lit a brilliant gold. I watch the ground, keeping my eyes diverted from the glare. My sunglasses must have been taken in the robbery. Next shopping trip, I'll have to replace them.

"Still," he says. "You have it narrowed down to blue. Good work."

"Are you patronizing me?"

"Never."

I'm not sure about that. "Why is it whenever you talk about me, I always sound so high maintenance?"

"Because you are, Clem. Trust me, I've dated enough women to know the difference." His brows draw in all thoughtful like. "You're not a take-it-easy, whatever-comes-is-fine kind of girl. Not saying you don't know how to relax, but that's not your normal setting. You're a little high strung, which requires some extra care, might as well embrace the fact."

"Hmm. I think your bias is showing."

This time, he actually does smile. So dreamy. Full-blown tingles in the pants area.

I turn away. It's safer not to look. "Have you ever

been friends with an ex before? And yes, I know we're not friends, that you're just being kind, et cetera."

"I don't know what the hell we are," he says, sounding weary. "But yes, I've been friends with exes before. Kind of depends on the breakup, though."

I nod, turning over his words in my mind.

"When it's a drift apart or you're just not right for each other, then it's no big deal to maybe keep in touch. But when it's Godzilla leveling Tokyo, like we were . . . not a whole lot left to build anything on. Sure as hell no trust in either direction."

While I don't get the reference, the general meaning is loud and clear. "Right. Though you did come and help me at the hospital."

"Don't read too much into that," he says. "Frances only called me because she had no other options, and I was hardly going to leave you there on your own for hours on end. No matter what shit went down between us."

"It was still kind of you, and I wasn't particularly nice to you at the time. Sorry about that."

I'm pretty sure behind the sunglasses he's giving me side eyes. "Whatever."

We walk a block in silence, Gordon doing his happy doggy thing. The quiet between Ed and me is strangely peaceful as opposed to awkward. An occasional car zips past and a few people are out and about enjoying their weekend. One man is in his small front garden, planting some daisies. That he does this wearing white long johns is a little different.

"I've never actually seen him dressed," whispers Ed

once we're a suitable distance past. "Only ever wearing those thermals."

"Have to admire his dedication to comfort."

"True."

"Interesting neighborhood," I say.

"You picked it."

"I did?"

Ed nods. "I was sharing an apartment with friends on the other side of the city and your rental was up. Figured we might as well move in together."

"I figured or you figured?"

"We both figured. It was mutual."

"Okay."

"You thought with my hours it would be better if we were close to the shop. We looked around for a while, lucked out and found this place."

"It's a nice place."

"It is." His hands flex and tense at his sides before he realizes what he's doing and stops. I've strayed into forbidden territory yet again.

Times such as these, I always wonder what he's thinking, what he's remembering that's set him on edge. Probably he's dwelling on the good old days. Back before he did or didn't cheat on me. But even I know better than to ask what's on his mind. This is exactly why I avoid contacting him. Why I didn't text him after Monday's hospital brouhaha. Because occasional communication with him feels safest. He's less likely to turn his back on me if I don't push. Though I really want to push.

As if sensing my curiosity about things best left unsaid, he speeds up, his long legs stretching, leaving me behind.

"Frances and I did some girl bonding this week," I say as he turns the corner and we cross the road to enter the large green expanse of the park. I think our pace borders on power walking. At any rate, Gordon seems content to follow and I do my best to keep up. "We're getting along better. I feel like progress has been made."

"Good."

"Did you have a busy week at work?"

"Yeah."

All right. So everything is horribly awkward again. But I can fix this. "Resting and staying in was annoying. But it gave me a chance to start rereading the books."

A nod.

"Got a fair way into *The Stand* by Stephen King. It's awesome."

A grunt.

Okay, I can't fix this. The man is in unhappy land and I'm lost at sea. Instead, I give up on Ed for the moment and focus on the dog. This involves me crouching down to deliver belly rubs followed by a brief discussion on the merits of various things for peeing on. Chain link fence was a bit of a bitch, but wooden picket appeared to be quite satisfying. In the park, he's mostly moved on to trees. Gordon seizes the opportunity to overwhelm me with doggy kisses, knocking me on my ass in his exuberance.

"Jesus." Ed grabs me under the arms, lifting me back onto my feet with ease. "Are you hurt?"

"No, I'm fine. Thanks."

"Be careful. He's stronger than he looks."

"Meh. He's a lover, not a fighter." I wipe dog spit off my chin. "Too much tongue, Gordy. You got to take it easy on the ladies. Ease them into things."

"Clem, I'm serious. You need to be more careful." He pushes his sunglasses up on top of his head, worried eyes looking me over. My ass is given a quick light brushing, his capable hands running over my body with obvious familiarity. I'm being manhandled—and I like it. It's as if he hit my ON switch and boom. My skin becomes hypersensitive, my breathing is faster, and the want for more is real. More contact. More him.

Feeling this much, however, is a little scary. Cold and clinical are safer. I just can't seem to reach that state of mind.

"Enough bruises on you already," he carries on, unaware of my ongoing lust/fear.

"Don't treat me like I'm made of glass."

"Then don't take stupid risks."

"Are you kidding me?" I ask, voice rising in volume. "I can't pet a dog. I can't leave the house. I can't do a fucking thing without it being a risk. But the bad thing already happened, Ed, and guess what? I survived. I could have died, but I didn't. And I am not going to live the rest of my life in fear. So back the hell up. Stop touching me."

Mouth slightly open, he just watches me, his hands retreating back to his sides.

It takes me a good minute to calm down and get a handle on things. I didn't exactly mean to rant. In all honesty, I'm not sure where it all came from. Frances irritates me now and then with her caution and things not said, but generally I handle it okay. At least, I don't verbally abuse her in public. Thankfully, the party in my pants has calmed down.

"You okay now?" he asks, sounding subdued.

"Yes."

He moves the sunglasses back into place, covering his eyes. "All right, then."

Gordon looks between us before taking a step or two onward. A bee crosses his path and he of course sniffs at it with interest.

"Gordy, irritate the bee and you're going to get stung," I say, leading him onward, away from temptation. "Not a good life choice."

"I think there's something in that for all of us."

Though I'm pretty sure he's teasing, I don't dare speak.

"You were enjoying yourself and I overreacted," he says, a late-afternoon breeze ruffling his hair. He's like something out of an ad, too perfect, too pretty, too much in general. "I'm sorry, Clem. Shouldn't have touched you without your permission either. When we're together like this, sometimes I forget."

I snort. "You forget? Try being me."

At this, he laughs, shaking his head. "How can you make jokes about it?"

"Dark humor has its place. God knows, being depressed all the damn time would just be boring."

"Fair enough." The corner of his lips creeps up.

"Wow. You sure told me. You know, you wouldn't have done that before. Or at least, not until you'd stewed on it for about three days, making us both miserable in the process."

"And again, I sound awful."

"Nah. Neither of us were all that great at saying what we meant."

"You have flaws?"

"Shocking, isn't it?" He walks alongside me, taking smaller steps so I no longer get left behind. It's a start.

"Next you'll be saying you used to hog all the covers and always wanted to be on top."

His head snaps around to face me, the tension palpable.

Shit. "Sorry. Shouldn't have gone there. The doctors say my frontal lobe will eventually start working properly again. But then again, my filter can't be trusted."

He sighs. "This is getting us nowhere. How about we both stop saying sorry to each other all the damn time?"

"I don't know. Given the situation, is that even possible?"

A thick shoulder lifts. "Never know until we try."

"All right. I'm not sorry."

"Yeah, well, I'm not sorry either. So there."

I smile. "You know, I'm really not. There are so many questions about sex and more personal stuff I'm dying to ask you. I mean, I'm twenty-five years old and I don't even know my favorite sex position."

"Don't do it," he answers, shaking his head. "Shit. Seriously, Clem?"

"Sorry."

When we get back to the building, two people are sitting on the front steps waiting. The female tattoo artist from the shop is holding hands with a man. Even in a simple yellow dress, she's beautiful enough to give me a severe case of the dowdies. My hand immediately reaches up to adjust my hair so my scar is covered. I hate getting all self-conscious.

"Are you kidding me?" is all the woman says, getting to her feet.

Ed stiffens at my side while Gordon wags his tail, happy to have more visitors.

"Beautiful. Relax." The man still sitting on the steps tugs on the woman's hand.

"Relax?" she responds.

"Come on," says Ed, ushering me forward with a hand to my lower back. We go in ahead of the couple on the stairs, keys jangling as Ed unlocks the front door and then the door to his condo. "Calm down, Tessa. I told you the situation."

Off his leash, Gordon trots over to his water bowl on the floor at the end of the kitchen counter. The living room seemed big before, but Tessa's anger fills it up fast.

"I just . . . how could you, Ed?" she says, pacing.

"Babe, have a heart," the man she came with says, collapsing onto one of the sofas with a nod in my direction.

"You really don't remember anything, huh?"

"No, nothing," I answer, lingering near the door.

Tessa mutters something along the lines of, "Have a heart, my ass."

"Clem, this is Nevin and Tessa. Friends of mine." Ed's in the kitchen, pulling beers out of the fridge. "Take a seat, it's fine."

If he says so. I perch on the edge of the unoccupied couch, grateful when I get passed a cold bottle. Not only am I in need of a drink, but it gives my hands something to do. Because this whole scene is beyond uncomfortable.

Eventually, Tessa sits down, her arms and legs crossed. I ignore her glare to the best of my ability. Gordon comes over and sits on my feet. Bless him for his loyalty. Dogs really are a girl's best friend.

"So what happened?" asks Nevin, watching me with interest. He's a good-looking man, lean and muscular with brown skin. Indian descent, perhaps. "How'd you get amnesia?"

Ed groans. "Man, she doesn't want to talk about it. Stop and think. You're complete strangers to her and you want her to just open up about bad shit like that?"

Tessa harrumphs.

"What did I do to you?" I ask. Not hostile, just curious.

The woman doesn't hesitate. "You broke Ed's heart and then you tried to drag Nevin and me into your shit storm, and I am not interested in forgiving you."

"Okay."

"Okay?"

There's not really anything else I can say. Curiosity makes me want more details about how on earth I entangled the two of them in my and Ed's implosion. But given Tessa's hostility, asking for more information would not be constructive. So I set my beer aside, ease my feet out from beneath Gordon's butt, and give Ed a smile. "Thanks for letting me visit."

He just nods, rising to his feet. "I'll wait outside with you."

"That's not necessary."

"Yes, it is."

No point arguing. I give Nevin and Tessa a strained smile. Tessa ignores me, but Nevin lifts his hand in a friendly enough wave. Someone should really write a guide for what to say in these situations. Etiquette for reconnecting with an ex after suffering amnesia. That would be quite useful.

Gordon whines unhappily when Ed tells him to stay inside. After giving the dog a pat and a hug goodbye, I get the hell out of there. Outside on the street, I can at least breathe easy. Ed stands beside me in silence as I pull out my cell and request an Uber. Everything between us is now cold and distant. I hate it. In all honesty, I'd rather be bewildered by desire than left bereft like this.

So I'm not emotionally empty when it comes to him. Now I know.

"Sorry for making things awkward with your friends," I say.

"Thought we weren't going to say sorry anymore." Arms crossed, he stares off into the distance. "You and

Tessa used to be close."

"Really?"

"Yeah. That's why she's so mad at you. Mostly."

I don't know what to say.

In this part of the city, at this hour of the day, it only takes three minutes for my ride to arrive. I climb into the backseat, still searching for words. Something to take the edge off what happened. I should thank him, I should . . .

"Take care," says Ed, shutting the car door.

And we're done.

CHAPTER FOUR

"Amnesia chick?"

The barista grins, handing over my drink with this new nickname scrawled on the side. What a fucking comedian. I guess having a seizure on the café floor has made me mildly famous. Whatever. At least the coffee is good here; they don't burn the beans.

"Thanks." I meet his grin with a small smile. Nothing to do but take the nickname in relative good grace. I take the cup over to the side to pour in some sugar. Let's face facts: I need all of the sweetening up I can get.

It's been over a week since I last spoke to Ed. I try not to think about him. Try not to remember the way he looks and the sound of his voice. Definitely try not to dwell on everything he's ever said to me. Though given the silence, I'd say he's far better at ignoring my existence than I am his.

Also, the bank broke up with me this morning. No

more job. The good news is, the small amount of holiday pay I'm owed, combined with severance, means there's more money in my account.

So mostly my life has consisted of me attempting to be useful and keeping myself occupied. I clean my sister's small ranch-style house, cook most of our meals, read books, go for walks, and attend doctors' appointments. Everyone (the good doctor and Frances) says to take things slow. To let myself heal. But I feel like I'm stagnating and it sucks. No past and no future.

Apart from the occasional headache, I suffer from acute anxiety. Just because I can't remember the attack, apparently doesn't mean I'm not dealing with the trauma. It's a bitch because you can never quite tell what will set it off. The crowd in the coffee shop, for instance, is not great. People bumping into me, all of the noise . . . the sooner I get back outside, the easier I'm breathing.

"Clem?" a woman asks with a wary smile. She's smallish, has very short hair, and is vaguely familiar. "Clementine?"

"Yes."

"I, um . . . this is weird. I don't know what to say."

"Why don't you start by telling me who you are," I say, taking a sip of scalding-hot coffee.

"Right." Her smile widens. "You won't remember, of course, but we used to be friends. Good friends."

I just wait.

"My name's Shannon."

"You're from Ed's shop, right?"

"Exactly. I'm the receptionist, assistant, whatever's

needed really." She bops on her feet with excessive energy. "I didn't get to say hi when you came in the other week. I mean, none of us even knew this had happened to you. It was such a shock."

"So you and I were friends back when I was with Ed?"

She nods. "Yeah. When the breakup happened . . . well, it was messy. You just kind of needed time out from everyone attached to him. I understood completely."

"Right, okay. Ed had mentioned something like that happened, but it's good to know for certain."

"Yeah. When I heard what happened to you, and I just wanted to reach out and see that you were all right."

"That's nice of you." I tip my head. "Do you live in the area? I haven't seen you here before."

"No. I was driving to your sister's place and happened to see you heading in here, so I just . . ."

I nod.

Her smile finally waivers. "Should we grab a table? Have you got time to sit down for a minute? I'd really like to know how you're doing . . ."

"Sure. Outside would be good."

I lead the way, finding one at the end situated against the shop window. There are a couple of men in work clothes. Probably belonging to the French Town Electrical van parked nearby. Some women in athleisure wear. Several of them look askance at Shannon's shaved head and tattooed limbs. Ah, life in the suburbs.

"So I met you through Ed?" I ask, carefully prying off the lid to my coffee and blowing on the liquid to try to cool it down.

"That's right."

I just wait. When the amnesia first struck, and I was around people I was meant to know but didn't, I'd often stay silent because I had no idea what to say. But it turns out keeping your mouth shut is actually a good technique for getting information out of people. If you wait for people to fill the silence, they usually do. They just can't help themselves.

"It was sad, I mean . . . you and he tried so hard to make it work, but there were just some fundamental differences, you know?"

"Not really. Why don't you tell me?"

"God." She giggles and rolls her eyes. Like my lack of memory makes her uncomfortable. "Whatever you want to know."

"You and I were that close?"

One of her shoulders rises. "Well, yeah."

Previous me's life continues to make little sense to me. The way she disappeared on people who supposedly mattered to her. But I'll take all the information I can get.

A bird pecks at the remains of a muffin on a nearby table. The sounds of chatter from patrons and the noise from an occasional passing car fill the air. Shannon rests her elbows on the table, leaning in. There's a certain wide-eyed innocence to her. I don't trust it, but then again, I'm paranoid. Or maybe I'm just having a shitty day and am jealous that she gets to spend quality time in Ed's presence while I've been exiled.

"I'd like to hear your take on it all," I say, settling into the chair. "If you don't mind."

"Of course."

And the girl opens her mouth and talks for over an hour, while I listen.

Seems there are two types of people in this situation. People who probably do know you better than you know yourself yet manage not to rub it in. And people who think they know you and have plenty of opinions about you and are more than happy to shove it all in your face. Shannon belongs to the latter.

Operation Get a Life starts with me enrolling in a self-defense course in the city. Something I'd been wanting to do ever since the police informed me of how I'd wound up in the hospital. Not even Frances can object to me leaving the house for the sole purpose of better learning how to defend myself. Though she does try. With her on night shift, I continue to Uber around. Suits me fine. I can't take part in all the physical aspects of the classes, but I sit and watch, soaking it all in.

The instructor, Gavin, a fit-looking Korean-American guy, tells us to look at any odd thing we hear or see when we're out and about. To let anyone following us know they've been spotted. To let them know that we're not an easy target through confident body language. He also talks about things in our handbags, such as keys or a ball-point pen, that could be used as a weapon. Step three is to remove yourself from the area as swiftly as possible. During the next lesson, we'll move on to the three key attack areas: eyes, throat, and groin. Gavin doesn't mess around.

He spends a fair bit of time making sure I'm following everything. Maybe he's just a good teacher, making the new student feel welcome. Or maybe it's more than that. The bruises on my face haven't gone away yet. And sharp enough eyes might even make out the scar on my forehead, not completely hidden beneath my bangs. Easy for Gavin to conclude that my interest in self-defense is not an idle one.

After class, I walk from the West End where class is held down to Old Port. It's only about eight o'clock and there are plenty of streetlights and people around. But I can't stop looking behind me, my small can of mace held tightly in my hand. Being out and about is good.

Fuck being always afraid. I won't do it. I can't live that way. The mace goes back in the bag, and I swing my arms as I walk. I stop thinking about eyes-throat-groin, and force my attention to the surroundings.

Pavement turns into cobblestones and there's a more touristy feel to the shops in Old Port. Lots of beautiful, over-a-century-old brick buildings. I'm almost tempted by a waterfront lobster place, but continue on, looking for Vito's—the Italian restaurant Ed recommended I try.

And I'm glad I did. It smells amazing and has heavy wooden tables and dark red napkins, silver cutlery glinting in the low light. There are plenty of shadowy nooks and atmosphere aplenty, despite the crowd.

Just when I think I'm going to get turned away, the maître d' smiles, obviously recognizing me on sight, and leads me to the only available table.

I feel comfortable here. Maybe it's the warm welcome. Or maybe some part of me deep down recognizes this place. Unlike the froufrou clothing, Vito's still fits. Though I should probably dress up more next time. Black yoga pants and a T-shirt is a bit slummy.

"Clem?" asks a familiar deep voice.

I raise my eyes from the menu to find Ed staring down at me. He looks good. But then, he always does. More dressed up than normal in gray slacks and a white button-down shirt with his hair slicked back. God, he's so handsome and smooth looking, like a movie star out of an old black and white movie. Just behind him is a woman with wavy shoulder-length dark hair. She's beautiful too. Of course she is. They make a great looking couple, dammit.

Meanwhile, the maître d' stands nearby, visibly flustered. "I'm so sorry. I just assumed . . ."

"Shit," I say, realization dawning. "This is your table."

Ed clears his throat. "Yeah."

"Awkward. Okay." I slide out of the chair, grabbing my usual bag with money, cell, and book inside. God. The brunette is dressed in a sexy off-the-shoulder number and I look like crap. "What a coincidence, huh? Enjoy your meal."

And I'm out of there, pronto. Not even the cooler air outside can take the heat out of my face. It's just as well that I'm wearing sneakers and not heels. Otherwise, there would be no chance of moving fast on the cobblestone streets. The usual ache/awkwardness caused by the thought of Ed escalates into an agonizing kind of pain. I think I'm having a heart attack. Or maybe my heart just hurts. Which makes no sense at all because he's not mine. Not in any way, shape, or form. The man doesn't even like me. And I definitely don't enjoy the riot of feelings he inspires.

"Clem, wait!" Ed runs after me, his expression tense. "Are you all right?"

"Sure. Why wouldn't I be?"

He just looks at me.

"That was unfortunate, them thinking we were still together and meeting for dinner. I mean, what were the chances of me turning up here tonight?" I babble, staring at his shoes. Much easier than meeting his face.

"Random," he says.

"It's just that you told me to try this restaurant and I was in the area, so . . ."

"Yeah? What were you doing?"

"Taking a self-defense class."

"Good. That's good."

I cross my arms over my chest. Only it feels defensive, best to just let them hang at my sides. He's freshly shaved, the strong line of his jaw dramatic in the low lighting. All of the planes and angles of his face are so perfect. Also, he smells incredibly good. Probably some expensive cologne or just his general coolness leaking from his pores. I don't know. But at such a close distance, I can almost believe the emotion in his eyes is something other than annoyance or pity.

"Anyway," I say, taking a deep breath. "You should get back. I guess I'll try the place another time. Make my own reservation next time."

"It was always your favorite."

That stops me. "You're taking your date to my favorite restaurant?"

"I happen to like the place too." Lines crease his brow. "What, we need to divvy up the town now?"

"No, just . . . my favorite? Really? Isn't it weird, going somewhere we made memories?" I raise the corner of my lips in distaste. "Obviously not, or you wouldn't be here with her and this wouldn't have just happened. Never mind."

Now the lines have spread to beside his beautiful eyes.

"Though maybe that's the point, you want to overwrite everything we did together. Make newer and better memories."

"You know, maybe I do."

"Fantastic. Awesome. Best of luck with that." My voice rises in volume. "I hope she's everything for you that I never could be. A paragon of female worthiness. A lady on the streets, a wildcat between the sheets, and all that shit."

A couple passes by, darting looks at us. Fair enough.

"And I'm yelling at you on street corners now like a deranged person. Great."

"Please continue, Clem," he bites out. "I for one am enjoying the hell out of all this honesty for once."

"Oh, fuck off back to your *date*, Ed."

His shoulders rise on an exceptionally heavy sigh and honest to God, I feel exactly the same way. Apparently this city isn't big enough for both my ex and me. Not tonight, at least. I might have forgotten the initial breakup. But we were sure making up for the loss of those memories now. And I barely even know the guy. It shouldn't have mattered where he went, let alone with whom. It shouldn't hurt. Empty was so much safer.

"I don't want to yell at you. I don't want to be this person. Give my love to Gordon," I say, sounding much calmer than I feel. "Hope you have a nice night."

"Clem . . ."

I don't stop walking and I don't turn back.

Frances laughs so hard when I tell her about the showdown with Ed that she nearly falls off the kitchen chair. "It's like you're an evil twin of your former self or something."

"So glad my trauma amuses you."

"Oh come on, you're not really upset about this, are you?"

I finish making our sandwiches, putting a bit of extra oomph into the knife work. Bright early afternoon sun shines in through the window, a lawnmower roars in the distance.

"God, you are." She frowns. "I warned you not to get too close to him. It was bound to be confusing, given your history."

"I didn't get too close to him."

"Don't lie to me. You sat up crying last night after you got home, didn't you?"

"No."

She just waits.

"Maybe. A little." I place our lunch on the table, pulling out a chair and taking a seat. "But I was dealing with the death of Matthew Cuthbert as well. It was very sad."

"Who is Matthew Cuthbert?"

"*Anne of Green Gables.*"

"One of your fictional friends. Right. Sorry for your loss." My sister takes a bite and chews, talking all the while, because we're classy like that. "You always put Ed on a pedestal and thought you weren't good enough for him. Which is absolute bullshit. I don't like that he's hurting you again."

"He's not doing it on purpose. At least, I don't think he's doing it on purpose." I turn it over inside my head. "No. Mostly he's not doing it on purpose. It's pretty much just me and the remnants of my messed-up mind."

"How is he even upsetting you if you don't remember him?"

"I don't know. I guess I grew new feelings for him . . . sort of."

She chews on, raising her eyebrows to display her disbelief.

"We probably won't even see each other again, so this discussion isn't required."

"Pretty sure that's what you said last time."

"Guess Shannon was right. There were fundamental problems in my and Ed's relationship."

"The chick from the tattoo parlor?"

"Yeah." I rip the crust off one of the pieces of bread and tear it into little pieces. Heartache deserves chocolate cake. Not Swiss, turkey, and lettuce on rye. "She's the receptionist. Apparently we were close."

"Makes me feel like a crappy sister for not knowing all your friends from back then." A trace of a scowl hardens her eyes. "Thought you said she gave you bad vibes."

I raise a shoulder. "Everyone gives me bad vibes. My head is a catastrophe. I can't even trust myself, so how can I trust anyone else?"

"Huh."

"Don't you think that was a dick move on his part, though? Taking a woman to my favorite restaurant?"

Frances just shrugs. "They do have really good cannoli. Met you there for your birthday last year. Much as I don't like to defend Ed, once you've found a place like that, it's tough to give it up."

I scowl. Desserts shouldn't come before sibling loyalty. Not when matters of the heart are at stake.

"What are you doing with your day, apart from hating on Ed Larsen?" she asks.

"I'm not hating on him. I'm just openly expressing disappointment in his life choices."

"Got it."

"Why do I have to deal with the fallout from a relationship I don't even remember being a part of?"

"Just plain dumb luck, I guess."

"It's not fair. And I don't want to be attracted to him either. It's inconvenient."

Frances laughs. "No time for romance in your planner?"

"Hardly. What do I even have to plan? When to clean the toilet next? My life sucks."

"Things will get better," she says. "Give it time. You're recovering from a serious injury."

"I know." I sigh all the sighs. "Maybe he's not inconvenient so much as he is extremely confusing."

She nods. "I can see that. You are, after all, a born-again virgin."

"True."

"You're also quite bitchy and whiny today. Did you want to get out and do something this afternoon or not? I'm feeling you could use the distraction."

"Don't you have stuff to do?" I pick up the sandwich, give it a long hard look, and put it back down. My stomach just isn't interested. It's probably evening out the pack of Oreos I comfort ate last night. "Shouldn't you be out spending time with your friends or maybe getting laid? One of us should have something resembling a fully functioning existence. I feel like me and my problems chew up all of your time."

As usual, Frances remains nonplussed by my outburst. "This again? Clem, when Mom was sick, you just dropped everything to look after her."

"Huh."

My sister stretches her neck, first to one side, then the other. "I was adjusting to a new job and dealing with a marriage that was falling apart at a startling rate. You didn't bitch about having to be the person to put your life on hold and move back home to look after Mom. You just did it. I always admired you for that."

"Okay."

"Basically, what I'm saying is, let me be here for you now."

"All right. Though it feels weird inheriting all this baggage, both the good stuff I did and the bad." I shrug. "Thanks."

"No problem." She flashes me a brief smile. "What's the next step in figuring out the contents of your head/getting a life type plans?"

I push my plate away, brushing off my hands. "We should get a dog. If we had a dog, he or she could eat this sandwich."

"We're not getting a dog. Focus, please."

"Fine." I sigh. "Some of the books have a stamp on the inside cover from a secondhand bookstore. I'd like to check the place out."

"Still seeing if anything is familiar?" she asks. "Makes sense. And let me guess, this place is downtown."

I just smile. Or maybe it's a wince.

Braun's Books is a couple of blocks away from Ed's shop. In a city of over sixty-thousand people, however, surely I can go a day without running into him. Surely. Frances drives us in. It's another sister-outing type thing, which is nice.

Behind the counter is a woman with long white and gray hair tied back into a braid. At the sight of me, her whole face lights up. "Well, about time! Where on earth have you been? I was getting worried about you."

Apparently we have the sort of relationship where hugging is required. Before I know what's going on, she's out from behind the counter and squeezing me tight. I stand there mildly stunned while Frances watches in amusement.

"Got a couple of things put aside for you," the woman says, rushing back to her counter. "Including a beaten-up but original copy of *The Flower and The Flame*. Awesome, right? I knew you wouldn't care if it had a little wear and tear. You're lucky I didn't decide to keep it for myself. New Alyssa Cole came in last week too and I knew you'd be all over that."

"I'm sure she'll be delighted with them," says Frances, barely holding back a grin. "But she doesn't know who you are."

The woman raises her brows. "What?"

She holds out her hand for shaking. "I'm Frances, her sister. Clem was attacked a month back and sustained some damage to her frontal lobe. She has amnesia."

"No."

"Unfortunately, yes."

I lift my bangs to flash the scar at her. It makes for great evidence.

Immediately, the woman's jaw drops. "Holy cow."

"That's part of why we're here," explains Frances. "Revisiting places to see if anything's familiar to her. Figuring out parts of her life. You know."

"Goodness . . . I don't know what to say." She huffs out a breath, her shoulders slumping. She seems so gutted by my misfortune. So genuine. "Honey, I'm sorry that happened to you. I'm Iris, by the way. You've been coming here for years, ever since you started working in the bank on Spring Street. You're one of my best customers and, well, I like to think we're friends too."

I lift my hand in greeting. "Hi, Iris. Nice to meet you."

"Did they catch the son of a bitch who did this to you?"

"Not yet," says Frances, her voice hardening. "But we will."

"Good. We need coffee, that's what we need." Iris gets busy with a collection of mugs and the coffeepot sitting on a side table. "Take a seat, girls. Get comfortable. Sounds like we've got a lot of catching up to do."

"Can I help?" I ask.

"No. Sit."

I do as told and so does Frances.

The bookstore has a large arched front window, the walls lined with shelving. In the middle of the space is a big table covered in haphazard stacks of books. A comfy-looking red sofa, a couple of wingback chairs, and an ottoman. Over against the right-hand wall is a high old-fashioned counter. Lord knows how long this place has been here. The air of permanence, the scent of paper and ink is real. It's a great shop.

"I had good taste in hangout places," I say, looking around.

Frances laughs. "Oh you're owning this one, are you?"

"What?"

"Please," Frances says, her legs crossed, foot bopping. "You've been constantly down on the first twenty-five years of your life. Apart from Ed, maybe. You seem okay with having been there and done that."

"Well, he's a very pretty man," I say. "Besides, you try having a lifetime's worth of choices dumped on you with little to no explanation available as to why you did the things you did. I feel sorry for me."

"I've noticed."

I smile. Either my sister's dry sense of humor is rubbing off on me or the halfhearted bitching at each other feels a lot like actual affection these days. I don't know. But I like it.

"We were in the middle of planning a monthly romance book club," says Iris, arriving back and setting a tray down on the coffee table. "That's why I was so surprised when you up and disappeared on me."

"Romance?" I ask, sitting up straighter. "I didn't realize I read that too. I've got a lot to catch up on."

"I'll make you a list, honey."

"Thanks."

"And where's that big strong man of yours? He's a fine specimen." Iris winks at me.

"We broke up. Before the thing happened."

"What a pity. He was always so patient when you brought him in, following you around and carrying your books for you."

It's a pretty picture. Ed being my bookstore beck-and-call boy. The muscles in his arms flexing as he carries around my stacks of reading material. Sounds like a perfect boyfriend. A part of me misses him. A big part of me. Or maybe it's just the idea of him, since it's hard to miss something you have no actual happy memories of. Hard to tell which exactly. And what with him dating other people, it's not like my opinion of him or our previous relationship is going to matter anytime soon.

"Oh, get that look off your face," chides Frances.

"What?"

"The sad-girl thing doesn't suit you."

Iris watches us with interest. "She misses him. Sometimes our hearts are wiser than our heads."

My sister scoffs. "Don't get her started on him. There's a whole world of angst and bewilderment better left alone."

"True enough," I say.

Frances sighs. "I agree he did always seem to treat her well. Right up until he didn't. But either way, it's over, time to move on."

"Still not totally convinced he cheated," I admit.

"Nine out of ten men will be assholes given the opportunity."

"You're making that up." I frown. "That can't be scientifically proven."

"Experience dictates . . ."

"You're a police officer," I object. "Your experience is bound to be skewed. After all, you're always having to deal with the asshole contingent of the world. That's basically your job description."

"No," Frances says. "My job allows me to properly see the asshole contingent of the world that everyone else would prefer doesn't exist. *That's* my job description."

"I think I better make you a list of required reading as well, Frances," says Iris.

"I'm not into romance, neither the genre nor the state of being."

"Have you ever read one?"

"Well, no, but I've tried a few real-life romances and I have to say—"

"Of course you have to find the right one. The story that speaks to you." Iris sips her coffee, somehow appearing both serene and stern. It's quite a trick. "At the heart, romance is about hope, and that's what keeps us going, dear. The eternal quest to improve ourselves, our lives, our world." Suddenly, she snaps her fingers in front of her face. "Ah, I have it. Just the one."

Now Frances looks vaguely worried. "It's fine, really. Don't trouble yourself."

In a flash, the coffee is back on the little table and Iris is off to the bookshelves, moving like a woman on a mission. "No trouble at all. Romance isn't all kissing and bedroom action, you know. Though there's often some of that too. Don't be a mindless slave to misogynistic prejudices. That's never a good look. Think for yourself, form your own opinions. These are stories about women standing up for themselves and what they believe in. Women working to be whole and demanding what they deserve. Here we go!"

I'm pretty sure Frances would climb under the chair if there was a chance she'd fit.

In a moment, Iris is striding back and handing Frances her prize. "I get the feeling you've suffered some hurts, but it wouldn't do to grow bitter and closed-minded. I think you deserve better than that, don't you?"

"I guess it wouldn't hurt to try just one." Frances closes her mouth, her brow furrowed as she takes the book. I peek at the title: *Sweet Dreams* by Kristen Ashley.

"Excellent." Iris's smile is beatific. She sits back down, picks up her coffee, and turns her attention to me. "Now, what are we going to do about you, Clementine?"

"Me? I'll read the books you tell me to." After her impassioned spiel to my sister, I wouldn't dare do otherwise. "Promise."

"I meant about your situation, but I'm delighted to hear that you continue to love reading."

"Oh, there's not much we can do on that score. The bank let me go since I can't remember what my job is and that's not going to change anytime soon," I report. "And I'm supposed to be taking it easy, though I've been doing that for weeks, and it's boring as all hell. It just means I have more time to spend alone, fixating on everything I don't know and getting stressed out."

"You're lost." Iris sighs. "I don't like seeing you like this."

"She'll figure things out eventually," says Frances. "There's no rush."

I set my mug back on the tray. "I need something to

do with myself before I drive what's left of my mind insane. Maybe I should volunteer somewhere."

Iris tips her head. "Well, I could certainly do with some help here. I can't afford to pay much, but you'd be very welcome and the work wouldn't be overly cumbersome. No need to take on more than you're ready for."

"Really? That would be great!"

"You're supposed to be resting," says my sister, face tight. Definitely not pleased with the plan at all. "Doctors don't give out orders just for shits and giggles. It freaks me out enough that you wander the streets on your own, going out for coffee."

"Come on, Frances. I need to start rebuilding. Look around you. This is as soft a start in as safe an environment as I'm going to get."

"I'd be able to keep an eye on her if she was here, make sure she's not overdoing things. Surely that's better than her being on her own?" Iris sounds so calm and reasonable, making it hard to disagree. "Why, there's even the sofa if she needs to rest. She wouldn't be in anybody's way."

Frances looks between the older woman and me, her mouth little more than a thin worried line. "I don't know; it's so soon."

"This is an awesome opportunity, and I'll be fine." I meet her scowl with one of my own. She won't win this fight. She has to know that. I needed my own space, my own life. And I want to do this.

"It's not like I can stop you," she mutters. "I guess."

That's about as good as it's going to get.

Iris and I grin. Look out world, I am gainfully employed.

CHAPTER FIVE

Noise startles me awake. The glowing green digits of the alarm clock indicate it's around three in the morning. The crash of glass breaking. A thump and groan followed by metallic screeching. It's all jarringly loud in the dark. I almost fall off the mattress, frantically searching for my cell on the bedside table.

Close by, a dog starts barking. A man yells from somewhere across the street. Frances isn't due home for another hour or two so I'm on my own. My head's so fuzzy from sleep, it doesn't occur to me to be scared. Not yet.

I stumble out into the quiet of the house, pulling back the curtains on one of the front living room windows.

Huh. Everything outside seems to be as it should be. With the exception of the dude across the road standing on his front porch in his robe. So I'm not the only person who heard something. At least that means it wasn't just a dream.

But wait . . . my older-model hatchback sits parked at the curb, moonlight reflecting off the sharp edges of shattered windows.

"What the hell?"

I put down my cell and grab my sister's baseball bat (definitely intended more for home security than sports) out of the hallway closet. I shove my feet into some sneakers, flick on the outside light, and unlock the front door. Two days ago, I had my second self-defense lesson. Gavin probably didn't have a baseball bat in mind when he was giving us the eyes-throat-groin talk, but a dark part of my mind kind of liked where the combination might lead. My grip on the bat strong, I stride out into the night.

The man from across the street is checking out my car with a heavy scowl on his face. His bathrobe is white and he has fluffy slippers on. They're quite fetching.

"Did you see anything?" he asks, eyeing my baseball bat a little warily.

I just shake my head.

"Me neither. Thought I heard an engine start up down the street, but . . ." He mutters on under his breath. "Jesus, they did a hell of a job, and they were fast too. Is this yours?"

I nod. Though it looks more wreck than actual vehicle now. A piece of postapocalyptic art, maybe. Just as well I wasn't relying on it to get anywhere anytime soon. Shadows darken the indents in the door and hood. Lines of silver show where the paint's been cracked or removed. The windshield is a shattered ruin. It's almost pretty, the way the light traces the web of broken glass.

"Kids, probably," he says. "Your sister's a cop, right?"

"Yeah, she's at work. I'll go call her now."

He nods, crosses his arms, and settles in to wait with me. Nice of him. "Sorry about your car."

I just keep staring at the car in disbelief. Who could have done this? One thing is for certain. My vehicle is well and truly fucked. "Yeah, me too."

Once daybreak and business hours arrive, I make a detailed (not that I have any actual details) report for the police, then start in on the insurance side of things. Frances talked me through what to say and what to expect at the police station. The insurance company keeps me on the phone answering questions for roughly three and a half years. At the end of the interrogation, I'm told an assessor will be out in a day or two to decide if it's even worth fixing. Given the vehicle's age and the damage, it's apparently unlikely. The inside is full of glass. But my new friend from across the road, Martin, and I managed to get a tarp tied over it to protect the interior from inclement weather.

"There've been some small acts of vandalism at the school, and a car parked on the street a few blocks over got rammed a month or two back by joyriders," says

Frances. "Unlikely either of those events have anything to do with this, though."

"So I either have shit luck or I'm being targeted. Those are the two options here."

"Let's not jump to conclusions. This could very well be about my job. Someone who had a bad experience with the police and decided to take it out on a vehicle parked out front of an officer's house." She sighs. "It happens, unfortunately."

"Maybe. Who knows?"

"I am sorry this happened, Clem."

"Me too," I say. "But I mean . . . let's face facts. It was most likely just a random malicious attack by some local troubled youths out to relieve their boredom at odd hours of the morning. Or people who really hate hatchbacks, I don't know. Maybe they had bad sex in one once. Pulled a hamstring or something trying to get a leg over."

"This isn't funny."

I sigh. "No, it's not. Making jokes is apparently my new coping mechanism."

My sister ravages her thumbnail cuticle for a while, a glass of orange juice sitting forgotten in front of her. She's probably wondering what would have happened if they'd taken the crowbar to one of the house windows. What might have occurred if Martin across the street hadn't likely scared them off by getting out there so quickly.

"Frances, it's not your fault I was here on my own. You were at work. You're allowed to work. Indeed, money-wise, you kind of have to." I yawn, beyond tired. "I do not need to be constantly watched. So please stop being anxious. You're making *me* anxious, and this is just a whole new circle of hell I'm not up to dealing with on limited sleep."

My sister takes a deep breath and sets her hands in her lap. "I take it you're still determined to work in the bookshop?"

"Yes. I told Iris I wouldn't be in today given all this. But tomorrow . . ."

"Okay. I'll give you a lift in the morning."

"Okay?" I repeat, a little startled.

She just shrugs.

"I'm just used to you fighting me on things. Not that supporting my choices isn't nice."

"You're a grown adult. There's only so much I can do with my work hours the way they are at present." She sits back, crossing her legs. "Life goes on, et cetera and so on. Right?"

"Yes, right."

"Still aiming to go in five days a week?"

"Seems best. Iris says she can only pay me for three, but God knows I need the experience, and it's not like I've got anything else going on."

She nods, gaze thoughtful. "Okay. All right, then."

It's nice, not fighting with my sister about my welfare. I have to admit, however, I'm surprised. If anything, I'd have thought the incident with my car would have made her double down on the security side of things. But no.

Great. I smile, she smiles, we all smile. Maybe this day isn't so completely shit after all.

New releases take up the front half of the shop. Secondhand books and a range of literary themed items and locally made handcrafted giftware—such as T-shirts, coffee mugs, and sea glass pendants—inhabit the other half. Of course, there's also the counter area off to the side and a staff bathroom and storage area out back. To say Iris is happy to have me there would be an understatement. I think she gets lonely. How you could feel isolated with people coming and going, I'm not sure, but everyone's different. I find the semi-constant stream of customers a little overwhelming. It's a good opportunity to work on my next-to-nonexistent conversation skills.

I asked Iris why she wants someone working in her shop who only remembers ever actually finishing a couple of books. She said because I was trustworthy and still loved books, just needed to catch up on my reading.

All day, the pile of books sitting at the end of the counter waiting for me has been growing. I'm only borrowing them. Guess it's a staff-bonus type thing. Otherwise, I'd be further in debt as opposed to actually moving forward financially. Which, let's face facts, I'm still barely achieving. But at least I'm not bored.

The door jingles and I quickly straighten up from the fluffing and strategic placing of cushions on the couch. Because having your ass in the air when someone walks in is such a good look. And oh shit. "Ed, what are you doing here?"

"She means hello and welcome," singsongs Iris.

The man stands just inside the doorway, face tense. Although, I'm not sure I've ever even seen his face un-tense. And it's probably not something likely to happen around me anytime soon. Sneakers, jeans, and a faded black T-shirt. Of course, he makes vaguely disheveled look good. Damn good. He licks his lips and my mind blanks; my heart stutters. I just stand there like an idiot.

Having a crush on my ex-boyfriend is problematic.

"We need to talk," he mutters, gaze fixed on me.

"What have I done now?"

"Clem . . ." His lips morph into a slightly lesser scowly type look. Rueful, I guess you could describe it. He nods at the couch, wandering over to take one of the wingbacks for himself. Not like I wanted to sit next to him anyway.

After getting the nod from Iris, I sit. Curious as per the usual. "So?"

"I called your sister just to check on you and she told me."

"What about?"

"'Bout what happened to your car, and how you're alone a lot with her doing shift work," he says.

"None of that concerns you."

"She's worried about you."

I shrug. "She's a worrier. It'll pass."

"Yeah, but I think she's got a point. There's every chance the target was your sister. From a distance, you two look a lot alike. But while Frances is armed and trained to handle this sort of thing, you're not. Plus, you're already recovering from head trauma. You being there on your own so much isn't good." He sits forward, elbows resting near his knees. "We had a talk and . . . you're going to move back into the condo. Just for a while."

"What?" I gasp. "Move in with you?"

He nods somberly. "With me, yes."

"And you two just decided this? How? Why?"

"Hear me out . . . legally, it's half your house anyway."

I shake my head. "No, Ed. Just so much no."

"My hours are eleven to six, so you won't be on your own so much. Just in case someone is messing with you," he says, face lined. "You'll be safer."

"Thank you so much for making decisions about my life for me. But us living together is just an all-round fantastically bad idea."

"Closer to your work here too, so the commute is easier. And I know you like the area."

"You do *not* want me living with you." My mind is officially blown. The man is already on the verge of outright hating me. This could tip him over the edge. I can't afford it. "I cannot believe . . . I mean, what on earth makes you think you're in any way responsible for my personal safety?"

"Calm down."

"I don't want to calm down!"

Iris clears her throat in a rather distinct manner over at the counter.

"Sorry, I'll calm down." I turn back to Ed and hiss, "No. Absolutely not."

"I'll clear out the spare room. You'll have your own

space. It won't be so bad."

"Who are you trying to convince, me or you?"

"Look, I don't want you getting hurt again," he says, eyes serious. "This shit happening now with your car, I've got to admit, Clem. I'm a little freaked."

"It could be nothing."

"Or it could be something. We don't know."

I'm pretty sure I'm wearing his trademark scowl times a hundred.

"It's still your place too, that's the fact of the matter." He swallows, turns away. "We'll just be roommates for a while. It doesn't have to be a big deal."

"Great. Do I get to spend time with your new girlfriend too?"

He just gives me a dry look. "Want to turn the sarcasm down a little? I'm trying to do the right thing here."

"Making decisions behind my back is not the answer."

He lifts one shoulder. "Look, I know it's not going to be easy. But it just feels like the best choice to me. I don't want anything happening to you, okay?"

"Ed, nothing's going to happen to me. Probably. Frances shouldn't have agreed to this." I pull my cell out of my back pocket and bring up her number. It rings approximately twice before the call is cut off. I growl in frustration. "She's not answering. Why am I not surprised?"

A moment later, a text arrives.

Frances: *Consider yourself evicted.*

Clem: *What the hell is going on?*

Frances: *I hate to say it but the man made sense. You're on your own too much. It's not safe. Not if there is some cop-hater out there who knows my address. This is for your own good.*

Frances: *Besides, you're already moved in. You're welcome.*

"I'm already moved in?" I ask, bewildered.

"She dropped off your stuff earlier," he says. "I had a break, stopped by home to let her in. Your things are all waiting. We've just got to get the second bedroom sorted."

"Fuck." I slump back in the chair, cell lying forgotten in my lap. "You two are treating me like a child."

He sighs. "We care about you. And think about it. If there *is* something going on, it dates at least back to the first attack when you lost your memory. And maybe it dates further back, when we were together and . . ."

"And when my safety would have been your business."

"My responsibility, yes."

"So this is some misguided macho thing."

His lips press together hard. When he speaks, it's clear he's making an effort to be calm and reasonable. "You would feel the same way if something happened to me when we were together. Exactly the same. We both looked out for each other; it's what couples do. So I owe you some help in making this right."

"Ed, this is not a good idea."

"Look," he says, shifting tactics, "you're working in

town now and don't need to be commuting when you should be taking it easy, recuperating and everything. Plus, there's no need to be spending that money on rides. This will be better. You'll also be close to where you have your self-defense classes too, right? There're a lot of reasons why this is a good idea."

I am not convinced. "Not for you, there isn't."

"Don't worry about me," he says. "And on the bright side, you'll get to spend more time with Gordon."

"He's a good dog."

"It won't be so bad." Ed frowns. "It's only until things calm down and we know you're safe."

My head falls against the back of the couch and I stare at the ceiling. "But I really don't like the idea of putting you out like this."

"Eh. No big deal."

"Yes, it is."

He doesn't bother to respond.

While some of his arguments may have substance, it still isn't right, this dumping of me upon his fine self in a domestic setting. Same goes for the bizarre collusion between him and my sister. Guess the attack on my car scared her worse than she let on. It seems so random, though, bashing in a windshield and dinging up some doors. So petty and stupid. Surely it doesn't mean anything?

"Maybe just for a few days while things calm down," I say, thinking it all through. "But I don't need you accompanying me everywhere and playing bodyguard. That's unnecessary."

"Okay," he says, all easygoing like.

"And you'll tell me if it gets to be too much. If I'm doing something wrong or that you don't like."

A nod.

"Or if I'm just generally irritating you and you need your space or whatever."

Another nod.

"I promise not to yell at you again."

"That would be nice."

"All right." I take a breath. "Don't you have some ground rules for me?"

"Why don't we just work it out as we go along?"

And I'm back to staring at him again. Maybe I'm just irritated by how much, deep down in the mire of my subconscious and soul, I actually want to be close to this man. To be in his house and part of his everyday life. When it all goes wrong and is taken away from me—an inevitability, given our history and how easily I tend to piss him off . . . well, it's going to suck.

"She's finished for the day," calls out Iris, looking much too pleased by this turn of events. "You can take her home."

Home. I'm not sure where the hell that is anymore, if I ever even had a clue to begin with.

Ed moves his easel and art supplies into a corner of the now somewhat crowded den. A surprisingly comfortable futon mattress thingy lies unrolled on the floor of the spare bedroom. My suitcase sits nearby, along with the stack of books Iris sent me home with. I didn't let Ed carry them, either. Scattering my few things around is about as much commitment as I dare make to this new living situation.

At least there is one creature in the universe genuinely pleased with the new arrangement. Gordon is ecstatic, following me around constantly. Even going to the toilet without him is a challenge. It's not that I don't love him, but peeing in private is kind of a thing for me, apparently. When we sit down to eat dinner, he sits on the floor beside my chair, watching me with eager eyes.

"Don't feed him from the table," says Ed without looking up from his bowl of beef panang with jasmine rice. I have a green papaya salad with shrimp and vermicelli noodles. He ordered. It seemed easiest.

"I wasn't going to."

"Sure you were."

"Stop pretending you can read my mind."

The side of his mouth inches up. "I'm not reading your mind, Clem. I just know you, and as soon as he starts begging and making those eyes at you, you can't help yourself."

"Did you want some?" I nod at my bowl.

"There's cilantro in it. Stuff tastes fucking horrible."

"Huh. So I don't eat coconut and you don't eat cilantro."

A grunt from Ed.

"Learn something new every day."

Gordon whines ever so softly, his gaze shifting cautiously from my food to his owner. Not the most subtle of pups.

"Bad dog," mutters Ed.

"That's emotional abuse." I turn to him. "I'll be your witness, Gordy. I saw it all."

This time Ed snorts. At this rate, who exactly is the bigger animal could be debatable.

"So, what do you normally do at night?"

He takes a swig of beer, shoulders just about up around his ears. Like he's trying to make himself disappear in plain sight. Like my presence requires him to be permanently bracing for something. "I don't know . . . watch TV, do some work, hit the gym."

> Note: he refrains from mentioning restaurants and possible amorous female companionship of the brunette variety. It's a considerate, polite omission.

The following silence is broken only by Gordon's continued near-silent yet heartbreaking pleas. If Ed wasn't sitting right there just waiting for me to fuck up, I would totally feed the dog from the table. He was right about that much. Not that I would ever admit it out loud.

Maybe I should ask if we can put on some music. Anything would be better than this. On the walk home, the lack of communication didn't seem so explicit and all-consuming. There were other people passing by, traffic on the street, and myriad things to make up for our lack of noise. But now, not so much.

"You know, I might finish eating in my room." I start to rise, gathering up the bowl, utensils, and beer. "Do a bit more unpacking. Get organized for tomorrow."

"Clem, sit." He sighs. "You don't have to hide in your room."

My butt hovers above the chair, undecided. "Are you sure you haven't had enough awkward for one evening? Because I kind of have. It's been a long day and—"

"Please."

I sit.

"Sorry. It's just weird having you here."

"Hmm." No shit. I down some beer, searching for something non-offensive and noninvasive to say, and of course come up empty. "Shannon from your work came to see me the other week."

He raises a brow. "She did? Guess you two used to get along okay."

"Apparently we were real close."

"Don't know if I'd go that far. But I might be wrong." His elbows rest on the table, making it hard not to ogle his shoulders. It's sad how I objectify this man. Sad for me, at least, since my chances of ever touching him are nil to none. I tear my gaze away from him. Much safer to stick to my food.

"Anyway, she had a lot to say about everything. Especially when it came to us. Not that there *is* an us now. I didn't mean—"

"Such as?"

"Such as what she was saying? Umm, well, apparently

we were fundamentally flawed. This appeared to be based on you thinking I was a delicate creature in need of much careful handling on account of my mother's long illness and death and all." I frown. "That's come up in a couple of conversations. I mean, it had to have been a big thing in my life, right?"

"Yeah," is all he says.

"Who are you when all of your formative moments are gone?"

He finishes chewing what's in his mouth, washes it down with beer. "Like I've said before, you're still you, just different. Guess she has a point, losing your mom . . . you'd been sad for a long time. Watching someone you love fade away couldn't help but mess with your head. And since I knew that, I guess I did try to be careful with you. Maybe to the point of being too careful. Too cautious, not open enough."

"Mm."

"What else did she have to say?"

"Sure you want to hear it?"

"I'm asking, aren't I?" He loads up his mouth again with food, but his gaze remains on me, waiting. Only the kitchen lights behind him and a lamp in the den are on. And in this low light, his eyes are darker. Mysterious, even.

"She said I tried," I continue. "But I never really fit into your world and that's what made me insecure. She made me sound like some pretty pathetic, clueless kid from the suburbs who got out of her depth, actually. I mean, she phrased it nicely, but still."

His brow creases. All of this is dangerous ground. “That’s bullshit. You fit in with me and my family and friends just fine. I never expected you to change for me. Was surprised when you said you wanted the tattoo, actually.”

“Really?”

“Yeah. You liked ink on me, but it wasn’t really your thing. Until you decided it was. Anyway, Shannon’s way off,” he says. “My life isn’t edgy or some such bullshit. I go to work, come home and walk my dog, do laundry on the weekends. It’s a long way from anarchy and mayhem.”

“But do you separate the colors when you’re washing? Because if you don’t . . . whoa. That’s really flouting the rules right there.”

“Is it now?”

“Oh yeah. Chaos, pandemonium, total bad-boy territory. Chicks go wild for that sort of thing.”

His gaze is amused.

It warms me. “Believe me or not.”

“I think not.”

“Tell me something formative about you,” I say. Then rush to soften the demand for information before the inevitable wariness enters his eyes. “Roomie. Ed. Friend.”

“That what we are, huh?” He sighs. The question seems to be hypothetical, so I keep my mouth shut. Maybe he’s not sure what label to slap on us either. “Okay. Let me think.”

I eat. Harder to blurt out silly random crap with a full mouth. Or messier at the very least.

“I didn’t have my growth spurt till senior year. I was

always one of the shortest in class up until then," he says. "Never got picked for sports or anything. Some of the other kids gave me so much shit for it. Then, suddenly, I shot up like a foot within six months or so. I guess that counts as formative. It didn't make any difference to my friends, but some people really started treating me differently."

"Girls?"

"Yeah, some of them were girls." Out comes a hint of a smirk. "It was like all of a sudden I existed for a reason other than for piling crap on."

"Did you score?"

"I don't kiss and tell."

I smile. Maybe not, but I bet he kisses well. The tingles are back.

"It was a good lesson in not falling for people's false perceptions of you, you know?"

"Do you mean just because you were pretty all of a sudden didn't mean who you were as a person changed?" I ask.

He licks his lips, eyes a little wary now. Or assessing, maybe. I don't know.

"What? You're a pretty man; you must know you are. How is that a big deal? Am I not supposed to say that?"

"It's considered bad form to hit on your ex."

"I'm not hitting on you; I'm stating a fact. Oh my God, Ed." I scoff. "Also, I know full and well that using exes for back-up sex is a thing, so don't try that with me."

He stands so suddenly his chair screeches back against the floor. "For your information, I don't fuck around with my exes. Ever."

Bowl and empty beer bottle in hand, he stomps over to the kitchen. His movements stiff, brutal. The man is mad.

"I hit a nerve," I say, realization weighing me down the same as dread.

"No shit."

"I'm sorry. I didn't mean to."

The stiff line of his back is like an insurmountable wall as he rinses off his bowl and cutlery in the sink. And for a couple of minutes, I'd actually been doing okay there.

Conversation apparently over, I finish up at the table and wait in line to wash up. Gordon follows behind hopefully. If anything, my nearness seems to make Ed seize up even more.

No way, no how, can we live together like this. I feel as if, when it comes to him, I'm surrounded by emotional landmines. Never knowing when my dumb ass is going to stumble across another one and yet again blow things to hell. For all the talking she did, Shannon didn't exactly go into specifics about the breakup. She mostly just dwelled on how ill-suited Ed and I were and how inevitable the implosion of our relationship had been. Or at least, I think that's all she said. My mind wandered a time or ten. Being talked at is the worst.

God, coming here was such a bad idea. "That's what our breakup was about, huh?" I ask. "Me thinking you'd cheated on me with an ex?"

Movements brisk, he shuts off the tap and wipes his hands on a tea towel. Basically confirming my query.

Much as I might hate it, part of me revels in the newly acquired information. Another piece of the puzzle no one had previously deigned to mention. Then he's gone, heading for his bedroom. "Sweet dreams, Clem."

And the door is shut, locking me out.

"I don't think he meant that," I say, picking out the remaining shrimp for Gordon. Since we're no longer at the table, there's no breaking the rules. "Not really. What do you think, beautiful boy?"

Given the way his tail is beating against the hardwood floor, Gordon agrees.

"Oh, you're the best puppy. It's nice to have you on my side."

He laps up the treats right out of the palm of my hand. Little grunting noises of delight spilling out of him the entire time. I choose not to see this as bribery. More of a waste-not, want-not situation.

"Want to sleep on my bed with me?" I ask, patting his head. "I bet that's breaking the rules too and I don't even care."

Turns out, neither does Gordon. I finish up in the kitchen and turn out the lights. Brush my teeth, put on my pajamas, and get comfortable on the futon. Fortunately, Gordon is a very good dog and doesn't hog more than his half. It's nice not to be alone.

CHAPTER SIX

As a peace offering, I make Ed a thermos of hot coffee and leave it sitting on the kitchen counter. Since I don't know how he takes his coffee, I don't put in any milk or sugar. No idea what time he gets out of bed, either. Perhaps he's in there, listening to my footsteps, waiting for me to leave. Though he might also be fast asleep, completely unconcerned with me and not planning on waking up for hours yet. Gordon, meanwhile, is curled up on his designated dog bed over by the couch being absolutely no help. He's already been outside for a short walk so he could pee on the local flora and is now ready for a nap. With around twenty hours of beauty sleep a day, no wonder he looks so good.

I should probably leave Ed a note explaining not only the lack of dairy and any sweetening additions to the brew, but also what time I made it. It would be a nice touch.

Problem is, I don't seem to own a pen. The guy who robbed me really took everything that made me who I was. Memory. Phone. Handbag.

My cool new library-card-style cotton tote (got it from work) doesn't contain much. Money, cell, lip balm, and a book. The book is a fantasy this time, *Uprooted* by Naomi Novik.

But yeah . . . about that pen.

None in the kitchen drawers or lurking around the table and mostly tidy countertop. His art supplies include a case of pencils, though they look both special and expensive. I doubt he wants me using them to write silly notes.

The only place left I can think of is the desk in the spare room. Nothing on the top apart from a couple of folders filled with bills and receipts. A slither of guilt warns me against going through his shit, but my intentions are pure. I'm not reading up on his financials or anything. His privacy is mostly being maintained. I just want to leave him a note, and it *is* my temporary room, and he did tell me to make myself at home.

Time's a-wasting, and I'm due at work. My kingdom for a pen.

In the top drawer are scissors, tape, some Post-its, an eraser, and—gasp, oh yes, at long last—a couple of pens. One looks crusty and about ten years dead. I test the second against the palm of my hand and bingo. We're good to go.

Only, wait . . . an old, slightly worn, small blue velvet box sits near the back of the drawer. Half hidden from sight.

Without thought, I lift it out, carefully cracking the lid.

"Holy shit," I mutter.

Because there, sitting on a bed of white satin, is the most beautiful thing I've ever seen. Jewelry-wise, at least. It's white gold with a round diamond and decorative metal lacework. Antique, obviously. An engagement ring, equally as obvious. It's sweet and pretty and all of the things I'm not.

"Give me that." Ed snatches the jewelry box out of my hand, his jaw set. He's only wearing loose sleep pants—and holy shit, his chest. So much skin and ink. Half-naked Ed is wildly distracting. Lots of unhappy on his face, however. "The fuck were you doing going through my things?"

"I'm sorry. I wasn't spying or anything; I was just looking for a pen," I say, holding up my graffitied hand. "See?"

"What the hell . . . to draw on yourself?"

"To leave you a note to go with the coffee I made you."

He just shakes his head, the box gripped tight in his fist. "Just stay out of my things."

"O-of course. Sorry. Again."

The man about-faces, heading straight toward the bathroom. I wisely do not say another word as he slams the door shut.

After this, I go to work. Kind of, sort of wondering if the locks will be changed by the time I return. It might be for the best.

"If sorting it out in bed isn't an option, then filling his stomach is always your next best bet."

I wince. "I don't know. It was making him coffee that got me into this mess."

"No, it was sticking your nose where it had no business being that got you into this mess," says Iris, sounding far surer and wiser than I.

"But—"

"You were just looking for a pen. Yes." She clucks her tongue. "And when you found the pen, did you stop looking? No, you did not. Now go over to the recipe section and get busy."

"I feel judged."

"I don't know," says Frances, sipping coffee on the couch. "Seems like she kind of has a point there."

I just flip her the bird.

"Real mature, Clem."

"What if I buy him something?" I ask.

"Why don't you try making something with your own two hands?" asks my sister. Two against one isn't fair. "Invest some time and effort into your apology."

With a heavy sigh, I sit on the floor in front of the cookbooks. "Who do you think the ring was for, anyway? I mean, I doubt it was for me, right?"

After a minute or so of silence, I finally look up to find them both gazing at me with wonder. Maybe a little horror too.

Iris just blinks. "Honey, you cannot possibly be that stupid. Tell me you're not."

"Maybe they hit her harder than we realized," says Frances.

Give me strength. These two are theoretically meant to be on my side, but some days it really doesn't feel like it. Though I guess their version of the truth is better than having people try to feed me bullshit. Still . . . "I know we probably haven't been broken up long enough for him to be proposing to the brunette I saw him with at the restaurant. But the ring could have been meant for someone he dated before me."

Frances shakes her head. "No. He actually asked me if I thought you'd like an antique ring or if you'd prefer a new one. Wanted to be sure you got what you wanted."

"When did this happen?"

"Must have been about three months ago. Guess he was just waiting for the right moment to pop the question," she says. "And then everything kind of imploded."

"He wanted to marry me?" My shoulders slump. This was one piece of my history I could have done without ever learning. "Marriage . . . holy shit. That's big. Huge. I didn't realize we were anywhere near that stage. I mean, I knew we were serious and everything, but . . . I feel like the biggest asshole alive."

"Now you're just being dramatic," chides Iris.

"You shouldn't have agreed with his idea about me moving in, Frances."

"Please." My sister groans. "You know you were desperate to spend more time with the man. I pretty much did you a favor."

I admit to nothing. The thought of Ed and me planning a long-term future together, possibly involving white picket fences and two-point-five children, has blown my mind. Till death do us part and all that. There are no words. No wonder I broke his heart, thinking he'd cheated on me. Everything considered, the man couldn't have been more serious about our relationship if he'd tried.

"But your safety had to come first anyway. On the off chance you're being targeted, changing your location and making sure you're not alone more of the time is best."

I disagree, but keep my mouth shut. Instead, I pull out a book.

Ed's opinion matters to me. He matters to me. So it's time to take charge. Even if that means groveling.

It's a bit after six o'clock when Ed walks in the door, keys jangling in his hand. Gordon walks over to greet him for a pat, his tail wagging double time. The table is set, the scent of roast chicken and vegetables in the air. Along with a fainter hint of lemon cleanser. I've been busy.

This would be easier if my heart didn't get overexcited at the sight of him. If I didn't want his approval and affection. But you can't demand shit from people. You can only give of yourself and hope for it to be reciprocated.

Ed stops cold, head cocked. "What's going on?"

"I, uh . . . we need to talk. Can we talk?"

"We're already talking." His gorgeous face is like stone. All strong angles and no nonsense. "What's up, Clem? You made dinner?"

"Yeah, I got off work early."

"Obviously." His gaze moves around the room. "See you did some tidying up too."

I just nod. He can witness the glory of his now shining toilet and bathroom tiles later. Every possible inch of his pad has been scrubbed, wiped, swept, mopped, or dusted. And no drawers or cupboards were looked into. I've learned my lesson. The goal here is to undo what harm I've done, unintentional and otherwise. If I haven't quite accomplished that, at least I tried.

"And you packed your bags."

I stare down at the suitcase at my feet. "This wasn't a good idea, me being here. It was generous of you to open your home to me, but this place should be your sanctuary and that doesn't work with me here."

He says nothing.

"My ride will be along soon." I attempt a smile. It's doesn't really happen. "I'm going to go stay at this old B&B I found in the West End. Reasonably close to work, good security, there's always someone at the front desk, and they gave me a great deal since I booked in for a couple of weeks. Since my payout from the bank came in, I can afford it for a while."

His gaze narrows. "You've already organized all this?"

"Yes."

His fingers slowly curl in on themselves, gripping the keys tight. Gordon whines softly, picking up on the weird vibe in the room. Poor puppy.

"I've never lived on my own. Not so that I remember, anyway. I'm kind of looking forward to it. Dinner's in the oven when you're ready."

He looks toward the kitchen and frowns. "How much cleaning did you do, exactly?"

"Quite a lot. Iris let me off work early." I just shrug. "This is my way of apologizing and saying thank you."

"I have a bad feeling I'm being an overly sensitive asshole."

I laugh. "I have a bad feeling I've been an asshole in general, so . . ."

At this, he laughs too, and maybe things aren't so bad. I made the right decision for both of us, I think. No, I know it. How the hell am I ever going to figure out who I am if I'm always being protected and monitored? There hasn't been another seizure. No crazy person followed me home. Not that Ed's place is home. But I'll be fine.

"Let me help you with the bags," he says.

"Thanks."

He takes the suitcase and box of books, leaving me with nothing to do except open the door. Gordon does not want to stay inside. The dog yips at me once in protest. Earlier, we had hugs and many pats. I even took some photos of him with my cell.

"You told Frances about this?" asks Ed.

"Not yet."

He raises his eyebrows in response.

"Clementine," a voice crawls down the dimly lit common hallway, coming from the front door. If I'd been on my own, it would have freaked me right out. A dude grins at me, gaze creeping over me in a way I do *not* like. "You're back? Or you're leaving again already? Damn. That was quick."

"Tim," Ed says, muscling past the man.

"Good to see you." Tim holds out his arms, coming toward me. And he's a nice-enough looking guy, but he's also a complete stranger.

Given how I feel about being touched in general, no fucking way am I letting him get close. So instead, I hold my hand out in the universal sign for stop and his arms flop back to his sides. The look on his face changes to surprise with a hint of resentment. But I don't want to tell my story to this random person. Something about him just feels off. Probably the creeper-gaze thing. Like talking to my tits is okay.

"Leave her alone, man," says Ed.

"What?" Tim sort of half-laughs. Like he knows he's being called out on something yet isn't willing to admit to it. "Thought we were friends."

"We're in a rush," Ed continues. "Come on, Clem."

He shrugs. "Fine. Just being neighborly."

Sidestepping the man, I follow Ed out. And the look he gives Tim back over his shoulder isn't happy.

Soon we're standing out on the curb, the night closing in. The air is crisp, a little cooler than it was a few weeks ago. Already I feel lighter, better. Not only about getting out of sight of Tim the creeper, but about knowing that giving Ed his space is the right thing to do.

"Who was that guy?" I ask.

"Rents one of the other condos on our floor. Always was a bit overly friendly toward you. Ignore him. Are you sure about this?"

"Yeah."

"You know you're breaking Gordon's heart." Ed hands my suitcase and then the box of books over to the driver to be put into the trunk.

"I'll miss him."

"You can still come visit."

"Maybe in a few months. Once things are more settled and I know what I'm doing."

"Okay. Be careful and don't lose my number."

"I won't," I say, weirdly gratified.

He opens the back door of the vehicle for me without comment. Gallant to the bitter end. The world doesn't deserve Ed Larsen. Or maybe it's just me who doesn't, because my mouth betrays me one last time. "For what it's worth, I don't think you cheated on me. I don't know how I reached that conclusion back then, how it happened exactly. But—"

"Thank you," he says, cutting me off. His eyes seem darker, more serious than ever. "I mean it, Clem. That was good to hear."

I nod, pleased that I got something right at last.

He closes the door, taking a step back. Ed and I don't say goodbye. But then, we've done this dance before, after his friend Tessa ripped into me the first time I visited. It felt final that time too, if I recall correctly. Though, this go-around, I know for certain that an era of my new life is over, the one where he was lingering on the fringes. It couldn't have ever worked. An ex that you dumped on suspicion of cheating. Total amnesia wiping out all memory of a person. Either of those things is capable of destroying a relationship. Add them together, and you get a perfect storm of don't-even-go-there.

From now on, if I want friends, I'm going to have to make them. If I want a man in my life, then I'm going to have to date. Eventually. There's no rush.

Before the car can pull away from the curb, Ed shouts out, "Wait!"

I turn toward him, confused.

He opens my door, mouth set and forehead furrowed. "Stay."

"What?"

"I'm asking you to stay."

I just blink. "Why?"

In the front seat, the driver turns around, giving us both tired looks.

"We just need a minute," says Ed, his jawline tense. "Because you're different now. I mean, you're still a pain in the ass, don't get me wrong. But you're a different kind of pain in the ass . . . one I think, given everything, I can deal with a bit better."

"I don't know . . ."

He swallows hard, gaze conflicted. "Look, what it comes down to is, if anything happened to you, I'd never forgive myself, okay? So I want you to stay."

"Make your mind up, people," growls the driver, shaking his head.

"I'm going to screw up again, Ed. It's a given."

He nods. "I know."

My mouth opens, but nothing comes out.

"You're a fucking mess, and honestly I don't know that I'm much better. But you going off on your own isn't the answer," he says, holding his hand out to me. "C'mon."

I still hesitate.

"Please, Clem."

Me and my bags are back on the sidewalk in no time with the driver happily disappearing into the night care of a twenty-dollar tip. I give Ed a worried look and he gives me one in return.

"Thank you," I say. "I hope you know what you're doing."

He just nods. "Yeah. Me too."

CHAPTER SEVEN

Life with Ed goes like this . . . I stumble out into the hallway the next morning to find him brushing his teeth. Only wearing a pair of soft navy sleep pants. Oral hygiene has never been so erotic. It's a lot to deal with first thing. My hormones don't quite know how to take it. And I don't mean to stare at his nipples, pecs, and all of the glory that is his chest region, but it happens. Oh boy does it happen.

"Um, hey," I say. "Hi."

Gordy wanders out of the room right after me. At the sight of Ed, his tail happily yet sleepily wags back and forth.

"Are you letting him crash on the futon with you?" Ed asks amid much white froth. "Clem?"

"No."

"Liar."

To avoid incriminating myself, I stay silent. It's possible that he's right. Eventually, I say, "I'm going to take this very good dog outside so he can do his business."

The half-naked man shakes his head at me before walking back into the bathroom. I go fetch Gordy's leash and a doggy poop bag to get the job done. We didn't talk much after my aborted attempt to leave last night. Both of us were on edge. Wary and cautious and other emotions like that. Instead, we ate dinner and watched *Die Hard* while sitting at opposite ends of the sofa. Awesome movie. Previous me had good taste in films. And men.

"You're off early," I say once I'm back inside and Gordy is wolfing down dog biscuits.

Ed is sadly now fully dressed in gray jeans, a white tee, and sneakers. "I'm walking you to work. If you hurry, we can go by the waterfront. It's a little out of the way, but you used to love it down there."

"That sounds great, but you don't have to."

"I'll take you to work and pick you up again. The book shop opens at ten and closes at six thirty, right?"

"Right, but—"

"It's fine, Clem." He shoves at me one of the two cups of coffee he'd been making. "Here, drink this, then go get ready."

"Okay. Thanks." I turn toward the hallway, then stop. "Is this what we used to be like in the morning? You making coffee and us sorting out our day?"

"Yeah, pretty much." He doesn't look up from the counter. "Sometimes I work late. So walking you to work at the bank was a way of fitting in more time together during the week."

"Right."

"You always took fucking forever in the bathroom."

"Guess I had more hair back then."

"Yeah. If I didn't get up first and get sorted, you'd be pissed at me for showering and fogging up the mirror while you were trying to do stuff."

"Sounds like a heinous crime to me. I don't know how you live with yourself."

The man almost smiles.

"Now tell me something good about when we were together."

"Hmm." He tosses the teaspoon into the sink. "I got to wake up to your face every morning. I used to like that."

I cup the warm mug in my hands, not sure what to say.

"Sometimes on your lunch break you'd go over to The Holy Donut," he says. "Pick up a box to bring into the parlor. Everyone loved you those days."

My stomach does some weird upside-down type thing. It's the sound of his voice, deep and a little rough. Kind of distant, but not in a bad way. As if these memories are good ones for a change. Positive memories that include previous me not being high-maintenance or hellish or something similar. Amazing.

Even so, I feel conflicted about the ease with which he stirs all these emotions and desires within me. I try and keep reminding myself it has all gone south before. True, maybe he didn't cheat, but there must have been something wrong between us if it was possible for me to believe that he had. Or maybe I wanted out and the cheating accusation was just what I used to escape. Or maybe Ed was getting cold feet about proposing and my accusation was a good excuse to let me go. Either way, there's a nagging feeling in the back of my brain that I've been down this path before and it didn't end well for either of us.

And I wonder if he's thinking it too.

"Better get ready or we'll run out of time," he says, lifting the coffee to his lips. A clear indication he's done with this dialogue.

I swallow. "Right. Sure."

We walk along the waterfront down Commercial Street to get to work. It's a little longer, but the view is spectacular. The restaurants, hotels, and gift shops. The wharves, boats, and water. I enjoy being in the city and I love the smell of the ocean. Where Frances lives is nice, but it's not like this. Here there's a rush, a vitality, and loads of character. About what you'd expect for an old seaport with plenty of history.

Conversation goes back to being stilted following my question, but for once I don't mind. It's like we're making actual progress on moving past him not liking me. Maybe. It would be foolish to get carried away. There's a moment when he leaves me at the shop and pauses sort of leaning into me for a second. Like perhaps he was going to kiss me goodbye. Probably a leftover response from our coupledom days. I wouldn't have said no to a kiss, even something chaste and friendly-like on the cheek. It probably would have made things awkward for him, however.

So no kissing accidental or otherwise is best.

Frances comes in to visit. Interestingly enough, this occasion has less of a supervisory feel and more of a sisterly affection vibe for once. It's nice. We have lunch at an amazing oyster place on the waterfront. Iris even closes up the shop to come with us. Apparently she does this occasionally when cabin fever starts to settle in and she needs to get away from the books for an hour or two. With a few drinks in her, my boss tells the most amazing stories about her various ex-husbands. Despite having one die, one cheat, and one come out of the closet, she remains a hopeful romantic at heart. Currently, she's seeing the owner of a gelato shop a block over. He's a dapper Sicilian gent who's apparently killer in the sack—a detail I didn't need to know.

A little after six, Ed arrives to take me home. My insides sort of swoop at the sight of him. The want to not inconvenience him wars constantly within me against the need to be around him. If he knew, he'd be even quieter, more guarded. And he's being pretty damn silent as it is. I can barely get a word out of him. We pick up some more takeout, tacos this time. Turns out, I fucking love tacos. Then back at the condo, I watch another movie while he works. A pity. Because despite the whole clear division of areas on the couch and required physical space between us the night before, I enjoyed experiencing the movie with him. But tonight, not even Gordy's interested in hanging out with me. Maybe I smell funny or something.

"Oh my God." I sigh when it's over, relaxing back on the couch with my stress cushion still clutched tight against my chest. "I loved that movie so much."

"Yeah?" Ed sits at the table, drawing on a computer tablet. "It used to be another one of your favorites."

"It was a really great love story."

"Clem, you do know the movie's called *Terminator*? It's about a killer robot."

"I don't care. I mean, it's not a romance because strictly speaking it doesn't have a happy ending, but the love story in it is superb."

"Those are the rules, huh?"

"Those are the rules."

"The second one's pretty good too. I kind of envy you being able to watch them all over again for the first time."

I smile grimly. "Gotta be some perks to my situation."

"After the second one, though, the quality drops off. At least, that was what you always insisted. I asked you once what you had against movies made this century."

"Yeah?"

He nods. "You said these ones from the eighties were all your mother's favorites. That you used to watch them with her."

"Oh."

"Mind if I ask, have you been to see her grave?"

"No, I don't mind. But no," I say. "I suggested it to Frances once, but she shot the idea down pretty quickly. I think it's weird for her, still mourning Mom when I don't even remember."

He nods.

"Did you want to watch it with me? The second movie, I mean . . . if you feel like it." Hope is such a bitch. "No big deal if you don't. I was just thinking, it's only nine and—"

His jaw firms. "Pretty busy right now."

"Right. Sure."

Silence.

"What are you working on?"

"Just a piece for a client."

I wait, but no further information is forthcoming.

Gordon sleeps on in the corner on his bed. The very picture of doggy contentment. When someone hammers on the door, however, he bounds instantly to his feet. His ears start twitching, nose sniffing.

Ed frowns.

"Were you expecting someone?" I ask.

"No."

When he opens the door, all hell breaks loose. Or at least it sounds that way. A deep voice shouts out greetings followed by much manly hugging and slapping of backs. Gordy shuffles elatedly around the newcomer's feet, tail wagging like mad. I just wait on the couch.

"'the hell are you doing here?" asks Ed, not unhappily.

The new guy is about as tall as Ed with dark hair. Lots of ink. He has a motorbike helmet in one hand and a six-pack of beer in the other. "Heard you and Clem broke up. Figured you'd need cheering up."

"That happened a while back."

A shrug from the stranger. "Well, I've been busy on the West Coast. Hadn't talked to Mom for a while so I only just heard. How are you doing? Never did like that girl, too fucking high-strung."

"Man—"

"I'm telling you, you can do much better."

"Really? 'Cause I seem to remember you trying to come on to her a time or two."

"I'd had a few drinks. I was just being friendly!"

Ed grabs the back of his neck. "Right."

"I mean, at least you didn't marry her and then have everything go to hell. Imagine if you two had kids. It would have been a damn mess," he says. "Better to get out now when things aren't so complicated. Or is she being a bitch about this place?"

Ed just turns and looks at me. His face is drawn, expression distinctly pained.

Then the man also turns, taking me in with surprise. "Ah, shit. Hey, Clem. Good to see you."

I lift a hand in greeting. "Hi."

"Sorry about calling you a bitch. And high-strung. And the other stuff."

"No worries," I say with a somewhat forced smile.

"Clem, this is my little brother, Leif." Ed takes the helmet off of him, placing it on the table. Next he gets busy with the beer. "Leif, Clem sustained a head injury a short while back resulting in amnesia. She doesn't know you. She barely knows me. So go easy, okay? And probably stop speaking shit about her—that might be nice."

"You're messing with me, right?" asks Leif, accepting a beer and taking a seat opposite me. The resemblance between them is obvious now. They're both tall and built along the same lean but hard lines. The same high cheekbones and beautiful eyes. Masculine pretty. But sized so that you wouldn't want to mess with them if you had half a brain. The internet said Larsen was a Danish name. Maybe they have Viking blood in them.

"No, he's not fucking with you," I say.

Leif turns back to his brother. "Jesus, Ed, you haven't told Mom?"

"I'll tell her when I'm ready. Things have been complicated enough."

Leif exhales hard. "Okay. So was it a car accident or what?"

"You don't have to talk about it if you don't want to." Ed intervenes, handing me a beer as well.

"It's fine," I say. "Someone tried to kill me. Well . . . they were robbing me, you know? Hit me over the head and took my bag."

"Shit."

"Yeah."

Ed settles once again at the opposite end of the couch. It's like I have cooties. Or ex-girlfriend germs. "Clem's staying here for a while. It's closer to her work and stuff."

"No problem." Leif takes a swig of beer while scratching Gordy behind the ears. "I'll sleep on the sofa."

"That your way of asking if you can stay?" asks Ed with a faint smile.

Leif grins. "You bastard. I haven't seen you in almost half a year and you don't want to spend time with me? Your own brother? Hell, I came back to the East Coast just for you."

"No you didn't," says Ed, his smile broader now. Cue the tingles. So attractive. "Tell the truth, asshole."

Now Leif grimaces, making a show out of holding out on the answer. "I may have slept with someone I perhaps shouldn't have slept with. Several times, in fact. It happens."

"Told you, don't fuck where you work."

"Oh that's rich coming from you." His brother laughs. "Besides, I was only a guest artist there. It was never meant to be permanent. You got room for me at the parlor or not?"

"Of course I do. Did you tell your old clients you were coming back to town?"

"I put something on Instagram."

"Good."

"You're a tattoo artist as well?" I ask. "And what do you mean, that's rich coming from Ed?"

Leif studies me, gaze curious. Or maybe just a little stunned.

"Yeah, Clem, he tattoos as well," says Ed. "We both apprenticed with my uncle. He used to own the parlor."

"Christ, this is weird," mumbles Leif, studying me.

"Shut up, you idiot. Don't make her feel uncomfortable."

"Sorry, sorry. It's just . . . amnesia. Shit."

"You already said that." I drink my beer. As much as I'd like to press the point about the other question, Ed is relaxed and happy. He's even sitting on the same item of furniture as me again. Questions can wait. I'm so hungry for his words, for his attention. Not that it stops my brain from turning things over. "Hold up. It says *and sons* on the shop window."

"Uncle Karl thought it sounded better than *and nephews*," says Ed. "I used to hang around so much he told me to pick up a broom or get out. That's pretty much how I started. Then Leif got interested too and he had both of us annoying the hell out of him every chance we got."

Leif gets up, heading into the kitchen. "Good times. Whiskey?"

"Above the fridge."

"In case I forget to mention it later, I was always your favorite Larsen, Clementine. You absolutely adored me, okay?"

After the whole high-strung bitch thing it's just not so believable. "Got it, Leif. Thanks for the information."

"Not that it was ever awkward or anything. Nothing like that. Entirely platonic. For you, I was basically an unattainable object of adoration."

"I can see why you had to flee the West Coast," said Ed, shaking his head but grinning all the same. "You've been here less than ten minutes and we're already realizing how good we had it before you showed up."

"What do you both specialize in?" I might have flipped through a few books on tattooing at the shop. What can I say? Everything about the man makes me curious. And if having his brother here gets him talking, then Leif can have the futon and whatever the hell else he wants. "Traditional or realism or water color or—"

"I do neotraditional," answers Ed. "Like the piece on your shoulder."

"Same as what's on your arms?"

"Some of it is." He displays the blue rose on the back

of his right hand. "On my back there's a more traditional Japanese piece and there's some fine line work on my side that Leif did. That's what he does. But I've got a few different styles on me."

"Did you do any of them yourself?"

Leif laughs, carrying over three glasses with a couple of fingers' worth of liquor in each.

"Yeah." Ed takes his glass of whiskey, smiling again. "On my thigh, when I was starting out."

"What did you do?"

"An anchor and a Celtic knot and some other stuff. My legs are a bit of a mess. Leif's are the same."

Leif nodded. "It's not all our doing. We both let a couple of apprentices practice on us over the years. So yeah, the legs get to be a bit of a dog's breakfast."

"Is your uncle still alive?"

"No. He passed away a while back. Cancer, the same as your mom," Ed says. "Only his was lung cancer from smoking a pack of cigarettes a day his whole damn life. The man was lucky to last as long as he did."

"I'm sorry."

"Thanks."

"To Uncle Karl." Leif raises his glass and Ed and I do likewise. We all drink.

"So." Leif settles back into his chair once again. "You two aren't together, but you're living together? How does that work? Because from what I heard from Mom, the breakup was like Death Star levels of . . ." He mimes something exploding with his hands, throwing in some rather disturbing and violent noises as accompaniment.

"Death Star?" I ask.

"Sci-fi movie. We'll watch it sometime," says Ed.

"And I'm not talking the original version either," Leif continues. "No sir. The digitally remastered one, where you can feel the explosion's shock wave through your whole body."

His exuberance only makes me frown harder. "I think I get the picture."

"It's just while I get Clem her down payment back and have the deed changed and everything," said Ed, returning to his brother's question.

Leif's brows pull together. "Thought Mom said you had that sorted?"

The expression on Ed's face . . .

"Jesus," says Leif, looking to Ed's face, and mine, and back again. "Brother, my apologies. But I cannot even begin to keep up with what you are and aren't telling our parents or your ex-girlfriend these days."

"It's done?" I ask, setting my glass down on the coffee table.

After swearing under his breath, Ed shoots his brother another foul look. Leif swallows down his whiskey and looks elsewhere. Anywhere that's not me or Ed.

"Well?" I ask.

He relents. "The money's in the bank as of a few days ago; I just have to transfer it over to your account. I'll do it tomorrow. Paperwork's not ready yet, though. I was waiting on that, but I guess it doesn't matter."

"No, we should do it the right way. Wait on the paperwork and everything."

"So fucking complicated," mutters Leif. "Remind me to never have a serious girlfriend."

"Thing is, Clem, I didn't want you using it as an excuse to leave," Ed says, gaze troubled. "I know this is awkward, but you're still safer here with me."

I frown.

"We're getting on okay, aren't we? Basically?"

I don't know what to say. The truth doesn't seem wise. And yay me for not blurting it out for once.

"Wait, she's in danger?" asks Leif.

"We don't know, and I don't want to risk it." Ed downs his drink in one go before rising to go get the bottle. "It's not a big deal. The reasons for you staying here haven't changed."

Leif sits up straight. "What the hell's going on?"

"Someone trashed my car," I say. "Took a tire iron to it or something. We don't know who or why. It may be about Frances being a cop and have nothing to do with me being assaulted at all. But your brother has kindly been babysitting me just in case there's a big bad dude out to get me." I look him over and realize something. "You know, you're not going to fit on the sofa; you're too tall."

"I'm six foot two and I'm the runt of the family." Leif smiles, but it's a distracted and small thing. "I'll be okay—don't worry about me. I'm more worried about you, right now."

"I can take the sofa. You have the futon in the spare room."

Ed tops up everyone's drinks before sitting back down. "You're not sleeping on the sofa. You heard him:

he'll be fine. And you're staying here for as long as it takes to make sure you're safe and okay."

"We don't even know if there is a problem."

"We don't know that there's not. Didn't we just have this argument?"

"That was like twenty-four hours ago," I say. "It's clearly time for us to revisit the topic."

He downs half his drink. "No, we're good."

"We're not. You're not. You've been avoiding me since you walked me to work this morning. You know you have." Okay, so my gift of blurting has obviously returned.

Leif's gaze jumps back and forth between us while Gordy whines slightly.

"That's crazy." Ed scoffs. "How could I possibly be avoiding you while walking you to work and picking you up again? We've been in the same room for the last few hours!"

"Mentally and emotionally you are avoiding me. Not that I blame you." I hold up a hand. "I do not blame you. But ever since you made me coffee this morning and I asked you a question about us and you answered it honestly and openly, which I really appreciated, by the way. But, well, ever since then, things have been a little weird again."

Ed looks at me.

"Not that we're in a relationship. I didn't mean it like that."

Ed just looks at me some more. He's really not happy.

"It's just that I thought we were going to be friends. If you've changed your mind about that, then I guess I'd like to know," I say. "Promise I won't get upset or anything."

Nothing from Ed.

"I've annoyed you again. Sorry."

"Don't be sorry. He'll get over it," says Leif. "In the meantime, I'll be your friend."

"Leif," growls Ed.

His brother, however, does not take the warning. "Why don't I share the futon with you, Clem? You'll be extra safe and we can be as friendly as you like. I like the short hair, by the way. Very cool and edgy."

My hand goes to my fringe, checking it's still in place hiding the scar. "Ed said it was punk rock."

"Totally."

Meanwhile, Ed's lips disappear into a fine pissed-off line, then he gulps down the rest of his whiskey.

"Lucky I'm back," his brother continues. "Since you two are broken up and not getting along particularly well, why don't I start taking Clem to work and picking her up on the bike?"

"A motorcycle?" I ask with interest. "I've never been on one of those. Well, not that I remember, anyway."

"It's great. You'll love it." He frowns. "Wait a minute. Would you have forgotten ever having sex as well? Hell, you must be like an emotional virgin. All I can say is that it's a good thing for you I have a particular specialty—"

"You are not putting a woman recovering from a recent head injury on the back of your bike, dickhead." Ed's still growling. "It's not safe. And stop flirting with her."

"Shouldn't that be her choice?" asks Leif. "The bike and the flirting?"

I sigh. "He probably has a point about the bike and I'm not actually interested in you that way. Thanks, though."

Ed just looks to heaven. No help, however, appears to be forthcoming.

"C'mon, what about at least sharing the futon?" Leif winks at me, not the least bit put off. "Seriously, if you've sat on that couch for more than an hour you know it's impossible to sleep on. You don't mind, do you, Clem?"

"Whatever's easiest," I answer honestly. But it's apparently the wrong answer because Ed's jaw starts doing the tensing thing times about a thousand. Much more pressure and his teeth are going to break. My bad, again. "I'll take the sofa."

"Enough of this," says Ed. "You're sleeping with me and I'm still taking you to work."

"What?"

"You heard me. I'll keep taking you to work."

"Um. Can we please revisit the first bit again, please?"

"We can share my room. That'll be easiest." Ed fills up his glass once more. I'm not sure if it's me or his brother driving him to drink. Both, maybe?

"I guess the mattress is really big," I say, tone most dubious. Me and Ed in the same bed. I pick up my glass and down the lot, letting it burn my throat out. Whoa. Tears of whiskey joy leak down my cheeks. Alcoholic courage come to me. Fill me with your faux bravery.

"Take it easy," says Ed. "Just sip it."

I nod. "Okay. Good idea."

He refills both his glass and mine. His brother, however, he very much ignores. "You said I wasn't talking to you, so what do you want to talk about?"

"Oh, no, I'm fine for now. Thanks. I kind of just used up all of my words for the time being. You two should catch up, though, you haven't seen each other in a while."

Meanwhile, Leif is hiding a smile behind his own glass of liquor. "Fuck this is bizarre. She's so different to how she used to be."

"She's right here." I wave. "Why do people do that, talk about you as if you're not there? It's so rude."

"I figure you're about fifty-three percent different," says Ed with a softer smile.

"Really?"

"Yep. I did the math. You only react the way I expect you to about half of the time, so . . ."

"Huh." I don't say anything else, instead pondering the ramifications of his statement. It could possibly mean I'm still horrible, but best not to take it that way. All in all, I think I'm okay with who I am so far. Most of the time.

"She's a shitload more fun than she used to be," continues Leif.

"So glad I can entertain you," I say. "Is there just the two of you or do you have other siblings?"

"We've also got an older brother, Niels. He's the strong silent type."

My gaze moves tellingly to Ed.

"Nah," says Leif. "Eddy's actually pretty happy and easygoing most of the time. But I'm guessing the breakup kind of messed with his whole joie de vivre. I mean, you and he were—"

"You're right, Clem," interrupts Ed. "It is rude when people talk about you as if you're not in the room."

"Sorry," I say.

Leif just laughs.

They start talking shop then. Discussing mutual tattooing acquaintances Leif saw during his time over in the Pacific Northwest. I slowly sip my whiskey and pat Gordy when he comes over to say hi before retiring once more to his doggy bed. Such a good dog.

Leif's comment about Instagram has me thinking. If previous me had social media accounts, she must have deleted them after the breakup. I've done multiple searches and checked with Frances just to be sure. Time to fix that. It'd be nice to dip my toe into something. To have some sort of digital record of my life. Playing with my phone, I settle on Instagram. Of course, I'll have no followers, but never mind. This would be for me, not other people. Putting a photo in a public place makes my existence more real than just carrying them around on my cell. And more permanent. Phones can be stolen. Memories can be lost. But once it's out there and online, it'll take more than just a random mugging to lose it all.

Sitting on the couch, with Ed and Leif's banter in the background forming a comforting white noise, it takes me barely five minutes to set up the account. And just like that I have a digital footprint. It makes me strangely relaxed. Like I've just taken out insurance somehow.

Safety wise, my account is locked, but still probably best not to use my real name. So instead I go for @amnesia_chick. Might as well own it . . . in secret. I start with a picture of my Adidas Originals blue suede sneakers. I may or may not have bought them because they're similar to the ones Ed wears, only his are green. But the shoes give a hint of my aesthetic or style or whatever the hell you want to call it while also suggesting that I'm perhaps going places. Not sure where yet, but never mind. It's a nice message.

There. I have a social media presence now. Nothing can stop me.

Eventually, I guess the lull of conversation sends me to sleep. The soothing sound of Ed's voice. I wake up the next morning alone in his bed. Oh, God, Ed carried me to bed. Iris would say this is an act of high romance and I'm not sure I disagree. If I wasn't already lying down, I might even swoon. Though I doubt Ed would see it as any sort of romantic thing. Never mind. His sheets and pillows smell wonderful. And I try not to dwell overly long on the part where he must have slept next to me all night of his own free will or I'd never actually get up. Just lie there dreaming all day.

For the first time, I take a little longer getting ready, trying out some basics. A bit of concealer, mascara, and a tinted lip gloss. The shade is called Dolce Vida. No particular reason for the extra effort. It just seems like if previous me used to be immaculate in her morning routine, then it won't hurt me to give it a try and see how I like it. After all, I don't need to do the exact opposite of everything she did. I don't need to strip myself back to the bare bones. That would just be silly. While I suspect she and I have some basic differences, we can have the occasional thing in common as well. Same name, vagina, attraction to Ed . . . it's not a big deal. Despite not understanding why she made certain decisions, it's not like I hate her or anything.

And the makeup looks good.

CHAPTER EIGHT

"You're mooning again," says Iris, handing me a cloth. "Dust while you dream."

"I'm neither mooning nor dreaming."

She snorts. "Oh, honey. If daydreams had frequent flier miles you'd be halfway around the world by now from all of your ruminating over a certain someone."

"No idea what you're talking about." I get busy cleaning. "I'm focusing solely on my job."

"Are you now?"

"Did you know there's a coffee-table book dedicated solely to genital piercings here?"

"Of course I'm aware of it," she says. "Don't think I don't know you're trying to change the subject, either. But there's nothing wrong with a Prince Albert proudly displayed. As long as it's not in public, of course."

"Huh."

She smirks. "You're very judgmental for one so

young."

"I'm not judgmental. Just a little surprised."

"Why shouldn't I stock books on sex and the human body? Both are beautiful natural things worth celebrating."

Not knowing what to say, I dust my heart out.

"Good Lord, are you embarrassed by intimacy and the naked form?" She clucks her tongue. "Clementine, for shame."

"What do you want from me?" Leif's words the other night may have been said in jest, but the truth was a serious reality lay behind them. "Care of the assault, I may have well have regrown my hymen. I have nil practical experience and I've never even seen someone in the flesh totally naked apart from myself. It is on my to-do list, though."

"You know, I never thought of it that way."

"It's the truth. While I know that I've definitely done it, I don't actually remember doing it, so . . ."

"Maybe you should ask Ed to help you with that." There's an evil sparkle in her eye. "See, you're frowning. I say his name and you frown, every time."

"Pretty sure he'd be too busy schtupping the brunette from the restaurant to be worrying about my sexual needs regardless of where I'm sleeping."

"Hmm."

"And I look after myself. I masturbate."

A young guy who just walked in the door stops and blinks.

"Welcome to Braun Books," I say with a smile. "Let

me know if there's anything I can help you with."

He blinks again, still staring.

"To do with books."

With a jerky nod, he heads back to the secondhand section. I'm rocking this work and socializing thing. Just ask me.

"Well, I should hope you're able to see to your own needs," says Iris, picking up the conversation. "Did you watch porn to learn how?"

"Masturbation doesn't really fall under episodic memory. Its more things like personal facts and details of events that were wiped out. Muscle memory works just fine."

"Ah. Well, if you need a little help or are just after some variety, there's a wonderful selection of vibrators and other toys at Delilah's just a short walk from here."

"Sounds interesting. I might check it out sometime. Thanks."

"Personally, I've found a Lelo Lily to be a wonderful investment," she continues. "But you have to take the time to find a personal massager that works for you."

The guy in the secondhand section obviously has issues with sex or at least discussions regarding same, because he all but flees the premises. Whatever. It's around about five o'clock. Time for the after-work crowd to hopefully be lured in for some literature. The woman who struts in, however, is very familiar and probably not a customer. And there's no other word for how she moves. I couldn't pull off such confidence if I tried.

"We need to talk," she announces.

"Hi, Tessa."

Iris just looks between me and the beautiful black woman with intricate tattoos swirling up her arms. Tessa wears ripped jeans and studded boots. A chunky knit top that falls off one shoulder. Runway models wished they had it so good. In my ballet flats, jeans, and *Where the Wild Things Are* tee (got it from the shop), I do not compare. Oh well. At least I made some effort this morning, or I'd be feeling even further out of my league. And while I've seen an instance in a movie where that tone of voice was being used affectionately and jokingly between people, this is not one of those times. Not even a little. But Iris is beaming so I guess she figures it is. I don't even think Tessa noticed her standing there at first.

"Iris, this is Tessa, a friend of Ed's," I say. "Tessa, my boss, Iris."

Tessa nods. "Ma'am."

"Hello!" Iris smiles before turning back to me. "Clementine, why don't you grab your bag and go have a drink with your friend? Try out that new little wine bar along the way!"

"Oh, we are not friends," says Tessa.

"We're really not," I agree. "Are you sure you don't want a hand closing up?"

"No, no. Antonio will be here soon to help me. You go." Iris flaps her hands at me. "See you tomorrow, dear."

I ditch my cloth and wash my hands, grab my bag and head back out to face the woman waiting. The very angry woman. No idea what it is she wants to discuss. After the last time we crossed paths at Ed's when she ripped me a new one, I'd have thought talking to me would be the last thing of interest. She and I were friends, once. But those days are clearly gone.

"Ready?" I ask, gesturing toward the door.

"Follow me," she orders.

Out into the street we go. Tessa cuts through the sidewalk traffic with style and grace while I try to keep up. A block and a half along, she abruptly turns and disappears down a narrow stairway. The wine bar is in the basement of a building, all low lighting and atmosphere. Behind the bar is a wall full of dark gleaming bottles. People occupy maybe half of the tables. Guess it's still a little early for the night crowd.

Tessa sits at a small table and gestures to a waiter. "Two of the house cabernet, thanks."

"I drink red wine?"

"You do now." Hands joined resting on the table, she just stares at me. "We have a problem, Clem."

I wait.

Eventually, she continues, with one word: "Ed."

"What about him? Is he okay?"

"He would be if you'd stay the hell out of his life," she says. "I get that you don't remember anything, so let me explain this clearly. Ed is more than my boss, he's my friend. We've known each other a long time and I am not going to stand by and watch while you mess with his head again. You are not good for him. So you need to get away from him."

"I tried to move out. He asked me to stay."

"Try harder."

I raised my brows. "Okay. Can we visit the part where I'm not convinced it's even any of your business?"

"I should just let you hurt him again?"

"What have I done now?"

"You told him you no longer think he cheated on you."

"He told you about that?"

"Eventually," she says. "Leif let it slip that you were staying with him and then it all came out. Clem, did you think for one moment how that might affect him? About what it would mean to him, you saying that?"

"Yeah, I thought he'd be relieved. A weight off his shoulders."

She glares back at me.

"So what? I should just move to Alaska? Would that suit you?"

"I was going to suggest somewhere a little farther, at least the Yukon. But Alaska might be okay."

Our drinks arrive and thank fuck for that. My throat is parched, my hackles riled, and my head even more confused than before. I down half of the glass in one gulp, the heavy tasting-room temperature aged grape juice going down a treat. Much better than whiskey. Tessa apparently feels much the same since she also throws back a good portion of her wine. Next I text Ed to tell him something's come up so I'll find my own way home today and not to worry.

"Look," I say, diving straight back in, "It's great that he has friends who care so much about him. But this is still none of your business."

Her lips are an unforgiving line. "You didn't see him after the breakup. You wrecked him."

"Yeah, well, apparently I wrecked me too."

"I'm not joking. I've never seen him like that before and I do not wish to ever again."

My shoulders tense. Maybe it's the thought of Ed hurting. Or maybe it's the hate I'm facing. Either way, perfect excuse to drink more wine. "Why do you think I offered to move out of his place? I could see it wasn't working. That he wasn't happy."

"And I'm supposed to thank you for behaving like a half-decent human for two seconds?"

"How about just acknowledging that he's an adult who can make his own choices?"

She casts the ceiling a pained glance before drinking more wine, all while signaling to the waiter for another round. "Grown-ass men are idiots. How have you not discovered this yet?"

I laugh.

"Seriously?"

"Look, Tessa, for what it's worth, I'm sorry for the trouble I caused you," I say. "And I have no intention of hurting Ed. I'm not . . . that's not something I want to see happen ever again."

She scoffs, sitting back and crossing her arms.

"I don't know what else to tell you."

"You're not going to get out of his life," she says, her words jagged and sharp.

"Let me check I'm following you on this." My voice matches her harsh tone perfectly. "Previously, you hated me because I broke up with Ed, believing that he'd cheated on me. Now you're pissed off with me for staying with him and believing that he didn't. You'll excuse me for not upending my world on the basis of your current mood. It's not your choice to make."

She shakes her head. "Give me strength. Anytime now he'll be back to chasing after your ass. He can't help himself when it comes to you. You're like an itch under his skin."

I've never been compared to a rash before, yet it doesn't sound like a wholly bad thing. "Really?"

"Stop smiling. This is not good."

"Sorry."

"God, look at you, acting all cute and dumb. Do you really believe this works on me?" she asks, head cocked. "Or is this honestly who you think you are now?"

I finish off my wine. "I'm still figuring out who I am. But whatever I decide, you hate me and think I'm full of shit. Message received loud and clear. In the future, though, if you want to rant at me, can you stay the hell away from my job? Text me, I'll meet you somewhere. I don't mind."

"You don't mind?" she repeats, disbelieving.

"Whatever. It's not like I have much of a social life." I shrug, turning to scope out the bar. "Why are they taking so long with our drinks?"

Tessa sips the last of her wine, assessing me over the rim of her glass. "Interesting."

"How so?"

"I'd have expected you to be storming off all butt hurt

by now. There's a reason why he always treated you like a precious doll."

"Why should I storm off?" I ask. "No offense, but I don't know you. Your opinion doesn't really mean a hell of a lot to me. Ed says you and I used to be close, though those days are clearly over."

"Damn right they are. Any trust I had in you is long gone and you destroyed it."

"That time at Ed's place, you said I tried to drag you into the break-up. I am sorry that happened."

"Save it."

"All right," I say. "You really think Ed still wants me?"

"Men just follow wherever their dicks lead them and his is like a compass needle when it comes to you."

Hope flares up inside me despite my best efforts. I think I'd like to be his true north. But no, that's a bad idea. Our history is beyond complicated. On the other hand, however, I'd dearly love the chance to crawl all over him naked. I mean, we must have done it hundreds of times. Maybe more. Afternoon sex. Drunk sex. Sunday morning sex. Angry sex. Lazy sex. Shower sex. Post argument make-up sex. And who knows what else? It seemed beyond unfair that I could have such a history and not enjoy the memories of it.

"What did you do to your hair?" asks Tessa, before nodding to the waiter who is placing full glasses in front of us.

"I cut it myself. I like it shorter." We each pick up our new drinks. I hold mine out. "So here's to not being friends."

"I can drink to that."

It's strange, but Tessa's animosity is actually kind of comforting. At least I know what she's thinking. She straight up tells me. Other people can be so hard to read. Tessa asks me about what it was like waking up at the hospital with no idea who I was. How I wound up working at the bookstore. What it's like to have no memories, no real history. I ask her about how we met (through Ed) and about her life in general. After some initial hesitation, she actually starts to open up. The wary gaze never goes away, but she talks to me about her life and her past. Maybe it's the wine. Or maybe it's just a leftover from our once upon a time friendship. I don't know. She tells me how she and Nevin also met through Ed. Nevin was a client of his, though she soon stole him and kept him. Nevin is a teacher who used to be in the army. Guess his experiences there scarred him some since he suffers from insomnia and often goes jogging at night to wear himself out. Explains why he's so buff, I guess. They've been talking about maybe having a child sometime soon and Nevin has volunteered to stay up with the baby when necessary. At least his insomnia will be serving a purpose. Also, they've been together for four years.

In the end, we sit there through one bottle of wine and then I order another because why not? I've never actually been drunk before and we're just two not-friends spending quality time together.

As foretold, Ed does indeed eventually appear. Though I prefer to believe it comes from concern more so than just chasing after my ass, as Tessa described. His displeased face is back in play. "Ladies."

"See," says Leif, stealing a couple of chairs from a neighboring table. "You completely overreacted. No one's even bleeding or wounded yet."

"You didn't say you were going to visit Clem." Ed gazes at Tessa. Oh dear, he's seriously not happy. Even I get served some of his cranky glare. "Iris had to tell me where I could find you two."

"Am I supposed to need your permission?" snaps Tessa.

"Wait," I say. "Am *I* supposed to need your permission?"

At this, Tessa laughs.

"Ed?" I cock my head.

"Of course not," he says. "I was just worried about you."

Tessa throws some money on the table. Then she slings her designer handbag over her shoulder before rising to her feet. "What did I tell you? Just like a compass."

"Not going to stay for a catch-up?" asks Leif, signally the waiter for more glasses.

"Another time. Nevin and I have dinner plans." She smacks a kiss on his cheek before heading for the door. Ed, she ignores completely. Guess she's still annoyed about him not telling her I was staying at his condo. Or something.

The bar is busier now as people get off work and go for a drink. Music plays and people talk. It's a nice place. I'll have to remember to tell Iris. The alcohol is a happy warm buzz inside of me. I feel good. I look at Ed while swirling the wine in my glass all contemplative like. Another woman in the bar was doing it earlier and I thought it looked cool. "Her concern for you is intense. Like, seriously extreme."

Leif's forehead furrows in confusion. "Doesn't Clem know you two used to date?"

"She does now," grits out Ed, taking my glass from me and downing the wine.

Huh. "You and Tessa?"

"Yes."

I don't like the thought of them together. Of course, I don't like the thought of Ed being with anyone. I even get a little jealous over previous me. But Ed and all of the beauty that is Tessa. Ouch. They'd look so good together. Though she's with Nevin now so it's all in the past. But how distant is that past?

And just like that, the pieces start to click into place. Only they're pointed and sharp, each cutting into each other's space all too perfectly.

"Who did I think you were cheating with?" I ask.

Ed turns away.

The waiter deposits two fresh glasses on the table with a smile.

"Fuck." Leif helps himself to a glass of wine. "She doesn't know anything? You didn't tell her?"

"He doesn't like to talk about it," I say.

Ed's hand on the table curls into a fist. "Can you blame me?"

"I thought you were cheating on me with Tessa, didn't I?"

He just looks at me. Then he looks right through me.

But it all makes sense. "That's why you reacted the way you did when I joked that time about using an ex for sex. And when Leif said last night that you were being rich about telling him not to fuck where he worked."

"Yes," snarls Ed.

Leif rubs his hands over his face. "You should have told her. Shit."

"Why does Tessa hate me?" I asked, although I probably knew the answer.

Ed's nostril's flare. "Because you didn't stop at just breaking my heart. You called Nevin and told him she was cheating on him with me. Nevin absolutely lost it and the two of them had this massive fight. She loves him and she was your best friend and you did your utmost to try and break them up too."

"Right. Of course, if I thought you were—"

"I wasn't," says Ed, his voice low and harsh. "But you wouldn't listen. You were absolutely convinced you were right and nothing I said mattered. I was about to ask you to marry me and you thought I would do that to you, disrespect you and hurt you that way. I loved you more than I've ever loved anyone and yet you believed I'd fucking betrayed you."

"Like I said. Death star explosion." Leif's voice is offhand, but its light tone sounds forced. Like he's trying to keep a lid on the whole thing. He half-fills one of the glasses, pushing it across the table to me. "Drink, Clem. You've gone all pale. Go on."

I do as instructed, though I'm not sure alcohol is the

answer. However, something has to help the strange empty feeling. You'd think an answer, actual knowledge, would fill the vacant spaces inside. But it doesn't. This time the definite hurts more than it helps. "Why did I think that? Where did I even get that idea?"

Ed's eyes are a little frightening. The anger. "I don't know. You wouldn't say. You were crying, but you were cold. Like I was dead to you. I tried to get you to talk to me, but you just . . ."

I nod.

Without another word he's on his feet and racing toward the door. Leif grabs my arm as if to halt me. Just in case I'd had a mind to follow. And say what exactly? Then he pats the back of my hand, giving me a sad smile.

"Let him go," says Leif.

"I didn't mean to upset him like that."

"I know. Anyway, he should have told you by now. That was stupid of him. Sooner or later, it was going to come out, and it's not like it isn't your history too."

"Yeah."

"For the record, there's no way he did it," says Leif, looking me dead in the eye. "I mean, he's always the one lecturing me: 'Don't screw married women,' 'Don't screw clients or work colleagues,' 'Are you sure they're both over twenty-one?' No way he'd risk getting knocked off his high horse."

He's trying to make me laugh, and I muster up the best smile I can.

"He would never have done it, Clem. You might not have known him for that long with your head and all. But my brother is one of the best people around and he was crazy about you."

"I know; I do. I just wished I understood why I . . . anyway. Sounds like I hurt a lot of people." I put another twenty on the table beside Tessa's. That should cover the wine. "You should go after him, Leif. He's upset. He shouldn't be on his own."

"I'll find him once you're safe and sound at home. Don't worry."

"Are you sure?"

He slips an arm around my shoulders. It feels brotherly. Affectionate. "Oh my darling, Clementine. He'll be fine. And there's nowhere in this town that idiot can hide that I can't find him."

"Maybe I should call Frances and go back to her place?"

"No, don't do that. Once he's calmed down he'll probably want to talk to you, check you're okay and everything."

"Probably? Great." I sigh. "Though talking about this isn't really his thing."

Slowly, we climb the stairs back up to the street level. "You have to remember, for him this all happened a pretty short time ago. He loved you a lot."

"I know. I found the ring."

Leif groans. "Yeah. Shit."

"What a mess." Then a thought occurs to me. "Did he ever want to marry Tessa?"

"Come here." Leif turns me to face him, then carefully wipes away my tears. Obviously it was just raining on my face or something. You can't be upset about something you don't even remember happening. He tuts. "Stop crying. Goodness gracious. Your face has gone all blotchy and pink. Is that really how you want to look?"

"No."

"He and Tessa were together for years, but they were a lot younger. Late teens, early twenties. Just kids, really. It wasn't serious in the same way it was between you two, you know?"

"I think it's safe to say I do not know shit."

Leif smiles. "No? Well, know that shit will sort itself out. It always does in the end."

"If you say so."

We head back to the condo. I don't tell him that's exactly what I'm afraid of . . . the end. But I've a feeling it's just gotten a lot closer.

CHAPTER NINE

I'm not exactly certain what wakes me, but it's late. One in the morning, at least. Gordy's been asleep for ages and I must have finally drifted off a while back too, despite the emotional turmoil. Ed is sitting in front of me on the coffee table, his head in his hands. The lighting is low and his hair is a mess, as if he's been shoving his fingers through it all agitated like for hours.

"Hey," I say. "Are you all right?"

With a sigh, he raises his gaze to me. "Clem, why are you sleeping on the couch?"

"Thought you might want your space." I sit up, pushing back the blanket. "Where did you go?"

"Just walked around for a while." He pauses. "Is that my shirt?"

"Yes."

His brows rise. "You're wearing my shirt?"

I'm too tired to be embarrassed. "It smells good. It's

comforting."

"Okay." He exhales and holds out a hand. "Come to bed."

"Are you sure? You don't have to do this just to be kind, you know?"

He twitches his fingers impatiently and I take them, letting him lead me into the hallway. The door to the spare room is shut so Leif must have already crashed. A bedside lamp is on in Ed's room. A good thing. Not sure I could handle the brighter glare of the overhead light right now. He closes the door, slips off his sneakers and socks before taking off his shirt. Undoes his jeans and slides them down his legs. Holy shit, the hard planes of his chest and the sight of his black boxer briefs. All of a sudden, I'm wide awake. His strong thighs, his knees, even the light hairs on his legs are sexy. I turn my back on the ridiculously unintendedly hot striptease before I spontaneously orgasm or something. So I now know Ed dresses to the left. There you go.

I climb onto my side of the bed and get comfortable. Maybe tomorrow I should just hide out in a closet. Take a mental health day and disappear from the world for a while. It might be best. Having all of the details about our breakup come out has been emotionally exhausting. Perhaps I should ask Ed if he wants to hide out with me. It's been hellish for him too.

"What are you thinking about?" he asks, lying down on his side of the bed.

"Hiding out in a closet for a while. Taking a minibreak from life tomorrow."

"Sounds good."

"Well, you'd be very welcome. We'd just have to find a closet big enough for both of us."

"Hmm."

I roll over to face him. "I'm not going to say I'm sorry again because I've said that so many times and past a certain point it doesn't really work, does it?"

"Still think I didn't cheat on you?"

"I know you didn't. It's just not you." So many feelings. It's a lot to deal with. I turn onto my back, staring at the ceiling and around the walls. "Wonder if we'll ever know what the hell was going on in my head back then?"

He makes a noise in his throat.

"Hey, is that Tessa?" I ask, pointing at the charcoal drawing of a woman's lower back. The curve of hips and rounds of her ass cheeks. Probably not the wisest question, but whatever.

"Of course not. It's you."

"Oh."

"Like I'd hang up a naked picture of another woman in our bedroom," he says, shaking his head. "Haven't been able to bring myself to take it down yet. First week after you left, I just drank. I was a fucking mess. Couldn't believe it, you know? You'd always been a little insecure, but I thought we had it under control. I thought you knew how I felt . . ."

"Then you started dating other women a week or two later," I add helpfully.

He cuts me a look. Not angry. Surprised maybe.

"All right. So maybe I'm a little upset about your swift

timeline for that particular decision. And I'm not even going to bring up the whole issue regarding taking someone to my favorite restaurant, because . . . well, just because."

"Clem, you left me," he says. "Whatever version of yourself you're currently operating as, you were the one that did the leaving. The dumping. So you don't get to be upset about that."

"Fine. Whatever."

Weirdly enough, he smiles. Like he enjoys me being jealous or something. Though Lord only knows what the man actually thinks. "Then Tessa and Nevin kicked my ass and reminded me that I had a business to run, regardless of where you were at. So I pulled my shit together and . . . yeah. The dating was like the drinking. Me trying to distract myself from being fucking miserable twenty-four seven."

"Frances said I was a mess too."

He nods.

I go back to staring at the ceiling. It's safer than ogling him. "Today was a big day. A lot happened and there is much to digest."

Silence.

"What are you thinking about now?" he asks, face open and unguarded for about the first time in forever. The man's even more beautiful this way. "Clem?"

"Lots of things. Beauty. Heartbreak. Loss. And sex, of course. I mean, we're lying in bed together so it's a bit hard not to be thinking about that on some level. It's that whole physical awareness thing, you know?"

He's quiet for a moment, then he says, "We fucked a

lot in this room. We fucked in pretty much every room."

Wow. "Really?"

"Didn't think I could out-truth you, did you?" The corner of his lip curls upwards. "Well, I can."

"What? It's a competition now?"

"Leif was right; I should have just told you everything. Only talking about that stuff—it's not easy. It's like making it real all over again. But I think we're both due a whole heaping lot of honesty, wouldn't you agree?"

"Yes, Ed, I would. Absolutely."

"Go on then, ask me your questions. I know you've got some. You've always got some."

"How many am I going to be allowed to ask?"

He considers this for a moment. "Not sure. Hit me with your worst one first and let's go from there."

"All right." If the man wants to push at the boundaries of complete disclosure, then I'm more than happy to oblige. "Is your dick pierced? Because there was this book today about genital piercings and Iris was going on about the majesty of a Prince Albert proudly displayed or something. I can't remember her exact wording. But it got me wondering."

"No." He laughs. "I'm obviously okay with needles in most places. Just not down there."

"I don't blame you. Must hurt like hell."

He shakes his head, grinning.

"What?"

"Nothing. What else have you got?"

"Um, how many times have you been in love?"

His expression clears. "A couple. You kind of fall in

and out of love, but to find something more lasting . . . that's different. Special."

"Iris said marriage was finding someone whose shit you could tolerate long-term. Someone you could imagine wanting to see and talk to every day for the rest of your life."

"She's not wrong."

"And you honestly thought you could do that with me? I mean, it just seems like from what you've said . . ."

He rolls onto his side, studying me. "Clem, you weren't as bad as I've been making it sound. I probably haven't been as positive about how you used to be as I could have. When everything goes to hell you tend to focus on the worst. Guess it's a method of self-preservation. A way to convince yourself you're better off without the other person in your life."

"That makes sense."

"But lots of people liked you. Don't think you were a bad person or something. After all, everyone has their faults." He takes a moment, like he's thinking things over. Choosing his words with care. "I guess you were less sure of yourself before. Now if you're thrown by something, you kind of just barrel on regardless most of the time. Things don't seem to worry you as much."

"I don't know about that."

"Not saying you don't get worried about things, but they don't weigh you down in the same way."

"Is that a good thing or a bad thing?"

He shrugs. "It's just you. And you used to be hopeless at admitting when you'd gotten something wrong. Stubborn as all hell. Forget about getting an apology out of you. Now you can't seem to stop apologizing."

"Wait. How does being a neurotic wreck fit with being a stubborn jerk?"

"I never said you were a neurotic wreck. Just that you tended to worry over things."

"And then never admit I was wrong."

"Basically."

Holy hell. "I must have been amazing in the sack."

Ed bursts out laughing.

"Quick, tell me something terrible about you. I need it."

"I was a shit boyfriend," he says, quieting once again. "Because something was obviously going on with you and had been for a while and I completely fucking missed it. Maybe if I hadn't been so busy with work, if I'd taken more time for us, things wouldn't have gone the way they did. We might have still been together. And you wouldn't have been out alone that night and you wouldn't have gotten hurt."

I don't know what to say.

"Who knows?"

"You can't take all of that on yourself."

He says nothing.

"Can I make a comment without it being weird?"

"Considering the dick piercing question, I'm not actually sure it's possible for things to get any weirder."

I smile a little. "Right. Well, I just wanted to say this is nice, us talking."

"Yes, it is." He exhales. "Did Tessa give you a hard

time?"

"It was fine. I handled it. She cares about you."

"We've been friends a long time. You two used to get along," he says. "It'd be nice if you could get back to something like that. Having your old friends back might be helpful."

I wince ever so slightly. Tessa is more likely to throttle me than want to swap pedicures anytime soon. But I'll let the man dream.

"I've started making some new friends. The other day, the guy from the café across the road from the bookstore asked me if I wanted to go to a movie sometime."

His gaze narrows. "What'd you say?"

"Told him I'd think about it. But I'm not sure that would be a good idea for me just yet. Unless he meant as just a friendship thing. That could be okay."

"Always good to have friends," he says.

"I agree. But actual relationships seem complicated and I'm confused enough the bulk of the time. As well as everything else, I lost about a decade's worth of knowledge about how dating works."

"Yeah, I guess you did. How's your reading going?"

"Good, I, ah . . . this one I'm into now is *Ice Blue* by Anne Stuart. Iris said it's a romantic suspense classic. Not to be missed."

"You'll have to let me know how that goes."

It doesn't escape me how our conversation has been steered toward safer subjects. Which is fine. We're talking like friends. Or people with a complicated past who might become friends. It's nice. Yet his hand lies on the mattress, close to me, though in all the ways that matter, still out of reach. His fingers are bigger than mine, his hand larger. My jealousy at previous me reaches an all-time high. She could have just touched him whenever she wanted. The memories she must have had. Lucky bitch.

"What are you thinking about now?" he asks, voice quiet. The night is so still. The whole world contained in this one room.

"You really care what I think about that much?"

"Maybe I shouldn't, but I do."

It feels both sweet and sour, this statement. Both painful and pleasing.

"I like how I ask and you tell me. No guessing. No wondering if I'm missing something again," he says. "You just let me know where you're at. It's good. Very good."

"Honestly, I think you short circuit my brain."

"The feeling's entirely mutual."

My gaze jumps from his fingers to his face. "Really?"

His small smile seems almost uncomfortable. A little grieved, perhaps. "Why do you think you're here in my apartment? In my bed wearing my shirt?"

"Well, I kind of just took the shirt without asking. As for the rest, because you were worried about my safety and then Leif annoyed you by flirting with me?" I suggest. "Though nothing would have happened if we'd shared the futon. Things are complicated enough and while he seems like a nice guy, there's nothing there."

"No?" He licks his top lip and everything low inside me squeezes tight. An enjoyable sensation. And not a particularly new one when it comes to him. The man is beautiful, inside and out. "I'm glad to hear that."

"Mm."

"But you're back in my life for a reason, Clem. Because on one level or another, I want you here. It'd be stupid of me to pretend otherwise." The warmth in his voice is dizzying. The closeness of him intoxicating. Perhaps my reaction to him is part Pavlovian. A response from previous me and the no doubt disgusting carnal things she did with him. Just that easily, I'm horribly jealous of her all over again. Or maybe when it came to Ed the feelings never stopped.

"You're staring at my mouth," he says.

I put my fingers up to my own lips. "I've never been kissed. Did you know that?"

"No, I didn't." His gaze drops to my lips. "Tell me more."

"Well, what worries me is, what do you do with the nose?"

He blinks. "With the what?"

"The nose. How do you decide who goes which way so no one's nose gets broken?"

"If you're going in so hard that someone's liable to break something, you're probably doing it wrong. Especially given your medical condition. No one should require a crash helmet to kiss."

"And what about the breathing? Do you hold your breath or mouth breathe through it or what?"

"I can see you've given this a lot of thought," he says. "You are aware that you kind of babble now when you're nervous?"

"Yeah, I know. And then there's the whole tongue or no tongue thing to consider."

"Okay, Clem. Now you've definitely given this too much thought. If there isn't at least a little spontaneity to the act, you're pretty much ruining the whole thing. Have you discussed your kissing theories with anyone else?"

I think it over. "No."

"Good. I don't want you going out with that other guy from the café, either."

"Well, what about the woman at my restaurant?"

"It's not *your* restaurant; it's *our* restaurant, and I'm not seeing her anymore," he says. "Honestly, I don't have a clue what this thing is between us or if it has a future. Or just a past. But my suggestion is that we spend some more time together and see how things go."

I take a deep breath. "You've thought this through."

"Tonight, when I was walking around. Wondering why I was so angry. Wondering why I'd been so reluctant to tell you anything about what happened. The truth is, my feelings for you are all fucked up. I can't make sense of them . . . not yet. But I realized, if I'd come home and you weren't here, I would have gone looking for you. Okay?"

"Uh, okay."

"Good." He rises up on one elbow, shifting across the bed until he's lying beside me. Right flush up against my body. Him against me. "Now for the kissing."

I can hardly wait.

Hands cup my face and his mouth is pressing against mine. There's no time to worry about noses or breathing or any of that nonsense. So he was right about that. My mind is elsewhere, on much more important things. His tongue slides against the seam of my lips and I open my mouth on a gasp. It feels nice. All of it, everything he's doing. It's hot and wet and perfect. Him biting me. The way he rubs his tongue against mine. He kisses me hard and deep, thumbs stroking the sides of my face. Our bodies are pressed against one another and his hands slide into my hair. If I didn't know better, I'd have said the man owned me. And I owned him. We fit together so well.

He doesn't stop until my lips are swollen and my head is spinning. The pad of his thumb slides over my bottom lip. I can feel the warmth of his breath on my face. Don't even get me started on the heat coming off of him. The way he's lying half on top of me, pressing me down into the mattress.

"What do you think?" he asks, voice about a dozen times deeper and rougher than normal. His hands are tangled in my hair. The knowledge that this man wants me has my toes curling.

"About kissing or spending time together?"

"Both."

"Your eyes are so pretty." I smile. He's dazzling, really. But maybe I've said enough for one evening.

He smiles back. "Kissing, yes or no?"

"Ah, yeah. Nice."

"Nice?" he asks, sneering ever so slightly.

"You don't like nice?"

"It's your first kiss. I wanted to do a little better than nice."

"It was very pleasant. I think I'd like to do it again

sometime. If you're amenable, of course."

"You're killing me." He laughs. "What about the spending time together part?"

"Well, Ed, I would be delighted to hang out with you."

"Glad to hear it."

My heart is still beating so hard. It must be his nearness, the heat in his eyes. And something has definitely happened in his pants. I can feel it pressing against my lower stomach. Perhaps if I ask nicely, he'll let me see.

"We'll just take it slow," he says. "No need to rush anything. Let's see what happens."

"We're not going to—"

"Not tonight."

"Oh, okay." I don't bother to keep the disappointment out of my voice.

He kisses my forehead and reaches out to turn off the bedside lamp, before returning to his far distant remote side of the mattress. So it's not really all that far, it just feels like it. My lips still tingle along with everything else. It was a pretty nice kiss.

"Night, Clem."

"Night."

I'd thought maybe we might cuddle or something, but perhaps guys with boners don't want to cuddle. They either want sex or space. I would have been fine with sex. Though taking it slow does make sense. Now it's some stupid hour of the morning and I'm wide awake overthinking our relationship. If it's even a relationship yet. I don't know.

"Stop thinking," he says. "Go to sleep, baby."

Baby. He called me baby. No one's ever called new me something like that before. An affectionate pet name or whatever. Talk about an extreme case of feeling warm and fuzzy. Remarkably enough, after a little while, I do in fact sleep.

CHAPTER TEN

The next morning goes well. Even despite the bed being empty again when I wake up. Leif informs me Ed's taken Gordon for a run. So I get showered and dressed for work. Along with a little makeup, I attempt to style my choppy hair today. I'll never be Tessa levels of glamour. But I can rock my own thing. The need to hide and watch as opposed to partaking of life isn't as overwhelming as it used to be when I first left the hospital. Maybe I'm getting braver or surer of myself in some way. I don't know.

"Tell me what you're thinking," Ed says as I approach him in the kitchen upon his return.

"Well, I was wondering if you were going to kiss me again. But then I was thinking that you looked especially handsome all covered in sweat and you smell really good. Before that, I think I was just enjoying the smell of the coffee and trying to remember what books I need to take back to the shop. That's pretty much it."

"Okay."

My lips still tingle along with everything else. Or maybe they started tingling again at the sight of him. Gordon leans his butt against my leg, does some scratching, stuff like that. The love life and verbal repartee of myself and his owner means nothing to the very good boy.

"See, not everything passing through my head is worth hearing about," I say, as he hands me a cup of coffee.

"I wouldn't say that. First bit in particular was pretty interesting."

"So what's on your mind?"

"Apart from kissing you?"

"I wouldn't want to distract you from that." I smile, taking a sip. "Though on the other hand, it was my thought first and not yours, leading me to believe that you mustn't want to kiss me all that badly. To be honest, that's kind of disappointing, Ed."

A sound of amusement from Leif over on the couch. "I knew you two would get back together."

"Did you really?" I ask with a grin.

In response, he blows me a kiss.

"Stop flirting with her, dammit," says Ed. "And we're taking it slow."

Leif sadly shakes his head. "You always did have middle child complex."

"He's perfectly fine the way he is, and we are taking it slow. That's true," I dutifully back Ed up because togetherness or whatever it is we're doing.

"Whatever you say," answers Leif. "Why was Gordon whining at my bedroom door all last night?"

I don't even blink. "Because he missed you while you were gone."

"Clem was letting him sleep on the futon with her," says Ed. "Despite me asking her not to."

"Ah." Leif nods.

My outrage is mostly feigned. "You have no proof."

"I don't need proof, baby. I know you when it comes to that dog."

"Thank you for the coffee."

"Nice change of subject, and no fair about the kiss."

"How so?"

"In my defense, I had plans."

"Such as?"

"Getting you caffeinated, for starters," he says.

"A noble quest, of which I fully approve."

"Then having a shower so I don't drip sweat all over you."

I frown slightly. "I said I don't mind that."

"Ah, but you used to. Now I know that you don't." Bless him, the man doesn't hesitate. First pressing his warm lips to my cheek, my jaw, even my chin. The salty, musky scent of sweat and man is a wonderful high.

"Ed, that's not my mouth. Do you need a map?"

"You're so impatient," he mumbles, bussing my cheek with his nose. The feel of his breath on my face, of him being right there . . . holy shit. Privacy matters not in the least. His lips trail down my neck, tongue sliding against my skin. It's like lights turning on inside of me. A hypersensitivity only he inspires. Teeth press into the lobe of my ear, teasing. Then he sucks on a particularly amazing section of skin between my neck and shoulder. Sweet baby Jesus. My mind blanks entirely, head falling to the side. Little shocks of electricity zap up my spine.

"That doesn't look slow," comments Leif from the couch.

Ed nibbles on my jawline before placing gentle kisses either side of my mouth. The man is a goddamn tease. "As much as it pains me to admit, he's right."

My eyes open slowly, reluctantly. "I'm beginning to think slow is highly overrated."

"Yeah. I'm pretty sure slow is going to kill me." He takes a breath, pulls back to look me in the eye. "But, Clem, I still think it's the only way to do this."

I don't like it, but he's probably right. Also, he's the one who remembers us hitting the wall and having to deal with heartbreak et cetera. However, it sucks to be the one who gets to stand by, hoping he doesn't change his mind and pull the rug out from underneath my feet. I suppose I should want to go slow as well. My rational mind knows perfectly well how badly we struck disaster before. Which should be a warning for what looms ahead. But without the actual memories of the breakdown, with all its pain and misery, I just can't feel it on an emotional level. My heart and body just want to rush forward into his arms and into his bed. Really into his bed, I mean, not just me perched on the opposite side throughout the night, like we've been doing.

What's that saying about people who can't remember

the past being doomed to repeat it?

"I'm getting in the shower, then we'll see about getting you to work," he says. "Later, baby."

"That's the third time you've called me baby."

"It won't be the last," he says with such certainty it warms not only my heart but everywhere.

"Did you used to call me that?"

"Yeah, I did. Is that a problem?"

"No." I shake my head. Maybe a moment came in our breakdown when any talk of 'baby' was no longer possible, but if the term of endearment relates to good memories for him then it's fine. "Not at all."

"Good to know." And he's gone, padding down the hallway toward the bathroom.

"You're the worst for interrupting and being sensible," I inform Leif, who doesn't even have the good grace to appear upset at the news.

"Sensible, shmensible," he says. "That was just good old-fashioned cock-blocking. It's pretty much the only enjoyable part of being a sibling."

He raises his cup of coffee to me in toast. I salute him back with my own cup. It doesn't seem worth holding a grudge over. Besides, he probably is right. Dammit. If only my heart would stop racing from all the overexcitement.

We hold hands on the walk to work. The sun is shining and I'm happy. Actually, I'm jam-packed full of joy, all of my worrying pushed aside for the moment. It's a warning sign in and of itself. Little in my new life up until now has been what you'd call easy. And the familiar old feeling of paranoia comes roaring back when I see Iris in a frenzy trying to clean the shop's front window, a rag and bottle of glass cleaner in hand. She's scowling heavily. Not her usual expression of contentment at all.

"That's my job," I say.

"Guess you're getting let off washing windows today."

A man who could only be Iris's beau Antonio comes out with a scraper type tool and holy shit. Now I see what the problem is. The glass has been covered in black. Not just the window but some of the pavement below. It's like they threw a whole can of paint at the shop front. A big can. It's one hell of a mess.

"What the fuck?" I gasp.

"What the fuck indeed," says Iris, giving me a dour smile. "Vandals these days. You know, at least when they spray their tag on something I can pretend its art. This, however . . ."

"What can we do to help?" asks Ed.

"Oh, nothing. It'll be fine." Iris sighs. "But thank you. A neighboring shop owner saw it and called me first thing this morning, so the police have already been by. Unfortunately, whoever did it was wearing a hoodie and had face coverage, so the security camera didn't get much. It appeared they might have been planning on doing more damage; there were a couple of attempts to kick the door in. Ridiculous, really, they just would have set off the alarm. Though I suppose they could have done some damage in the meantime. But thankfully it seems they got interrupted by late-night revelers or such. Clementine, are you all right, dear?"

Not really. Everything inside of me feels heavy with dread. "This is because of me."

"Well, it would seem someone disagreed with your display of gardening books. I did think at the time it was a little edgy." She smiles, but the attempt at humor feels strained.

"No. It really is about me, and not because of Frances being a cop at all. It's about who I am. Or who I was."

She pauses. "We don't know that."

"Hey, calm down. It's just paint." Ed's hand slides around behind my neck, rubbing at the suddenly rock-hard muscles. "Iris is right, baby. We don't know anything for sure."

"First the attack, then my car, and now this? Really?"

"Clem—"

"How many coincidences do you need?"

He grimaces.

Fair enough. My voice sounds shrill to my own ears. I take a deep breath and let it out slow. "Sorry, I didn't mean to yell. But it's a message, Ed, and it means that me being here is probably not safe. We don't know what they might do next. What if they come back? What if they get violent again and someone gets hurt?"

The expression on Iris's face is somewhere between concern and dismay. So I'm not being completely crazy. Some of this is making sense. That's even more concerning.

Ed, however, is shaking his head. "You need to calm down."

"No, I'm serious. What if next time you get hurt? I'd never forgive myself." I take a step back, putting myself out of reach. It's better for everyone. If whatever this is spills over onto the people I care about I'll never forgive myself. "This . . . this isn't good."

"Don't you dare," he says, grabbing my arms. His grip is strong. "I agree; this is a worry. I get why you're freaking out. But don't you dare use it as an excuse to disappear on me again."

"But maybe it would be best if I left for just a—"

"*No.*"

One of us is probably being unreasonable. With fear making my heart pound and mind race, I'm not sure which of us it is, however.

"Do you hear me?" he asks, leaning in close. "Absolutely fucking not. We'll deal with this together, okay?"

I don't know what to say or do.

"Nod your head, Clem."

After a moment, I do as I'm told. "Fine."

"Now breathe," he orders, arms coming around me, pulling me in against his hard body. The scent and heat of him all helps. For me, he's a living and breathing sanctuary and being wrapped up in him this way is heaven. It's a bit scary to need him this much. No, I only want him. Lots. But if he left, if he changed his mind, I'd manage. I just really fucking hope he doesn't. "Just breathe. It'll be okay."

"Why don't you take her home, Ed?" suggests Iris.

"Thank you, Iris. But I'm fine now and I'd rather stay and help." The worst thought occurred to me. "Unless you'd rather me not be here?"

"Of course not." She clicks her tongue in disapproval. "In that case, stop hanging off your lovely man and get to work."

"I'll cancel my appointments for today, stay here with you," says Ed.

I look up. "No, don't do that."

Some people make those appointments months in advance. Ed's tattooing talents are in high demand. Plus, I'm already complicating his home life. I'd rather not screw with his work life too.

"I'm not leaving you like this," he says.

"I'm okay. Really, Ed, it's broad daylight. Everything that's happened so far has all been at night."

Doubt fills his gaze.

"You're right; it's just paint. Whatever it does or doesn't mean, they've probably done all they're going to do for now. I'll be fine."

"Promise me you won't go off on your own."

"I promise I'll be safety conscious, yes." Up on tippy-toes, I give him a kiss. "Go to work. I'll be okay. If it is the same person, at least they seem to be sort of de-escalating. Perhaps next time they'll just send me a sternly worded letter."

"Glad you've still got your sense of humor, but I'm not ready to laugh about this yet."

Iris, however, is good to go. "A sonnet expressing their displeasure, perhaps?"

"Maybe a cutting limerick?"

She grins with glee. "How about an abrasive haiku?"

"A bad fortune cookie?"

"All right." Ed shakes his head. "If you need me, call me. You've got your cell?"

"Yes, and I will."

"I'll be back at six. On the dot. You better let Frances know about this as well or she'll lose her shit."

"True."

"And you're definitely not going off wandering on your own." His gaze is so serious. "I've got your word on that, right, Clem?"

"You make me sound like some out of control toddler," I half-joke. "What's wrong, don't you trust me?"

It's the sudden lack of expression on his face that clues me in. The careful blankness with which I'm now being regarded.

Beside us, Iris is suddenly occupied with the window.

"Hey," I say, attempting a smile. "You can trust me. If I say I'll do something, I'll do it."

He does not look convinced, though he's doing his best to hide it. "Sure. If you're okay here, I better get moving."

"See you tonight."

With a final kiss to my forehead and one final murmured "just be careful, baby" he's gone. So that didn't go so well. Guess the word *trust* should be shelved from all further conversation.

Iris shoves a paint scraper and a bottle of turpentine at me and I get busy cleaning up the mess. The paint is already half-dried. Iris and Antonio have washed away most of the still-moist stickiness, so we are now left with the hardened underside. After a while, Antonio has to go open the gelato shop and Iris is occupied with customers inside the bookstore, so I'm on my own. It's hard work. Of course it is. If you're going to vandalize a shop window by splashing paint on it, you're not going to use any nice water-based acrylic. No, sir. You're going to use some nasty oil-based enamel that only comes off with paint stripper, elbow grease, and what seems like an infinite amount of turpentine.

I pop in my earbuds and put on some music while, inch by inch, I reclaim Iris's shop windows from the vandal's work. Because fuck them. Whoever they might be and for whatever reason they might be doing this. I'm not running or going into hiding. Sure, flight might have been my first response. No way, however, will I give them the satisfaction. I'm building a life here. One hopefully including Ed. And that's worth fighting for. Though I should probably start hitting up the relationship section of the shop once we've got the glass sorted. Oh God, the drama of having a love life. I'm not sure my heart can take it. Organizing an existence with other people in it, especially a romantic interest, is so much harder than just hanging out with Frances and ordering pizza. Those were the days.

Also, if whoever is doing this is trying to scare me into doing some stupid, then taking off on my own probably definitely falls under that category, now that I stop and think about it. Ed was right. Of course Ed was right. He's a smart guy. Truth is, the man is worth any amount of emotional mayhem and occasional commotion.

Soon my life is consumed by the shop window, the awful smell of enamel paint, and the fine sounds of my playlist. It's the main song list that previous me made. I've listened to it a few times now and it's good. Just like her favorite movies, some of her music is from the eighties too. I guess that's what Mom grew up listening to. Songs like "When Doves Cry" by Prince, "Bizarre Love Triangle" by New Order, and "Love is a Battlefield" by Pat Benatar top the list. Maybe I'll never know my mother in the way that I used to. Actually, it's a definite, given she's dead. But I can still get a feeling for her through the photos and stories, the movies and songs. We don't have to be total strangers. Next the music moves onto more recent decades with songs like "The Scientist" by Cold Play, "Dancing on My Own" by Robyn, "Do I Wanna Know" by Arctic Monkeys, "Wasted on Each Other" by James Bay, and "River" by Bishop Briggs. A brief wrap-up of the last twenty or so years. But mostly, whether recent or ancient, it's all pretty new to me.

I wonder if I used to like dancing or if I'd ever learned to play an instrument. It would be cool to just sit down at a piano and know what to do. Though Frances probably would have mentioned something if I was a secret virtuoso. Every kid usually has a couple of hobbies, however. I'll have to ask. There had been a photo of me in a middle school play portraying a tree. But what with me not being particularly graceful, I doubt ballet or something cool like that would have been high on my list of after-school activities. Some sports, maybe? Gordy likes the way I throw a ball. Though even with the doggy slobber, he's still a way better catch than me.

At any rate, slowly but surely the worst of my worry is pushed back as the music and contemplating the past takes over. But it always lingers just a little. Fear of so many things, both the known and unknown, casting a shadow over my world. Maybe I'll never know what it's like to live without the anxiety. Maybe there'll always be things to be unsure of. Then again, maybe that's just a part of life.

Finally, the work is done. My arms ache, and the skin on my hands is splotched an ugly white and red, but I have erased the stain on Iris's life that had been put there because of me.

I make my way inside. It's time to attend to the real business of the morning. "I want to see the video, please."

Iris's lips tighten, but I can tell she's been expecting this request. "I told you everything that was in it. You can't see anything more."

"I know. But I have to see it anyway." My voice stays quiet and calm, not giving her any reason to deny me. "Is it here, or did the police take it?"

"It's still here." She sighs. "The police just copied it onto a flash drive."

Soon enough, I'm sitting in the back room, fast-forwarding through grainy black-and-white footage to get to 1:46 a.m. And then there it is: a figure walking past the entrance. All you can really see is the hoodie, with the hood up covering everything, and what looks like jeans or sneakers. For all my squinting into the screen, it's hard to make out much else. The figure looks kind of slim and tall, but with the weird camera angle, looking downwards at them, it's hard to tell with any certainty. So that's just great. I've narrowed down my list of suspects to everyone in the world with two arms and two legs. Good thing it was my sister who went into the police force and not me.

The figure has the can of paint already out, held by the handle. It's heavy, obviously. A big 20-liter one—but I knew that even without seeing the video, courtesy of having to bust my ass cleaning it all up.

Our friendly neighborhood vandal does a pretty good job of splashing the paint onto the window. Maybe this isn't their first rodeo. Then it goes up to the front door and tries to kick it in twice. No luck there. One hand disappears inside the big jacket, as if reaching for something, but then the head jerks hard left, as if the figure heard something. And then it's gone, picking up the empty paint can and slipping away into the night.

Iris told me I wouldn't be able to see anything more, and she was right. I rewind the tape and slo-mo through the moment where the figure hears the sound, and the hoodie twists as the head turns. I try and convince myself there's something visible there, perhaps a flash of chin or nose. But it's really just a couple of pale pixels in a sea of fuzzy gray.

But that doesn't stop me watching and rewatching the figure. Rewind. Play. Slo-mo.

My heart thumps in my chest as I stare into the footage. Maybe the figure is unrecognizable. But that doesn't seem to matter. Because for the first time I am actually seeing them, the person who's out to ruin me. It's not just some crazy paranoia or a figment of my imagination. I feel sure of it. It's a real human being out to get me and I'm watching them right now. A crazy cocktail of fear and anger swirls in my stomach.

Rewind. Play. Slo-mo.

"She's still here? What not a surprise." Tessa is sitting on the front steps to Ed's condo when we return that evening. Her boyfriend, Nevin, is rubbing her shoulders. The boy needs to work harder, however, because she still looks stressed as fuck. If she isn't, I sure as hell am.

"Clem," says Shannon, the receptionist from the parlor, leaning on the stair rail beside them. "Hey."

"Hi." I raise a hand in greeting.

"You're early," says Ed, calm as can be. Obviously he was expecting them and didn't warn me. I try to keep a blank face. Try.

"Damn." Nevin laughs. "She's just as happy to see us as we are to see her. This was a great idea, Ed. Seriously, man, good work."

"It's pizza night. This is what we always do." Ed frowns ever so slightly. "Clem, it's not a problem they're here, is it?"

"No. Absolutely not. All good."

Tessa laughs. "Oh, your fake smile is awful. You might want to work on that."

"It is fine. I just wasn't expecting . . ." The words trail off and I shut my mouth. Mostly, I feel tired.

"Tessa, give her a break," says Ed. "She's had a shit day, okay?"

Immediately, Tessa groans. "All right, all right. I heard about the paint thing at your work. Did you get it cleaned up okay?"

"Yeah." I nod. "Thanks."

Ed frowns. "Leif should be home."

"No answer when we buzzed." Nevin gets to his feet and holds out his hand. Ed throws the keys to him. Then the visitors head inside, giving Ed and I a moment alone.

"Sorry I didn't warn you," he says. "They're normally over once a week for dinner and drinks. I thought it might be a welcome distraction from everything that's been going on."

"It's okay. Really. Just a surprise. But is me being here okay?"

"Absolutely. You sure?"

"Yes. I mean, it's great that you have such close friends."

"They're your friends too."

I give him the look of much disbelief.

"All right, so there's some tension between you and Tessa right now. You'll work it out. Just give it a chance, okay?" His hand kneads the back of my neck, turning me into agreeable mush. No wonder Nevin had been doing it to Tessa. What a superpower. Such magical strong fingers put to great use. Lord only knows the sort of things Ed could make me agree to when he's touching me this way.

His lips brush over my jawline all warm and perfect like. "You with me, Clem? And then later, when they're gone . . ."

"Yes?"

Oh, his laugh is so low, faintly evil, and full of erotic promise. My blood surges hot at the sound.

And the potential for further kissing later on is more than sufficient to get me inside. As we walk down the apartment building hallway, a door opens up farther down. Our neighbor, Tim, sticks his head out, see's it's us, and then shuts the door. Though I could have sworn some leering/naked imagining was going on when his gaze swept over me. So gross. The man is a creeper. That's a definite.

Inside the condo, Gordon greets us with much sniffing, butt wiggling, and wagging of his tail. From one of the comfy chairs, Leif just smiles, his hair still wet from the shower. No wonder he didn't hear our guests buzz.

Honestly, I was a bit relieved when I realized Leif had just been in the shower. It shouldn't have meant anything, him not answering the door. But courtesy of this morning's shenanigans, my paranoia was on a hair trigger, and crazy scenarios shot through my mind the moment anything was out of place.

Shannon sits on the big couch with Tessa and Nevin sprawled out beside her. In Tessa's hands is her cell, thumbs busy on the screen. "I put in the days of yore regular order multiplied by two since Leif and Shannon are here. It shouldn't be long. I'm starving."

"What's the days of yore regular?" I ask.

"She means the pizza order from back when you used to live here last time. One mushroom and bacon, and one chicken and basil." In the kitchen, Ed takes the caps off four bottles of beer. Once they're handed out, he grabs a seat, drawing me onto his lap. I think it's a statement. It feels like a statement, one meant not only for his guests but to me also, the girl perched awkwardly on his knee. And sure enough, Tessa raises a brow at the move. Shannon just gives me a limp sort of smile, gaze shifting between me and Ed. Given how damning she was regarding mine and Ed's previous attempt at coupledom, this must be bizarre for her. Perhaps she's worried how much of her vaguely hostile and blathering point of view I've shared with her employer regarding his personal life. People have probably been fired for less. But like I even have the energy to stir such pointless shit.

"Look at you, being all protective," says Tessa. "I'll behave if she does."

"Everyone's going to behave." Nevin clicks his fingers and Gordon runs over to him for some behind-the-ear scratches. "Even you, hey, boy? Police have anything more to say about what happened at your work, Clem?"

"No." I shake my head. "Vandals, disenchanted youth, whatever . . ."

"Assholes," mutters Leif.

Shannon nods her head. "It's horrible."

"At least they didn't break the glass or damage any stock," says Nevin.

Tessa's nails tap against her leg. "Still, bad luck is certainly following her around lately."

"Indeed it is and this is my point, beautiful. Clem is already hurting." Just for a moment, Nevin's gaze on me seems to go cold, dark, and cruel. It's a little scary. But then suddenly he smiles and turns back to Tessa. As if it never even happened. "No reason for you not to forgive her."

"I already have Ed on at me at work," she says. "I don't need you lecturing me too."

"Okay. Just saying . . ."

"She and I will work it out when and if I'm ever ready."

"Whatever you say, beautiful."

Shannon stares at Ed, lips shut tight. Around her boss, she apparently keeps her opinions to herself. A far cry from the time she tracked me down at the café near Frances's place for a chat. Her top is cut low, showcasing a large tattooed chest piece of roses and ribbon. It flows above her breasts, along with dipping farther down out of sight.

"That's lovely," I say. "Did Tessa do that piece for you?"

Her smile remains hesitant. "Ah, no. Ed did it."

"Does that worry you, Ed regularly seeing other women's bodies?" asks Tessa. Not malicious exactly, just curious.

Behind me, I can feel Ed go still, listening with interest.

I shrug. "Kind of part of the job isn't it?"

"Interesting," says Tessa. "Because it used to bother you quite a bit."

Shannon says nothing. Lots of it.

"We also get to see lots of hairy asses and other bits," says Leif. "It is just part of the job, Clem. You're right. The thrill gets old real fast."

I must have responded to the question appropriately since Tessa moves on to other things and Ed's body sort of eases beneath me once more. And this is all beyond awkward, being put on trial in front of people I barely know. Most of the time, I can live with what's happened. With what I do and don't know and who I was before. But tonight, this is all a bit too much.

Via an arm around my waist, Ed pulls me back against his body. His hard chest to my back. My ass against his groin. Whoa. Guess this is how we used to sit back in our couple days. Lounging all over each other, treating the other's body like beloved and extremely hot furniture. But given it's been less than twenty-four hours ago since he kissed me for the first time this go-around, then that trust thing this morning, it seems kind of awkward for some reason. Or maybe it's just about being surrounded by people from my messy past. All of the differing emotions regarding and reactions toward me. I'm not sure my social skills are up to it. Hell, my ability to handle life in general is dubious right now.

"This okay?" he asks, voice low.

"Mm-hmm."

"Relax, then. You're stiff as a board."

I ease back against him, trying to get comfortable. The span of his hand sits across my stomach in a possessive and thrilling manner. And if anything, he smells even better today than his shirt did last night. You can't beat the real thing for authenticity. It's some sort of sandalwood-type cologne and him. I'm not entirely sure we'd have been all over one another again so soon if Tessa hadn't been giving me the stink eye. Ed's protective instincts are nice. Comforting. Suddenly sharing the evening with her and her obviously still angry at me despite his whole easygoing guy-shtick boyfriend feels like the best thing possible. Then there's Leif, who is always good company.

This is fine. This should be fine.

Leif, Tessa, Shannon, and Ed start talking about work things while Nevin and I drink our beers. At first, I try to ignore the throbbing inside my skull. But it's no good.

"Hey, I . . ." I start to say, wriggling off his lap.

"You okay?" asks Ed.

"Headache. I might take some Tylenol and lie down for a bit. I'll be fine."

"Are you sure? You don't need to see your doctor or something?"

Now Leif is all worried too. "What's up, Clem?"

"All of a sudden, you really don't look so good," says Tessa, expression genuinely concerned. "What's going on?"

"Just a headache. Really, I'm okay. It happens sometimes." I squeeze Ed's shoulder and give him a smile. "Save me some pizza?"

"Absolutely. I'll come check on you in a bit."

I nod and lift my hand in farewell. Even Gordy lifts his head off Nevin's lap, following my path with sad eyes.

He's a good dog, but his canine extrasensory perception is probably telling him there's pizza coming. I'd stay put if I were him too. In the bedroom, I shut the door and turn on the little lamp. Take two of the pills sitting on the bedside table. Next I shuck off my shoes, jeans, extract my bra, and climb into bed.

Conversation from the next room is only a distant, low noise. And in the almost quiet, things are better. Guess I just needed some space to give myself a chance to catch up with everything. Some alone time to process things. There's so much to think about, despite the pain in my head. It takes me a fair while to fall asleep.

CHAPTER ELEVEN

I wake up alone in the dark hours later. The condo is quiet, all traces of chatter gone. But I open the bedroom door silently, listening to be sure before heading on out in my tee and underwear. Ed is sitting at the table working. He's got a pair of those soft blue sleep pants on, slung low on slim hips. No shirt. All that beautiful inked flesh on display. I almost start to drool. And I am apparently feeling much better. It's not just the lust he inspires, it's him. He makes me happy. He makes me feel wonderful things. From all of the heat of desire and warmth of affection through to the way he fills the empty places inside of me and feeding my curiosity with thoughts and words and experiences. I can't lose this, and the bitch of it is, it could happen. Not just through mistakes we might make, but care of the asshole out there who has it in for me. Maybe I'm losing it, imagining some ticking clock, counting down the hours of my existence. The time I have left until

I'm ended again. Only this time for good.

"Hey," he says softly when he sees me coming toward him. "How are you feeling?"

"Good. What time is it?"

"Just after ten."

"Everyone's gone?" I slip my hand over his thick shoulder.

"Tessa and Nevin went home and Leif and Shannon headed out for a drink. I came in earlier to check on you, but you were out." He shifts his chair back, guiding me with a hand to the hip to stand between his legs. We're alone in the quiet gentle of the night, just me and him. This is quite possibly another favorite life moment happening right here right now. He slides my hair back from my forehead, urging me to lean over so he can kiss my scar. It agitates me a little, the effort to not stop him. To not instantly cover the wound back up with my fringe. But if this is going to work, I can't hide from him. "You feel like going back to sleep now or you want to talk for a while?"

"I feel like staring at you because you're so pretty."

"But you still respect me for my mind, right?" He smiles, my hands linked around his neck while his sit on my hips.

"Oh, totally. For sure. I don't *only* objectify you."

"I don't believe you at all," he murmurs.

Maybe it's the way my hand is already sliding over his hot skin, down his collarbones and over his chest. Or perhaps it's the lust in my eyes. But I don't really blame him for doubting. His face is all sharp lines like some film star out of an old black-and-white film. But with tatts and 'tude to bring him into the moment. To make him mine. God, I hope he's mine. It's fair to say my confidence regarding a lot of things has taken a hit today.

"What's on your mind, Clem?"

"I'm worried," I say, baring my soul. It's necessary. This all feels so tenuous between us. As if it could be snatched away at any moment. "I'm scared you want the life back that we used to have and I can't give that to you. I'm not the same person anymore and things have happened . . ."

His hand slips beneath my T-shirt, fingers tracing circles into my back. "It's different now. I know."

"Tessa and Nevin might never forgive me and they're obviously a big part of your life, Ed."

"They'll get over it eventually. Give it a chance."

I'm not convinced.

"Hey, come here." He pulls me in closer, resting the side of his face against the front of my shirt, against my breasts. Maybe he's listening for my heart the same way I like to listen to his. The palms of his hands slide down the back of my bare thighs, up and down. Having more access to him is heady stuff. Being allowed so close. I stroke his neck, rest my cheek against the top of his head. "You had a crappy day and it was bad timing having everyone over. That's on me. I'm sorry, baby."

"It's okay."

"Kiss me," he orders, lifting his face to mine.

And his mouth against mine is poetry. His kiss sublime. The heat and taste of him are perfect. Pretty sure he could kiss me into submission. Hands grip my ass cheeks, fingers digging into my flesh just a little. Then he slides his fingers over my hips, tracing the waistband of my panties before heading north. Ed knows my body, knows what he's doing. With his tongue in my mouth and his hands beneath my shirt, teasing and touching me so close to below my breasts but not quite. My stomach flips. What's going on lower down is even more appreciative of his efforts.

It's a definite. No matter how clever my fingers, they can't make me feel like this. Ed has it all over masturbation, bless him.

Our lips press hard against each other, getting as close as possible. And I want more. Much more. I want everything. I break contact for a moment, lifting my shirt off over my head and throwing it far, far away. Clothing has no place in this moment. For a second, it almost occurs to me to be a little shy, standing there in nothing but my panties. But forget that. I climb onto his lap, straddling his legs. Skin on skin, my chest against his.

"Shit . . ." His voice is low and rough. The heat in his eyes intensifies by about a thousand, his gaze shifting between my face and my now bare breasts. It's like there's a war going on inside of him. Want versus what's safe, what makes sense given everything that's happened. I know which side I hope will win. He, however, remains conflicted. "Maybe you should put your shirt back on."

"Why? This is still sort of slow," lies my lying tongue.

"It's really not, baby."

"Yeah, you're right. I'm actually kind of done with

slow." One hand slides around the back of his strong neck, the other grasping hold of his bicep. His skin is warm and smooth to the touch. And I plan to do a whole lot of touching.

"You weren't feeling so great earlier. Shouldn't we take it easy?"

"But I'm feeling amazing now."

Even his scowl is sexy. "You know I had plans for this. Taking you out on a date, going to our favorite restaurant, doing it all the right way."

"Aw, that's sweet."

"You like the sound of that? We don't have to rush."

"But nothing about this feels wrong and we can still go on dates. In fact, I'd like that a lot."

His gaze on me narrows. "Clem . . ."

"Woo me later. Fuck me now."

The noise in his throat is vaguely tortured with a hint of pissed off. But his mouth comes back to mine, our tongues rubbing against one another, teeth clashing just a little. Then his hot mouth travels down to my jawline and on to my neck. So damn good. I shove my hands through his hair, holding him to me. No way is he getting away now. If everything between us goes to shit sometime soon, at least I'll have this memory.

"You always get your way," he growls. A thrilling sound.

"Not even remotely."

"No?" His fingers expertly toy with my nipple, making me gasp and writhe on him. "Pretty damn sure you do."

His growing hard-on is caught between us, tenting

the sleep pants. Ed turned on is a thing of wonder. I've never been so excited, all five senses hitting overload. My breath hitches, heart pounding.

"Tell me, is this is a curiosity thing? You getting your answers again?" His teeth gently threaten my neck, his grip on my breast tightening to a sweet edge of pain. It would seem the man is part animal when it comes to sex. How awesome.

"It's a *you* thing and you know it," I say, panting slightly.

"Just as well."

In one swift motion he clears the table of drawing pad and pen. Then, with one hand on my ass and the other on my back, he surges up, placing me on the surface. Holy wow, the slightly feral look in his eyes as he stares down at me. I feel more alive than I ever have. Every inch of me bright with sensation. Though our underwear is an annoyance. An ache has started up between my legs, everything low inside of me feeling swollen and tight. Needy. He grinds his dick against me and I see stars. The long hard length of him pressing against the soaked gusset of my panties.

"Sure you don't want to calm things down? If you change your mind, we can stop anytime you want." Oh God, the hunger in his eyes. He doesn't want to stop any more than I do. So instead of answering, I wrap my legs around him. Actions speaking louder than words and all that.

His fingers thread through my hair, tugging just a little as he kisses me. The nerves in my scalp fire up along with the rest of my body. Being like this with Ed is pure sensation. Each kiss is deeper, wetter than the one before. Our need for each other building.

"How far do you want to take this, hmm?" he asks, before shifting lower, mouth covering a nipple, his tongue lashing over it, and yes. So good. When his teeth press in just so my back bows off the table. He bites my breast, my neck, my lower lip. Just enough each time to give me the sweet edge of his sting. "Answer me."

"Like I said, all the way," I say, voice breathy. "I want to know what we're like together."

"Is that so?"

His hand slips into my pants, fingers ever so gently stroking me there, building me up and up. Making me even wetter. Little wonder he's an expert at this too. A thick finger eases inside of me, pumping slowly. Then he adds a second, stretching me. He curves his fingers, rubbing at some sweet point inside of me, making me moan. Everything low in me coils tighter and tighter. If he just keeps doing exactly that for a while, I'll come for sure. Instead, he draws his fingers out and I almost cry at the loss. Undignified yet true.

"Are you listening to me, Clem?"

"Y-yes."

"I don't believe you." Then he lightly slaps my sex and fuck. My eyes and mouth pop wide open. His smile is all satisfaction and sharp teeth. "Look at me, baby."

I have nothing. I can barely catch my breath. The truth is, Ed's a little mean when it comes to sex and I love it. Hell. I'm pretty sure I love him. Or maybe I'm just wildly aroused beyond belief and my brain is melting. Hard to tell. It's all so overwhelming. Much more than I expected it to be.

"Okay." Sadly, he pulls his hand out of my underwear and licks them clean before lifting me up into his arms. "We'll do it your way for now. But the first time we fuck isn't going to be on a table. And tomorrow, we're having a long talk about you and your lack of patience."

I cling to him as he heads down the hallway and into his bedroom. The door shut and locked behind us.

"In the future, we make important decisions together beforehand and we discuss them fully clothed, not half naked. Understood?"

"Yes, Ed."

He mumbles something, sounding vaguely disgruntled. Doubtful of my easy compliance, no doubt. But whatever. I'm deposited on the bed then divested of my underwear in no time at all.

The man does not mess around.

Next, standing beside the big bed, he pushes down his sleep pants, stepping out of them, one hand stroking his hard cock as it points straight at the ceiling. Maybe it's the angle I'm viewing it on, from kind of below. Or perhaps it's just the faintly threatening size of him and how small and exposed I'm suddenly feeling. How emotionally out there all of this feels. But a flash of panic, of feeling like prey, triggers my fight or flight. And I'm rolling over and scrambling across the mattress. Which lasts exactly until my hands reach the edge and then I freeze because what the hell am I even doing anyway? Where is it I think

I'm going and why exactly—such a barrage of questions inside my mind. Which is also about when Ed grabs hold of my ankle.

"What's going on?" he asks, sounding somewhat justifiably bewildered. "Come back here a minute."

And I have nothing. So my brain really has melted. There you go. Slowly but surely, he gently drags me back across the sheets. I startled and tried to make a run for it. Not exactly my proudest moment.

"Hey, talk to me." He kneels on the bed beside me, rolling me over with his hands. "Clem, are you all right?"

"I'm fine. Totally humiliated, but fine." He gently pries my hands off my flushed face. "Hi."

"What happened?"

"I don't know. I just had a moment, a small freak out or something. But I'm all good now. Can we pretend it didn't happen?" I reached up for him, because hiding in his arms sounds like the best idea ever. His body is so big and comforting. A walking, talking security blanket just for me. Carefully, he rearranges us until my head is back up on one of the pillows. Arms and legs wrapped around him and face hidden in his neck, I basically just cling to him like a monkey the entire time.

"You took one look at my dick and bolted," he murmurs. "I'm not really sure what to do with that."

"Sorry."

"Don't be sorry. Nothing to apologize for. I probably shouldn't have grabbed you and pulled you back like that, you just scared me."

"It's okay. I'd already put the escape attempt on

hold," I say. "How big are you anyway?"

"What?" he asks, his tone one of complete confusion. He's lying on top of me, taking some of his weight on his elbows. This is a good position, much more soothing than him and his mammoth hard-on towering over me. But it's also quite stirring, us being plastered together with nothing between us. "We're talking about my size now? You want actual measurements?"

"Yes, please."

"Well, too bad, I can't give them to you," he says, sounding more amused now. "Last thing I'm interested in doing when I'm turned on is pulling out a ruler."

"Fine." I exhale hard. "I just . . . I freaked out for a moment. Not exactly sure why. But obviously the mechanics of your penis fitting into my vagina have been thoroughly explored on numerous occasions and the very small panic attack was totally unwarranted and thoroughly embarrassing. Not that I'm sure it was about that exactly, I just felt . . ."

He waits me out.

"Unsafe for a second, I guess. I'm not even sure why, exactly."

Now he just looks at me. "That's it, Clem. I knew we were rushing. We're calling this off till further notice."

"No." My hold on him tightens to strangler vine proportions. Whatever my subconscious concerns, I will not cheat myself out of this moment. "Absolutely not."

"Baby . . ." He sighs. "I know that you're worried about how we're going to work out. Not just in bed, but with putting our lives back together again and being a couple and everything. But rushing into this isn't the answer."

"Please, just listen." I take a deep breath and I let it out slow. Not easing back on my hold on him one iota. I can't afford to. "This is all new to me. Every single part of this life is new, and yes, some of it is a little scary sometimes. I get surprised by my own reactions to things sometimes. But that doesn't mean I want to stop or go backwards."

A little line appears between his brows.

"So if you want to stop or step back for your own reasons . . . then okay. But if you're stopping because I flipped out for a second, then don't. I'm going to weird out occasionally. Please be okay with that."

He says nothing.

"Stay with me, Ed."

"I don't know . . ."

"I do." I kiss him lightly on the lips, once, twice, three times. Because kissing him is my favorite thing. "You're the best thing in my life."

"Are you sure you're not just doing this to make me happy?" he asks.

And I give his question all due consideration. "No. I'm doing this because I want to make us both happy. But I guess I should be asking you, what would make you happy?"

His smile is slow but beautiful. "Just being with you doing whatever. I'm not that complicated."

How previous me ever left him is beyond me. I honestly feel a little bad for the girl. No wonder she was apparently so heartbroken. To lose Ed in all his wondrousness would be a terrible thing.

"Stay with me," I repeat.

"I'll stay with you whether you want to have sex right now or not. You know that right?"

"I know." The butterflies in my stomach swoop en masse. "But thanks for saying so. Do you have a condom?"

He hesitates.

"Yes, Ed. Yes again and again."

And the man is still not moving.

"Would you like me to write it down?"

"I am apparently still shit at saying no to you," he grumbles. "You get me with those beautiful eyes, and it's all over."

Fair enough. For him, it has to be a losing battle. Because I'm more than willing and he's still hard against me. The pressure of his body, the sound and scent and everything of him means I'm wet and aching. Though it's nicely aided by some slight hip wiggling. The sensation of sliding his hard length through my labia is mighty stimulating. He reaches out, hand rustling about, grabbing something from the bedside drawer.

Excellent.

Before he can attempt anything else, I kiss him deep and hard. Giving it my all. Getting us back to the good place. Hands clutching and hearts pounding. Where every touch is a thrill. We're tongues, teeth, and lips. Everything taken back to our basics. Skin sliding against skin, fingers endlessly exploring. I'm still a bundle of nerves, but I love it. He rolls us over, so I'm on top. Then he stops to tear open the wrapper, to roll the condom down the length of his cock. I, of course, watch with interest.

"You be on top," he says, voice deep and raw once again. "That way if you freak out or anything again, you're in control."

"Okay."

"Now I'm putting this on, but that doesn't mean we have to use it." He reaches back, gripping the wooden bars of the bedhead. "I'm just going to lie here. You're in charge. Promise."

"Right. Sounds good. Where should I start?"

"Why don't you kiss me, Clem?" He raises his chin, bringing my attention back to his kiss-swollen damp lips. "You could ride my face if you wanted."

A tantalizing idea. But I'm kind of stuck on the idea of my vagina and his penis getting together sometime soon. So I go for option one and kiss him instead. It's wet and messy and hot as hell. I never want it to end.

"You're so fucking pretty, baby," he tells me between kisses. "We can do whatever you want to do. Just take your time."

Guess he's forgotten about not only my lack of patience but general fascination for everything Ed. Because I go immediately for his cock, lining it up with my entrance and pushing back slowly. Very slowly. The way his gaze fixes on me, his pupils dilating . . . the man is hypnotic. Sweat beads on both of our skins. The musculature in his arms flexes, fingers tightening on the headboard as he groans. "Christ, I've missed you."

Maybe he's talking a little to her, to the previous version of me. But for once I don't mind. Truth be told, I'd kind of wondered how a girl like her managed to get a guy like him. Not just to get him but to have him. To own him. What had Tessa said about us? That I was like an itch under his skin. Maybe the answer is that old-me and Ed really had it going on once the bedroom doors were closed. And maybe I was about to find out.

Besides, it didn't make much sense to be jealous of her. After all, I get to be here now and she doesn't, the poor bitch. I get to have the wide blunt head of his cock pushing into me, his body beneath me. Deeper I take him in, feeling him moving slow but sure inside of me. Every muscle in his body tenses and, honestly, getting to sit astride him this way is divine. I am a fucking goddess in all the ways. And I don't stop until the whole length of his dick is in me completely. Eyelids closed, I just feel. The awareness of him so thick and solid inside of me . . . it's incredible.

"You okay?" he asks.

I nod.

With my hands on his chest, I start to move, taking my time. The slow glide of him out of me lights up some very special nerves. But then the harder push back onto him is kind of awesome too. Leisurely, I build up the pace, letting my body guide me. What position and speed feels best. We're well beyond tingles now. My whole body is electric, the charge building and building. And the expression on Ed's face, the exacting set of his mouth and the endless depths of his eyes. His rib cage rises and falls, nostrils flaring slightly as he struggles with the need to stay still. I'm guessing he doesn't usually lie passive in bed. Pretty sure he's the type to take charge and give orders. But it works for me. We're reaching for that high together. And when it hits . . . my insides lock onto him in both agony and bliss. It's so good it hurts. Every bit of me tenses before every atom's exploding.

Ed's hips buck beneath me, shoving his cock into me again and again. Then he makes this sound somewhere between a grunt and a growl. Something cracks loudly. Wood breaking, maybe? But I'm too high to care. My body goes liquid, collapsed across his chest. We're just two people smeared together with sweat and other bodily fluids. Meanwhile, my mind just keeps floating, reluctant to return.

"Hey," he eventually whispers, arms still raised above his head as promised. His heart beats strong and sure beneath my ear. "Clem, you okay? What are you thinking?"

"You broke the headboard." I rise slowly, still catching my breath, and I smile. "Cool. Let's do it again."

CHAPTER TWELVE

So it turns out Ed and I like to fuck. A lot. Whatever the issues in our relationship—past or present—sex is not one of them. I wake up with his hand between my legs, stroking me. He's lying behind me, his hard-on pressed against my ass.

"No wonder my dream was so good," I mumble.

"What were you dreaming about?" His teeth pinch at the sensitive skin of my neck, before he sucks and licks the sting away. I writhe against him. "Tell me, Clem."

"You."

"Good answer."

My leg is drawn back over his, opening me up for his attentions. Awesome way to wake up. I could quite happily do this every morning for the rest of my life.

"Is this okay?" he asks, nibbling on my jawline. "Tell me if you're too sore or anything."

"No, it's okay. Maybe just go easy."

"I can be gentle, baby."

He grabs another condom out of the drawer, pulling back slightly to get it on. Then he's moving me back into position, his dick prodding at me slightly before pushing inside. Fuck yes. My hands fist in the pillow. I can't get enough of him. Never want to get enough of him. And he's so damn good at it. Little wonder the thought of him doing this with anyone else drove previous me crazy.

I groan. "We should both quit our jobs and just do this all day."

His low laughter is glorious, making me shiver. That and the way he's ever slowly thrusting his wondrous cock into me. One big hand covers my breast, thumb brushing over my peaked nipple. While all the while his hot mouth devours me. My lips might never be the same. We can't seem to stop kissing. Then he licks my neck before biting lightly at my earlobe. On and on it goes, our lovemaking. It's too sweet and fine to be fucking. When his hand dips down to find my clit and circle it maddeningly, I know there's not long to go. He starts thrusting a little harder, the broken headboard squeaking. And inside of me, everything is on edge. Coiled tight enough to break. So that when he finally deigns to get direct with my clit, strumming it with his fingers, I can't help but come hard and fast. The wave of pure pleasure goes on and on. All encompassing. With him buried inside of me, hands gripping me tight as he comes too. It's all I'll ever need.

Good sex makes it easy to forget about the bad stuff. The complicated things. When your body's singing, flooded with happy hormones, it's almost impossible to care about anything else. A good place to be.

"Nice hickey, Clem." Leif grins at me across the table.

"Damn. I thought I covered it." I take another bite of toast with butter and blueberry jam. "Maybe I'll wear a scarf."

"I say be proud, girl."

"Thanks, Leif."

"Let me see." Ed lifts the edge of my tee, inspecting the work of his teeth. "Shit."

"Hmm?"

"If that's you two going slow, I don't want to see fast," says Leif, rising to go put his coffee mug in the sink. "In fact, I don't want to see anything to do with you guys at all. The new girl at the parlor, however, is pretty cute."

"I heard you went out for a drink with Shannon." I smile, momentarily distracted from Ed's unfortunate reaction to the love bite.

"Yeah, we had a good time," says Leif. "Not as good a time as you two, but then we can't all go so slow."

"Ha-ha."

"I'm hitting the shower." Leif disappears down the hallway, humming to himself. He seems in a most excellent mood. Guess they really did have a nice date or whatever it was.

Meanwhile, Ed's still staring at the mark on my neck. It's beginning to worry me. It's a decent size bruise and all, but still. His dismay is concerning.

"Hey," I say. "What's wrong?"

He shakes his head slightly. "I've never been that rough with you before . . . leaving marks."

"Really?" My brows rise high. "Huh."

"What?"

"Nothing, it's just when we first started fooling around here on the table you seemed pretty aggressive, I guess. A little edgy and dominant, sort of. Not in a bad way or anything. I liked it a lot."

On a scale of one to ten, it's a solid nine and a half of a frown on Ed's face.

Gordy finishes wolfing down biscuits to come rest his head on my knee. I'm not sure if it's me or the toast he's casting longing looks at. Though despite him being a very good dog, it's probably not me.

"After everything you've been through, getting hurt and everything . . ." Ed hangs his head, the frown ramping all the way up to eleven. "I should have been gentler with you. Fuck."

"You didn't hurt me, Ed. As I said, I liked it."

"But that's not how we are. I don't get physical with you like that in bed. Not in a way that leaves bruises."

"*Were*. That's not how we were, you mean."

He pushes back from the table, expression tense.

"Maybe I'm not the only one who's been changed by everything that happened. We've both probably got some things to work through, right?" I ask. "I mean, it just makes sense. But so long as we're working through them together, does it really matter?"

"Clem, I hurt you." He gestures at my neck, the movement sharp, agitated. "Are you not getting that?"

Now I'm frowning too. "No, you didn't."

"Yes, I did. The evidence is right there on your skin."

"No, I've been hurt before. I know what that feels like, believe me. This is not it."

Poor Gordy whines at the tension in our voices, leaning against my leg. I give him a pat. He doesn't like it when we fight. As for Ed, he just shakes his head, grabbing at the back of his neck. The usual stress pose.

So telling him about the blue thumb-sized bruises on my thighs probably won't help. A pity—I thought they were pretty. And I'm a little surprised by his reaction. I honestly am. "Have you never left a mark on a woman before? Never had, you know, rough sex?"

"Years ago, maybe. But . . ." He swears under his breath, getting up from the table. "I'm a big guy. I can't afford to get carried away."

"You were holding out on me?" I ask, aghast.

"I was not holding out on you."

"Oh my God."

His voice is flat and unamused. "Clem, we did not have any problems in bed."

"Then it's something new in our relationship. Okay."

"No. Not okay. Nothing that leaves you black and blue is okay."

I swallow, thinking it through. "When you talk about this the way you are it makes me feel like I have no say in our sex life. I was more than consenting, both last night and this morning."

Lines furrow his brow.

"I wonder if with our emotional dynamic being a little different now, that kind of affects how we relate physically as well. Because expressing your feelings regarding our breakup and everything we've been through with hot sex that I am fully consenting of is more than okay." I'll have to check with Google later. Google knows things.

Meanwhile, still nothing from Ed.

"After all, we can't expect things to automatically be all nice and neat just because we're spending time together," I say. "It's probably really healthy for us to be working through things like this in bed when you think about it."

His gaze is distant, shut down. Like he's already made up his mind and fuck what I think. So maybe it's time to take this to the next level.

"I liked it when you bit me."

"Clem . . ."

"And I liked it when you slapped my pussy."

Hands on hips, he scowls. "We're not talking about this anymore. I mean it."

"Being on top the first time was really good. But it was also hot as hell when you held me down the second time and just kind of made me take it, you know?" I shiver again at the thought, smiling not so shyly. "I came so hard I swear I saw stars. Then this morning, waking up with your hand between my legs . . ."

A strangling noise comes from the hallway, followed by his brother saying, "Please make her stop."

"This is a private discussion," I snap. "Go away, Leif."

Some muttering, then the door to the bathroom

shuts. Serves him right for eavesdropping. Meanwhile, Ed is still standing there, jaw rigid, worry coming off of him in waves. I'm done with being reasonable.

"Does it bother you that I'm not that pretty girl wearing floral prints who wants to have polite sex anymore?" I ask. "Because if that's going to be an ongoing problem, we should probably talk about it now."

His gaze cuts to me. "Clem. We did not have polite sex."

"Are you sure about that?"

"Very," the word is ground out in such a way that it might never recover. Finally, he tips his chin. "You're driving me crazy on purpose, aren't you?"

"Yes." I rise from the chair, walking over to him and slipping my arms around his waist. "Ed, I won't tolerate you thinking you're some kind of bully or that I'm a delicate little flower. That isn't fair to either of us, is it? Last night was special to me and I won't allow it to be turned into something wrong or shameful because in retrospect you're maybe a little uncomfortable with some elements."

"We didn't used to have polite sex," he grumbles because masculine pride clearly takes precedence over working on our relationship. Next his shoulders slump, hands sliding down my back, holding me to him. The worst of the fight is over.

"Whatever you say. But if we both like things a little different now, is that really such a problem? I don't want you second-guessing every thought and holding back. I like us the way we are now."

He wraps me up in his arms, holding on tight. Ever so

gently, he kisses the mark on my neck. "You'll tell me if you ever want me to stop or if you need things to calm down?"

"Absolutely."

"You had a fight about how rough you like sex?"

I shrug. "Well, yeah. Basically."

"Kinky," says Frances, the whites of her eyes on display. It's late in the afternoon and she's sitting on the couch in Braun's Books eating some of the gelato Antonio brought around earlier. Ed was right about me hating coconut. The whole taste and texture of it is just gross. Hazelnut gelato, however, is awesome. You learn something new every day. Frances took me to my doctor's appointment earlier. Despite the fact I could have easily gone on my own and all she did was sit in the waiting room. Pretty sure her and Ed are still texting behind my back, swapping babysitting duties so that I'm never alone. Still, it's nice to get some sibling time.

"Really, you think so?" I ask.

"It's not like you used to confide in me about your bedroom activities previously so I guess I can't cast judgment."

"Though Ed's reaction is telling, I guess."

My sister just nods.

"Nothing wrong with a little slap and tickle so long as it's consensual," says Iris. She always knows what to say.

"Exactly. Ed would never hurt me. The whole idea is ridiculous, and it pisses me off that he thinks I'm so fragile."

"Hmm. Maybe hold off on installing the sex swing until your doctor gives the okay for the really hardcore stuff, though." Frances licks her little spoon. "Who do you think he used to have the wild monkey sex with?"

"The doctor said I was fine and no idea." I re-shelve another book. Customers abandon stock all over the shop. Returning things to their proper places is a daily job. "So long as the only person Ed's biting and banging these days is me, does it matter?"

"You're not even curious?"

"Sure. I want to know everything about him. But I don't dwell on it or anything," I say. "That would be incredibly stupid considering my jealousy is what did us in last time."

Iris smiles. "Sounds very sensible of you, Clementine. We all have a history, but it's the here and now that's important."

Detective Chen called earlier to talk to me about the paint on the shop front. He agreed that this incident along with my car getting trashed was concerning. But apart from advising me to be security conscious and not go places alone, there's little they can say. As for my car, the insurance assessor has agreed to it being written off. To fix the damage to the body, paintwork, and windows would be more than the worth of the vehicle. Now we're just waiting for the paperwork and then eventually for the money to come through. Everything takes time.

"It's quiet, this evening," says Iris. "I should have told you not to worry about coming back after your appointment. Why don't you finish up early and go do more dreadful things with that lovely man of yours?"

It hasn't escaped my notice that Iris always refers to Ed as lovely. Pretty sure my boss has a crush on my boyfriend. Can't say I blame her.

"He'll still be at the parlor," I say.

Frances raises her head, the gelato all gone. "I can drop you off there on my way home if you like?"

"Sure. Why not?" I head behind the counter to grab my bag. "I've never really seen him in his work environment, doing his thing. Well, apart from that one time when I first showed up and he wanted to throw me out."

"A few weeks ago, you mean?"

"It's been longer than that." *Just.*

When I arrive at the parlor, Tessa is finishing up with a client, smiling and shaking hands. Not sure I've ever seen her actually happy before, since whenever I see her she is always in the presence of a major source of personal angst. Namely, me. Of course, her warm smile makes her even more beautiful than normal. Today, the green velvet chaise lounge is empty. Makes sense given they're getting close to finishing time. An old grandfather clock stands in the corner keeping time. Very vintage cool. Various drawings and pictures of tattoos hang framed on the otherwise pristine gray walls.

Tessa's smile dims slightly at the sight of me before she kind of reinforces it. It obviously doesn't come easy, but at least she's trying. "Clem. Hey, he's out back."

"Thanks."

Leif is bent over one of the massage-table-type things they use, working on a woman's calf muscle. She's looking a bit green and has her eyes firmly averted, attention riveted on the posters on the far wall. Blood wells to the surface of her newly inked skin, and Leif wipes it away with an expert hand as he works. It's easy to forget how much blood and pain must lie beneath the beauty and art in a place like this. Leif winks at me as I walk past. The sound of the tattoo gun is loud, but the music is louder. At the back of the shop, there's a hallway with a bathroom on one side and an office/work space on the other. Here's where I find Ed, seated at a table in front of a laptop. Shannon stands beside him, leaning in close, pointing at the screen. Any closer and her boobs will be touching him. In all honesty, I don't see how standing quite so close is necessary.

Annoyance shoots through me. Sad but true. And the feeling is every bit as dirty and unwanted as expected. But perhaps I'm being unreasonable, seeing things that aren't there. After all, there's my history to consider. Maybe this is how it started last time, innocuous interactions that I built up in my head and blew out of all proportion.

I school my face into a pleasant smile. "Ed?"

Immediately, Shannon takes a step back. Maybe she'd deliberately gotten too close. Though it might also be care of my previous reputation as a jealous bitch. The woman is, after all, possibly dating Leif. I'm pretty sure I'm overreacting and it's not pretty.

"Baby, hey. I didn't know you were coming in." He

lights up at the sight of me. Fuck the green-eyed monster. This man is mine. I'm like ninety-nine percent sure of it. Nine-eight-point-five at worst. Still pretty good odds. The usual fluttery feeling in my belly and warmth in my loins kicks in at the sight of him. "Did Frances drop you over?"

"Yeah."

"How'd it go at the doctor's?"

"All good," I say, moving to stand beside him. His arm slides around my waist, drawing me closer. "Hi, Shannon."

"Hey." Her smile is instantaneous. "We can talk about this later, Ed."

"Right," he says, his gaze never leaving my face. "Is that all I get about the doctor's, that it was all good?"

"My recovery is going as well as can be expected. If there was anything important to tell you, I would." I lean down, kissing him briefly on the mouth. "Promise."

"Okay. Give me some more of that," he says, nodding at my mouth.

"It would be my pleasure."

My mouth covers his, kissing him lightly, teasingly even. But he doesn't tolerate it for long. Before I know it, I'm in his lap with his hands in my hair. His mouth devours me in the best way possible. The man kisses me stupid. Honest, my brain is long gone. I'm all hormones, my fingers fisted in his T-shirt.

"Oh good God, at work?" A voice fills the room.

Ed clears his throat. "Tessa."

"I'm heading off. Behave, children."

"Have a good night."

"Bye," I say. Then, once I'm sure she's gone, I whisper,

"She almost sounded not completely in hate with me. It's a miracle!"

Ed just smiles. "Told you she'd come around."

"I thought I might get to see you doing some ink."

"Had a cancellation so I was just looking over some bookwork."

"Ah. By the way, I was wondering . . ."

"Hmm?"

"Would you be willing to do another tattoo for me sometime?" I ask, slipping my arms around his neck.

"Of course. I can do it whenever you want. What are you thinking?"

"You know how there's the dogwood tree outside the condo? Maybe a branch of that with some flowers."

His gaze turns thoughtful. "Are you sure about that? Tattoos are awful permanent."

"I know."

"Okay, I just want you to be certain. Not all of our time there has been good, you know."

Hard not to wonder if the unspoken thought there is that we may not last. But it's not like I'm asking him to tattoo his name on my forehead. I do have some limits.

"I know. It'll always be an important part of my life, though," I say. "Besides, I think the flowers are pretty."

"Where do you want it?"

"Below the violets?"

"Sounds good." He nods. "Pity you've got your self-defense class tonight or I could get started on it for you now."

"I could miss a class."

His brows rise. "You're serious about this?"

"Very. If you don't mind. I mean, you've been here all day. If you're not in the mood . . ."

"Working on you is not a chore, Clem." Suddenly enthused about the idea, he pats me on the butt, easing me off his lap. "Let me get something down on paper and you can see what you think."

It doesn't take him long and I love watching him work. The man is an extraordinarily talented artist. Something I already knew, but seeing him in action is still mind-blowing. His final drawing is perfect. Exactly what I had in mind.

"You're absolutely sure about this?" he asks, arms crossed over his chest.

"I'm sure."

A nod. "All right. Shirt off and lie down on the table."

"Why do I need to take my shirt off? It's short-sleeved." I ease it up over my head regardless, handing it to him so he can hang it over the back of the chair.

"It'll be in the way."

This doesn't entirely make sense since the violets cover my shoulder and this will be going lower on my upper arm, but whatever. He's the expert and we're in a private room out back of the parlor so it's not like me and my bra will be on view. Though lucky I wore a nice black lace number as opposed to plain old cotton. Because making a good impression is always important.

I climb onto the table, getting comfortable, and trying not to wonder how painful it might be, or whether I'll turn the same pallid shade of green as the girl getting her calf done. Next, the drawing is traced and turned into a sticker which he carefully places against my skin after shaving any hairs from the area and applying lotion. He's wearing gloves now. Once I okay the position, he pulls over a little stool on wheels and sets up the tattoo gun. This involves a rubber band and him selecting inks to go into little caps since I'm leaving him in charge of colors.

"What's going on?" asks Leif, arriving in as the gun starts up. "Nice bra."

"Clem's getting another tattoo and you keep your damn eyes off her." Ed is the picture of concentration.

"I'll have you know that once a client is in the chair, I am the very picture of professionalism," Leif objects, his voice haughty. "Is that lace edging?"

Ed's frown deepens. "Ready, baby?"

I nod.

The first touch of the needle is a bit of a shock and it does hurt a little. It's like a sort of cutting feeling as he does the outline. But the area soon numbs, and I relax.

"Okay?" he asks.

"Yes. Are you finished for the day, Leif?"

"Yeah, Shannon and I are heading out for dinner."

"Is this a first date sort of thing? How exciting."

He just winks. "We'll close up as we head out. Have fun, you two."

A grunt of acknowledgment from my beloved. His lips are set in a distinctly pissy line. "He shouldn't have been looking at your chest."

"You're the one who made me take my shirt off for no reason."

Now a small smile appears. He's so devious in his own sweet way. "That was for me. Not for him."

"Well lock the door next time."

"I will."

"Can't believe you lied to me."

"What?" He raises a brow. "I said it would be in the way, and it would be in the way. Of my view."

My eyes narrow.

"Well, you lied to me about letting Gordon sleep on the futon."

I just smile.

The added benefit of getting another piece of art from Ed on my skin is getting to watch him uninterrupted. Since the tattoo is roughly the span of my hand, it does take a couple of hours. He works seamlessly, interspersing the tattoo gun with a wipe of a paper cloth and some more of the ointment to apparently keep the skin moist and slow the flow of any blood.

"What are you thinking about?" he asks me at some stage.

"Um, how did we meet? You never told me that story."

He swallows, thinking it over. "Once upon a time, a very charming prince did the banking once a week. And this very charming prince, well he had a thing for one of the women who worked there. There was just something about her . . ."

"I like this story."

"Me too," he says.

"So what did the very charming prince do?"

"Ah, well . . . the prince didn't want to come off as some asshole harassing her in her workplace. So he took his time chatting to her, getting to know her a little more each visit. Of course, he had to start doing the banking more often for security reasons, you know?"

"Sounds legit."

"That's right," he says. "And actually, before the prince could find his balls and figure out a way to ask her on a date that wasn't sleazy, he saw her out one night. She was with her friends at a bar not too far from her work. Some going-away party for someone."

"Huh."

"So the prince just happened to bump into her and they got to talking. A funny thing happened, the prince forgot all about his friends and the girl forgot all about her workmates—"

"Why do you get to be the prince and I'm only the girl?"

"Sorry. The princess forgot all about hanging out with her friends and they talked for hours and hours."

"What about?"

"Everything and anything. We just talked. It was like we were in our own little world, just the two of us together. And by the time it occurred to us to check on our respective friends, they'd all disappeared. I mean, they'd texted us. But we were obviously very into each other and they hadn't wanted to interrupt. It wasn't like we'd been worrying about checking our phones, what with us being so caught up in talking to each other." When he meets my eyes, his gaze is tender. This is obviously a happy memory. "It was late, really late. So we swapped numbers and I asked you about having dinner with me a couple of nights later and you said yes. Then I walked you to your car."

"Did we kiss?"

"No, we didn't kiss until the end of our first date."

"When did we start having sex?"

"Second date. I made you dinner at my place. Told my roommate to get the hell out and not come back until as late as humanly possible." Now his smile turns vaguely wicked. It's a thrilling thing to see. "My poor baby. You couldn't keep your hands off me any longer. And there was no way I was keeping mine to myself."

"Sounds sensible. A princess can't be expected to perform superhuman feats of restraint all the time."

"Exactly."

"Can I ask another question?"

He nods. "Go for it."

"What's it like to love someone?"

His gaze meets mine for a moment before returning to his work. "That must be strange for you, not having feelings for anyone."

"Some have developed. I'm not completely unemotional . . . these days at least."

"But at first when you woke up in the hospital, not knowing anyone."

"Yeah. I didn't even recognize my own sister," I say. "Think I initially probably trusted the doctors and nurses more. I just saw them more often. Or maybe their roles in my life made more sense. I don't know."

"So you want to know what love feels like," he repeats, little lines appearing between his brows. "Of course, there's the love you have for your family and friends. It's pretty different to what you can feel for your significant other. I'm guessing the latter is what you're interested in?"

"Yes." And it's on the tip of my tongue to ask him if I fall under this heading. But I don't. Go self-restraint.

He's silent for a long time, the sound of the tattoo gun the only noise. "For me, it's more than just thinking about the person all the time, wanting to get into their pants."

"I'd hope so."

"But don't kid yourself, that's part of it as well."

I just smile.

"It's wanting to know what they're thinking, how they're feeling. Just keeping an eye on them and checking they're okay. Because if they're not okay, you want to fix it. Make life smoother for them. Put a smile on their face."

"That makes sense."

"The first stage is like, whenever you see them or hear their voice or hell . . . even just when someone says their name, it kind of causes this response in you. This automatic physical, mental, and emotional response. It makes you happy. It's exhilarating," he explains. Though I'm already familiar with stage one. Not that this is necessarily the right time to enlighten him as to this fact. "Then that grows into something more. Like, putting them and their needs first most of the time just starts to come naturally. You make what changes are necessary to fit your lives together because it's the right thing for both of you. Early on, their little quirks, idiosyncrasies, and shit like that are kind of cute and amusing."

"Let me guess, that doesn't last?"

The edge of his mouth moves upwards. "No, it doesn't. But you accept most of these things as being a part of them."

"Nobody's perfect."

"Exactly."

"You keep using the word *most*," I say. "Most of the time. Most of these things."

"If you're going to meld two lives together, there's got to be some willingness to change on both sides. You both have to want it equally. A big part of making it work is your willingness to compromise. Some things just are deal breakers. But *mostly* you accept and respect the person for who they are and they accept you."

I nod.

"What love means is probably pretty different for everyone, though. I feel like I only gave you a mechanical rundown. But there's all of the emotion behind it too."

"And you loved me." Just the thought of it staggers me. So maybe Frances is right about me putting him on a pedestal. Though I don't think I'm blind to the idea of him having flaws. We all have flaws. It's like he said about being willing to overlook certain things and work on others. Becoming a real live functioning couple sounds as difficult as I'd suspected. And despite us quasi-dating or whatever we're doing, there's every chance that at the end of the day Ed doesn't want to take such a mammoth risk on me again.

Who could blame him?

Then again, there might have very well been aspects of his behavior that fed my inner demons. All of previous me's insecurities and shit. He's open to talking to me about pretty much everything now. But he wasn't always. A habit that might go back much further than I know. He's already admitted to working too much, to not paying attention. Caution would be wise on both sides. It doesn't stop me from wanting to bleed my heart out all over him, however. Lately, when it comes to him, I always feel like I'm leaking emotions. Perhaps this tattoo will be as long-term as we get this time around.

"Yes, I loved you. Very much," he says matter-of-factly. "And before you ask, I don't know what I feel for you now, Clem. Okay?"

"Okay."

He turns off the tattoo gun, sitting back on the stool. "Right. We're done. What do you think?"

I smile. "I love it."

CHAPTER THIRTEEN

So it turns out that the internet can provide you with an absolute wealth of tips regarding the giving of blow jobs. One of the top suggestions is to just ask the guy what he wants and or likes. This, however, doesn't suit what I have in mind because it's the next morning and Ed is fast asleep and I kind of want it to be a surprise. We, of course, had sex the night before. Because he's gorgeous and hot and wants to fuck me, so ongoing inner emotional turmoil or no, why wouldn't we?

This is my point. Life is short.

Oh, and I'm pretty sure he held back using the excuse of watching out for my newly inked arm. Like I wouldn't see through that excuse. The jerk.

It's a good thing we slept nude and he's on his back. Otherwise, access could have been a real problem. I crouch beside his magnificently slumbering form admiring the ink, the art spread across his skin. My own freshly tattooed arm is a little tender, but no big deal. And it's tempting to take a picture of him, though it seems distinctly wrong and stalkerish without previously given permission. I'll just have to commit him to memory and hope this time it sticks.

I stroke him at first, working the morning wood into something more solid. The trail of light hair leading down from his belly button is nothing short of a delight. I kiss his chest, sliding my free hand over his pecs, up his shoulders, and then down his arm. When I reach his hand, his fingers mesh with mine for a moment.

"Clem." His voice is thick from sleep. "What are you up to?"

"Nothing."

"Mm. I don't believe you."

As the bulk of the internet articles advised, I start by getting his cockhead damp, care of my tongue. While I guess it's vaguely kind of like licking an ice cream, as advised. It's also kind of definitely a dick so I don't really get the correlation, but whatever. He smells and tastes of musk and sweat. It's unique, though not unpleasant. His pubic hairs are crisp and his balls are soft in my hand. Because all of the tip lists said some ball rolling action is recommended. Given the happy rumbling sound Ed's making, they were right. I hold his dick firmly with one hand while massaging his balls with the other. Occasionally slipping a finger back to rub his perineum, which is the bit immediately behind the balls. Apparently, this is quite important and experience enhancing for the dude.

Got it.

In all honesty, sucking cock isn't anywhere near as complicated as some of those websites made it out to be. Pretty sure men in general are just happy when the right person pays attention to their dick. Fair enough. Ed playing with my pussy is a thing of wonder. When I take half his length deep into my mouth, firm my lips around his width, and drag my mouth back up him, he groans. Then, when I have his cockhead in my mouth, interspersing lashing him with my tongue and sucking, he fists my hair, holding it tight.

Ha. So much for his treat Clementine like a delicate little doll bullshit. It only lasts as long as he thinks he's in charge. Now I know for certain.

His cock swells and I can only fit so much of him in my mouth. But all good. I lick him and suck him and stroke him with my hand. It's not exactly science so much as common sense. He reacts and I give him more of whatever made him happy. When the noises he makes get louder, his stomach muscles tensing. Just when I think he's probably about to come, however, things abruptly change. I find myself suddenly on my back with Ed crouched over me. He pumps his cock vigorously until warm come spills over my bare stomach. His hot face is buried in my neck, teeth sunk into my skin again as he comes and comes.

At least he's bit me on the other side this time. Both sides of my neck will match. His broad shoulders heave, the quiet of the room full of his panting. I totally nailed this. Honestly, I'd high-five myself if I thought I could get away with it without him noticing.

"Baby." He sighs all happy like. "Hell of a wake-up."

"Alarm clocks are so passé."

"I'd take your mouth any morning." He raises his head, fixing his lips to mine. There's no light and easy. We kiss slow but deep. Morning breath be damned. And meanwhile, he's spreading his seed over my body as if I'm a canvas or something. Pretty sure he even doodled a smiley face in it all.

"What are you doing?" I ask, looking down with a smile.

"Just marking what's mine."

"I see."

His gaze turns somewhat wry. "I bit you again."

"I know, and after all of your oh so gentle lovemaking last night." I sigh. "You're going to have to stop fighting it, Ed. Besides, I like you a little out of control."

He shakes his head. "Just like I said, you always get your way."

"But when we both win in the end, is that really such a bad thing?" I smile. "I match now. Got a love bite on both sides of my neck."

And yet his smile is fleeting. "Are you sure I didn't hurt your head or anything when I pushed you onto your back just now?"

"I'm fine."

"Okay, okay," he groans. "I'll try not to worry so much."

"Thank you."

"Thank *you*," he murmurs. "That was a great blow job."

"You're welcome. Though I kind of got carried away and forgot to do a few things. For instance, apparently outlining the cockhead with the tip of your tongue works well."

"You can save that for next time," he assures me with a grin. "Sounds like you've been doing some research."

"Oh, I have. Question, do you not like me swallowing?"

He lifts one shoulder. "Do what you like. I just felt like covering you in my come and went with it."

"Huh. Okay."

With a final kiss, he picks up a T-shirt off the floor (the one he stripped off last night when we were in a hurry to get naked) and wipes off my belly. I stretch and groan some when I get to my feet. Ed, meanwhile, strips the top sheet off the bed and proceeds to wrap me up in it.

"I kind of need my arms," I say.

"It's just to get you to the shower without my brother seeing anything interesting."

"You do realize he only pretends to flirt with me because it annoys you."

A grunt as he heads for the door au naturel.

The man's swaddled me so well I can barely walk, but I shuffle down the hallway with him close behind. From the kitchen comes the sound of feminine giggles. I raise my brows and once the bathroom door is shut behind us say, "I think Shannon had a sleepover with Leif."

Another grunt. Blow jobs or not, Ed's no more of a morning person than I am.

"And you're walking around bare-ass naked," I say. "Hope she didn't see anything."

He gets the water going, testing the temperature with his hand. "Shannon's not interested in seeing my ass."

"I don't know. It's a very attractive ass."

"You're funny." Glad he thinks so. I drop the sheet and follow him into the small space. "Turn around. I'll wash your hair."

"Thanks."

Few things compare to him rubbing shampoo into my scalp. Ed and his magical fingers. "Clem, you're not really worried, are you?"

"Worried?"

"About Shannon." There's a slight thread of tension running through his voice. And who can blame him, given the catastrophe my last bout of jealousy triggered? So I take my time, considering the question with all due seriousness. "No. If you were actually interested in her you'd tell me, we'd break up, then you'd make your move. And if she was interested in you, despite apparently banging your brother, I'd kick her ass with my newfound self-defense skills."

"Pretty sure self-defense doesn't mean kicking people's asses."

"Hmph. The best form of defense is attack."

"But your faith in me is humbling. Tip your head back."

I wipe some suds out of my eye. "Are you mocking me?"

"Absolutely not." He so was.

"I just mean . . . if you were into someone else you'd tell me, right?"

"Yes, baby. I'd tell you. But I'm not, okay?"

"Okay. Understood." Next comes the conditioner and more scalp massage. So damn good. Maybe I should grow my hair back. With longer hair it would take him longer to wash it and the whole experience could be drawn out further. A fine idea.

"You're not jealous, then?" he asks, the tension still lingering in his voice ever so faintly.

"I'd prefer I was the only one to see the glory that is your bare ass. If that's jealousy, then I guess I am a little. But when you think about it, it's no better or worse than you mummifying me with a sheet on the off chance Leif might see some skin."

He carefully rinses out the conditioner and we're sadly done. I pump some of the body wash into my hand and get good and clean while he does the same. There's something fascinating about watching the way his hand moves over his body, the way he handles his goods. So matter-of-fact about the way he washes himself, while here I am ready to write his dick bad poetry. Though to be fair, he does have a really great dick.

"You have a point," he finally concedes.

"I think a certain amount of jealousy is probably par for the course for the human condition."

"Agreed."

We finish up and turn off the water. He towels himself dry with the same efficiency while I dawdle. The thought of going out there and socializing with Shannon doesn't fill me with glee. It's just kind of weird to have her here this morning. Or any morning. Given her overabundance and very open (to me at least) opinions regarding previous me and Ed, I'd rather keep the woman at arm's length.

Obviously I'm not moving fast enough for him, because he wraps a towel around me, carefully tucking the end in above my breasts. Then he kisses my shoulder and leaves. At least he's wearing a towel around his waist this time. We have actual butt coverage. Sad but necessary.

I put some styling product in my hair and blow dry it. It's too short to do my makeup first. I learned this by trial and error. Once my scar is covered by my bangs, I apply some concealer, mascara, do my eyebrows, and add a little lip balm. Done. The girl in the mirror looks okay. Despite her matching hickeys, one fading but the other fresh. I'm half-disposed to keep them in clear view. Because Ed did that. Because I made Ed do that. But in the end, I decide that decorum requires the hiding of rough sex. A little concealer goes on either side of my neck.

And I'm delaying. Anxiety has soured my stomach. The question is, do I feel this way because it's Shannon or because someone new is in my personal space effectively? It feels mostly like the latter with a bit of the former thrown in for fun. Though I didn't freak out when Leif turned up, so . . .

Ugh to this. I ever so bravely speed walk back to the bedroom and quickly get dressed. There's conversation and laughter coming from the dining table. The chink of cutlery against china. When I get out there, my eyes no doubt go a little wild. She's made a stack of pancakes, scrambled eggs, and bacon. There's also sliced strawberries, banana, and blueberries. I'm pretty sure half of this stuff wasn't in the fridge. God knows what time she got up and went to the shops to get it all. Normally we just down a coffee, maybe eat a granola bar, and call it good. But oh no. Shannon has pulled out all the stops. The table is even set all pretty like with a blue-and-white-check tablecloth and matching napkins. I had no idea Ed even owned a tablecloth and napkins.

"Grab a seat, baby," he says, pouring me a cup of coffee as I sit. The way he looks after me makes me melt despite the morning's weirdness. It's far more important.

Gordy's tail beats against my legs. He's counting on me to get him some of the bacon. Not that he doesn't love me, but bacon.

Leif looks as happy as a king. A well-fucked and well-fed king.

"Morning, Clem," says Shannon, sitting on his lap. Her smile is so wide and doubtless genuine. I feel like a bit of a bitch.

"Morning." I attempt a smile. "You made all this? Wow."

"She's spoiling me." Leif grins, kissing her on the cheek.

"She sure is."

Despite shoveling pancake into his mouth, Ed doesn't seem so happy. "Just make sure nothing spills over into the workplace. I don't want shit getting weird with you two seeing each other."

"Nothing's going to get weird. My disciplined professionalism will be more than enough to quell Shannon's inevitable lustful advances." Shannon rolls her eyes as Leif shakes his head at Ed. "And you're worse than an old woman."

"That's sexist," I say, sliding a pancake and some berries onto a plate. Sort of healthy. Of course, drowning the whole thing in about a gallon of maple syrup makes it less so. Whatever.

"All right. He's worse than an old man, then."

"And ageist."

"I'm not going to win here, am I?"

"No."

Gordy rests his head on my knee, giving me the saddest of sad eyes. I can't blame him: the smell of bacon is pretty tempting and there's a heap even with Leif and Ed downing food like the end is nigh.

"Don't do it, Clem. You're teaching him bad habits," says Ed. "Go to your bed, Gordon. Go on. You know better than to beg for food."

With a heavy doggy sigh, Gordy goes. Oh, the cruelty. His life is a veil of tears. You can tell by the way he flops onto the giant comfy cushion and cuddles up to his stuffed toy friend, the slightly gnawed on squirrel. No dog has ever been treated worse. It's obvious. I send him a silent promise to sneak him some bacon later.

Shannon climbs off Leif's lap, picking up the half-empty coffeepot. "Let me make you some fresh, Ed. This has been sitting for a while."

"It's fine," he says.

"Oh, it's no worry."

Once I swallow what's in my mouth, I say, "You're a great cook."

"Isn't she?" Leif is all aglow.

Ah, young love/lust. I wonder if that's what I look like when I'm ogling Ed. All happy and silly and high on life. Probably. It's a nice way to be.

"You know, Clem, I wouldn't complain if you wanted to start making me breakfast like this every morning," says Ed with a sly sort of grin.

Leif just snorts while Shannon laughs.

I nod, choosing my words with care. "Here's the thing. I have a limited amount of energy in the a.m. to expend. So ask yourself, blow job or breakfast? What do you want more?"

At this, Leif cracks up laughing too. I didn't think it was that funny, but whatever. Two spots of pink appear high on Shannon's cheeks. Guess mentioning oral sex over the breakfast table is a no-no.

Ed, however, considers the question. "I get to choose every morning?"

"No. Somedays I might not feel like doing either."

He leans over, giving me a maple syrup flavored kiss. Yummy. As responses go, it's rather great. No words are needed. It's enthralling, all of his different types of smiles. Often the variations are quite subtle and reflected more in his eyes than his mouth. This time, it's the one that says I'm something to be cherished. A less observant or not so Ed-centric person might mistake this expression for amusement, but it's not. It's more.

Inside my chest is the now familiar sensation of warmth and overabundance. As if the amount of emotion he inspires inside of me is a dam bound to burst eventually. Every time a moment such as this takes place, I'm pushed closer to the edge. What will come out of my mouth the day this happens is a little frightening. Actually, it's terrifying. What it might mean and how he might react. But I can admit to myself that I'm no longer a stranger to falling in love or being in love or however you want to put it. He is my love. I know this now. Just as he explained last night, I want our lives entwined forever and ever and there's little I wouldn't do to make him happy. Frances is sort of right about me not knowing him that long. Though maybe loving him is an automatic thing for me, for this body. The not fucking it up, however, will probably take more effort.

"Seconds, Ed?" asks Shannon. "Or can I clear your plate?"

"It was great, but I'm good. You cooked; let me clean up."

Leif scoffs. "I was just about to offer to do the dishes. You're trying to make me look bad in front of the ladies."

"It doesn't take much."

His brother flips him the bird.

When you think about it, probably best not to declare my adoration for Ed, and all the rest, at the breakfast table in front of an audience. So instead, I finish up and take my plate over to the dishwasher where he's loading.

"Everything okay?" he asks, studying my face.

Care of practicing taking selfies for my Instagram account the other day, my carefree happy smile is at the top of its game. "Yes."

Ed, however, pauses. "What's on your mind?"

"Just work and stuff," I lie.

"Okay. We'll head off in a few, yeah?"

"Sounds good."

Shannon is holding out a fresh cup of coffee when I turn around. "Here you go, Clem."

"Thanks." More caffeine is always appreciated. "And thanks again for breakfast."

"Not a problem." Her teeth are so white. "Are you sure you're okay, you look a little . . . I don't know, off? How's your head and everything? Do they think you'll be back to normal soon?"

Normal is long gone. But I don't want to tell her that. "Um, no. I'm fine and my head's healing as best it can. But the chances I'll get my memory back aren't great."

"I'm sorry."

"Not your fault." I look elsewhere and chug down some coffee. Coffee makes everything better.

"Yeah, but . . . not knowing who you are and losing your past like that."

"I survived."

"Clem's not usually big on talking about it." Ed's hand rubs at my shoulder, giving it a quick squeeze. "Good to go?"

"Mm-hmm."

I add my empty coffee cup to the dishwasher and give Shannon a smile before following him into the bedroom to grab my bag. Time to get the day started and getting back into routine is good. The glance he gives me over his shoulder is questioning. Good that he knows I'm not one to open up about the messy insides of my skull to most people. It's confronting all of the medical stuff. While it's important, and I can see why others always inquire about it, dwelling on it doesn't feel like moving forward. I'd rather move forward. Ed grabs his wallet and sunglasses.

"Sure there's not something on your mind?" he asks, wrapping me up in his arms. "You seem a bit distracted."

"Do you prefer previous me or new me?"

"I like you both for different reasons, if that makes sense." He rests his forehead against mine. Quite possibly my favorite move of his. "I'll have a word with Shannon, make sure she doesn't question you again. People need to understand that you don't remember them the way they remember you. Relationships are different now. They need to respect your boundaries."

"It really is fine. I'm not that delicate."

"I know, but I have a vested interest in keeping you happy."

"Do you?"

"Absolutely," he says, a playful glint in his eye. "When you're in a good mood I get wake-up blow jobs."

"That's true."

"And I get your smile. The real one where your eyes get kind of lit up and it just . . . damn. Let's say I like it a lot."

"You're my favorite person in the whole wide world, did you know that?"

"Am I now?"

"Yes." I take a deep breath and I want to say something. I need to say something. "Ed, I don't want this to end."

Something flashes across his face, an expression there and gone so fast I can't read it. Doubt, maybe? Or hesitancy? But then it's nothing but a memory, and he says, "I know, baby. Me neither."

I exhale. There's reason to hope. "Okay, then. Good."

CHAPTER FOURTEEN

My day goes well until Detective Chen walks into the shop. There's nothing wrong with the man. He's been great. Honestly, however, apart from our phone call the other day, I'd done my best to shelve him. Willfully blanked his existence out of my life. It seemed easier. He brings back memories of those first scary days, waking up in the hospital and being so profoundly lost. And he's a walking reminder that someone, somewhere, might be out to get me.

But his being here also means something might have happened regarding my assault and robbery. Perhaps I should be elated, but I'm not. My stomach sinks through the floor.

"Miss Johns." He nods, slipping off his sunglasses. "Your sister mentioned you were working here. Hope you don't mind me stopping by."

I nod and hold onto myself. "No, of course not."

Fortunately, Iris is out having lunch with Antonio. Introducing the detective in charge of figuring out who tried to kill me would be a bit awkward. Despite the vandalism incident, the shop is a happy safe place for me. Maybe that's compartmentalizing my life in some unhealthy way. But I'd like to keep it that way just the same.

"There's been a development in the case," he says. "A man has pleaded guilty to the first attack in the area near where you were assaulted."

"Oh." I blink. "Only the first attack?"

"That's right."

"But . . . how does that make sense?"

He clears his throat softly. "We have reason to believe that the attack on yourself was committed by someone else. Who, exactly, we don't know yet."

"A copycat?"

"Perhaps, yes. Although it is also possible that they are entirely unrelated."

At first, I don't know what to think. But then, I realize I was wrong. It makes perfect sense. "Shit."

"The investigation is ongoing. Someone may still come forward with information relating to your case." He really needs to practice his selfie face, because his smile isn't soothing at all. "I just wanted to let you know."

"So I was right: it is personal. The attack, then my car, and the window here . . ."

"Without any solid evidence it would be unwise to jump to conclusions. We don't know anything for certain yet."

And I give a look that can only be interpreted as "Are

you fucking kidding me?"

"Your work colleagues and friends at the time were questioned."

"Few as they were."

"If you can think of anyone else we might want to have a word with, please feel free to contact me." His gaze is so sincere. Though Frances was so over all of that at the time. Tracking Ed on social media and God knows who else. "But, Miss Johns, it would be best to remain vigilant about your security. Don't go places alone if it can be avoided, okay?"

I nod.

"Hopefully we'll get a break in the case soon. I'll let you get back to your work."

"Thank you, Detective." He's half-turned away when my voice calls him back. "Actually. There is this one guy, maybe he's just a creeper, but . . . his name is Tim and he lives in our building. It's probably nothing . . ."

"I'll look into him."

"Thank you." I try to smile. It doesn't quite work.

Hope's a funny thing. To a large degree, it depends upon your ability to shove the shit aside and focus on the happy. To tell yourself everything is going to be okay. To play make-believe. I try my hardest, but underneath, anxiety rules the day. It's not so easy, knowing someone wants to kill you and has already tried once. The ferocity of hate involved in smashing a bottle against someone's skull must be huge.

And it's stupid because I basically knew this before. How the attack wasn't random. After the detective's visit, however, it's harder to ignore the evidence and slap on a happy face. Over the next couple of days, I start finding that loud noises make me jumpy. Getting my mind to still so I can sleep is next to impossible. Despite spending our one mutual day off a week having a sleep-in before wandering around the Portland Museum of Art (very cool) and hitting up The Holy Donut, my inner peace is trashed. After almost a week of this behavior, Ed sends me back to the doctor. Now I have pills. Some to help me sleep and others to keep me chill. There was also a big lecture about trying various non-narcotic calming techniques or risk being sent to a shrink. Because spending more time with doctors and sitting around in waiting rooms would be awesome. Not.

I take my pills, try to act serene, and fill my Instagram account with happy things. Pictures of book covers, videos of Gordon doing his doggy smile and wagging his tail, and the golden hairs atop of Ed's toes. God knows why his big ass feet amuse me so, but they do. My account now has two followers, Ed and Leif. They insisted, though, that my account stays locked against all others. It makes me a little self-conscious to know the Larsen brothers are watching, but whatever. I also don't miss another self-defense class because survival instinct. Ed suggests we try yoga sometime, learn some meditation. While the thought of watching him bend, stretch, and breathe is a good one, I kind of like us having a few nights free for TV and sex. You know, spending quality time together.

Despite the doctor's orders for tranquility, the movie watching stays true to the favorites of previous me. *The Lost Boys* and *Robocop* are my new favorites. Ed tries to calm things down a little with *When Harry Met Sally* and *Beaches*, but both left me in tears. Happy ever after tears for the first film and my heart has been torn out, stomped on, set aflame, and reduced to ash for the second. I swear, my eyes are still red the next morning. Though a good cry is kind of cathartic. Cleansing, almost. Ed, however, just yawned and generally looked pained. Leif fled the condo to go meet Shannon. So yeah, the movies stay mostly violent.

If I was occasionally chafing at the level of protection provided by Ed and Frances before, it's nothing compared to life post Detective Chen's update. I'm not even allowed to step foot out the shop door. Ed texts every hour or two to check I'm still both breathing and where he left me. Iris refuses to leave me alone. I can't even cross the street to get coffee in case my hater has decided to take up vehicular manslaughter or something. Imagine how messy that would be. So unless Frances is hovering/visiting, we have to wait until my friend from the café has time to make a delivery, something Iris totally talked the poor boy into. Every day he not so subtly asks how things with me and Ed are going. Just on the off chance we've broken up overnight and I'm now free to go on that date with him. The day after *Beaches*, my bloodshot eyes gave him such hope. Disappointing him daily just so I can get my caffeine fix seems harsh. But such is life.

"Hey," says a familiar voice late Saturday afternoon. "Get your bag."

I get off my knees, having finished helping my tiny customer and her mom find books about elephants. (I tried selling her on my personal favorite, *Curious George*, but she was adamant in her choice of animal so *Babar* it was.) "Tessa. What are you doing here?"

Behind the counter, Iris is beaming. "Your friend is here to take you out. Isn't that lovely?"

It would be rude to say no. Honest, but rude.

"We're getting your hair fixed and buying you something decent to wear." The expression on her face leaves no doubt as to her opinion regarding today's jeans and T-shirt combo. It's a *Jane Eyre* quote tee this time. My new favorite book. To be fair, though, the top pick changes at least weekly.

"Do I have any say in this?" I ask, curious. And yes, a little pissy.

Tessa sighs. "Don't be difficult. Ed and Leif need to get some stuff done and I'm pretty much only here as a favor to them. But let's face facts, your hair does need fixing. It was kind of cute, but now it's grown out a bit and it's not working at all."

"It has looked better," says Iris, tipping her head this way and that. "That's true."

My hand goes to my head in protest, but I don't bother to refute them. Beyond a certain point, not even some styling product can fix things.

"I promised I'd be nice." Tessa crosses her arms.

"Who knows, this might even wind up being fun."

"All right."

And I didn't even bother checking with Iris because this has all obviously been planned behind my back. I'm almost used to my life being organized by other people. It's crazy. The tension of living this way, of waiting for the next attack, is doing what remains of my head in. But I prefer to avoid the weird emotional distance the pills provide unless it's absolutely necessary.

Out on the street, Tessa doesn't stride ahead. This time, she sticks to my side, keeping an eye on our surroundings. Like something could happen at any moment. She's been well coached by the love of my life. Maybe I should be more appreciative of all the care they're taking. It means I'm loved or at least wanted. People care about me. But the burden of it, the lack of freedom involved, gets me down.

Still, I try to relax. No way anyone would dare attack me when I'm out with Tessa. She wears her elegance like a superpower.

The salon is only a few blocks away. My stylist is a gorgeous Latino lady named Margarita. Like Ed, she has magical fingers. My crappy mood and reservations last about two seconds beneath the scalp massage she delivers during the shampooing and conditioning process. The woman can do with me what she will. I am mush.

In the fancy black chair positioned in front of the mirror, she pats my shoulders. Her eyes go to my fringe. "Clementine, can I just fix this? Will you trust me to do that?"

"I need to be able to cover the scar."

"Not a problem."

"Then yes. Please."

"Thank God for that." Tessa sighs, slumped in the chair next to me. She makes even that position appear somehow glamorous and elegant. Today she's in a green floral halter neck dress. Silk, maybe. Even with my concerns regarding patterns, I can see its beauty. Chunky wooden bangles jangle on her arm. Guess she either didn't work today or got changed before she came and got me. The tattoo parlor seems to be more of a jeans atmosphere.

Funny how people's tastes change. How Ed went from dating her to me. Though I guess I used to be more like Tessa. More put together.

"What?" she asks, having caught me watching.

"Nothing. Just thinking."

For a moment she says nothing. "Ed says you need information, that you like asking questions . . . so ask."

"Really?"

"Sure. Go for it."

Margarita works on my hair without further comment. The click of her scissors and upbeat background music filling the air.

Huh.

"What now?" she says, meeting my eyes on the mirror with less patience this time.

"Nothing. I guess I just expected another lecture about staying away from Ed."

"Would it do any good?"

"No."

"Well then, I won't bother. Ask away . . ."

"Thank you. Did we used to do things like this together?"

"More like we'd have salon days, go get manicures and things. It was fun." Her smile is faint, but there. "We'd do a little shopping and have lunch somewhere nice in the city, have a few beers and talk smack about the boys. Sometimes all four of us would go see bands or just have a meal out. Often others from work would come too, guest artists passing through and so on. Ed used to be big on his team building, back when he had more time."

"Before getting caught up in my mess."

"As I understand it, you're in no way responsible for this current situation. Don't take on shit that isn't yours, Clem. That doesn't help anyone."

"Hmm...... Will you tell me a bit more about your background?"

"Like what?" she asks.

"Anything really . . . I'm just curious," I say as Margarita moves my head this way and that, still cutting.

Legs crossed, Tessa relaxes back in the chair. It turns out she's an only child and her parents are both lawyers. She rebelled by studying art and then moving into tattooing. While initially shocked, her folks are now fully supportive of what she does. Though they wouldn't mind if she wanted to get a degree in accounting or something just to be safe. She doesn't go anywhere near her romantic history with Ed and I don't ask.

"What do you think?" asks Margarita finally, hands sitting lightly on my shoulders.

I don't think I look too different, just neater. More stylish, somehow. With my hair shaped this way, my jaw doesn't look as heavy. As requested, my bangs have been left growing longer, sweeping across one side of my face to cover the scar before being tucked behind an ear. Or they will when my hair grows a bit more.

"It's still like a choppy layered crop only done right this time." Tessa nods. "I like it. Maybe in future, let Margarita cut your hair. Now for the makeup."

"We're doing makeup?" I ask.

"Girl, Ed gave me his card. We're doing everything."

It's a little disconcerting watching myself get another makeover. After all of the hacking at my hair and dumping of my wardrobe, I don't want to go back. Though I still mostly look like me, but with good hair. The multitalented Margarita does my makeup as well, which is good because I don't have to get used to someone new touching me. When I ask her to keep it reasonably simple and natural looking, Tessa snorts. But I get my way. So at the end of all the highlighting and application of various pencils, powers, and lotions, I look like me with good hair, cheekbones, a healthy glow, slightly bigger eyes, and pink lips.

"You're really good," I say to Margarita.

Tessa nods, pulling out a credit card. "Rest assured, your boyfriend's going to give her a great tip."

It's evening out on the street, the lights flickering on all around us. I stretch my neck, working out the kinks from holding so still. "Thank you. That was actually kind of fun."

"Oh," purrs Tessa with a crafty grin. "We're not finished yet."

I feel fear.

"We're having dinner?"

Tessa waves a hand in the direction of the restaurant. "Go on in."

I look between her and Vito's Italian. My favorite place, apparently. "The last time I was here I accidentally crashed Ed's date with this woman. It was really awkward."

"I heard. But you're invited this time."

"Are you coming too?" I ask, not against the idea. It's actually been a nice afternoon.

"Yes. Go on; you look good."

My hands smooth down the front of my jumpsuit. Except it's like a fancy jumpsuit. Black crepe, sleeveless with a high neckline. It's simple, but nice. Elegant, I think. Tessa tried to talk me into a pair of strappy high heels, however, I'm in black flats. I feel good. I like how I look.

"Thank you for taking me to the salon and hanging out with me," I say.

"Clem, you're delaying. Are we entering the restaurant sometime tonight or not?"

"Okay. Yes. We're going in." I stride forward with the kind of bravery only a new outfit and a professional makeup artist and hair stylist can give you.

Vito's is every bit as beautiful as the last time. Heavy

white tablecloths and dark red napkins. Candles flickering on the tables. And half the restaurant is filled with all of the people I know. Or just about. My sister Frances, Iris and Antonio, Leif and Shannon, Nevin. Even Walter and Jack who found me that night and Nurse Mike from my hospital stay are here. All of the important people from my short life are standing before me. It's unbelievable.

"Hey, baby," says Ed, dressed in a shit hot black suit. "You look beautiful."

"You organized this?"

He smiles and kisses me on the forehead. "Good to see you and Tessa managed not to kill each other."

"Ed, this is amazing."

"Frances helped. Doctor Patel is away at a conference and Detective Chen had to work. No way was I inviting the little shit from the café who keeps asking you out. But otherwise, I think we got pretty much everyone."

"This is amazing. But why?"

He just tips his chin. "Why not?"

Why not, indeed. We both know life is short. It doesn't need to be said. My eyes fill with tears and I blink them back furiously. The emotion teeming inside my chest is huge. Overwhelming.

"Hey, are you all right?"

"Yes," I say, managing a watery smile. "I love you."

There's the inevitable pause. His careful blank face. "Thank you, Clem. Why don't you go say hi to your friends?"

I just nod and do as he says. There's a goodly amount of hugs, pats on the back, and some kissing of cheeks involved in greeting all of the assembled. Ed's lack of a reaction to my declaration doesn't matter. I mean, it does. But it's okay. Everything's good.

If I'd stopped and thought about it for half a second, it was always going to be this way. The important thing is, we're together and there's always the possibility of a future. He might come around. It's what I tell myself through all of the smiling and the first two glasses of wine. (Just as well I hadn't taken any of my chill pills.) Alcohol takes the edge off my angst and we have a great night. Everything is fine.

As soon our bedroom door clicks closed, I kick off my shoes and undo the tie and zip on my jumpsuit. There's been a hesitancy to him since we left the restaurant. A troubled look in his eye. Like his mind's been busy all night concocting a speech, figuring out exactly what to say regarding my disturbing confession. Doubtless he has all sorts of sensible reasons for not saying it back or for wanting me to leave the L word out of things for now. But I don't want to hear it. Not yet.

"Clem . . ." He turns to me, a hand running agitatedly through his hair. His eyes widen slightly at the sight of me shrugging out of my clothes, stripping off my underwear. Or maybe it's the aggressiveness with which I'm doing it. While he might be conflicted, I know exactly what I want.

"No talking," I say.

"But—"

"No."

I grab the lapels of his suit jacket and go up on tip-toes, slamming my mouth against his. Surprise is on my side. Hands clutch at my waist, his lips opening to me. For all of tonight's emotional upheaval, it's pretty fucking hot, him wearing a slick black suit and me being naked. Only I'm not acting exposed or vulnerable. It doesn't take Ed long to get with the program. To take control. We war with tongue and teeth, greedy for each other as always. He backs me into the door, breathing heavy. Then he drops to his knees.

"Ed?"

"You said no talking." He nips at the soft skin of my belly in warning. A hand lifts one of my thighs over his shoulder, opening me to him. I grab hold of his hair for balance sake. His warm breath is right there.

My insides tighten in a most stimulating manner. Rivers have gushed less than my pussy.

His free hand kneads one of my ass cheeks, angling me just so. And the tip of his nose brushes against my mound as he plants soft kisses. "Surely you know when someone wants to go down on you."

Excitement takes over and my mind is empty. I really have nothing to say. The long flat of his tongue drags through me, up toward my clit. Just that easy, my legs start trembling. In the low lighting of his bedroom, his gaze is so dark and hungry. The man can eat me alive. I'd be totally fine with that. Next, he sucks at the lips of my labia, making my blood surge. He teases my clit with flicks of the tip of his tongue. I'm a wet writhing mess in no time, grinding my pussy against his face. And the sound he's making. The sucking noises and groans of appreciation as if he doesn't just like how I taste and how wanton I'm acting. He fucking loves it. When he concentrates on my clit, sucking on it, and even nibbling gently, I explode. My legs go weak, my whole body shaking. If he wasn't holding me up, I'd have hit the ground. Somewhere out in the universe, my mind flies free. It's a heavenly experience getting head from Ed.

Before my insides have stopped quaking he's up and on his feet, pulling a condom out of the wallet in his back pocket. I'm only vaguely aware of what's going on. Still trying to catch my breath. But he lifts me in his arms, pinning me against the wall. It's just natural for my legs and arms to go around him. Then he lines up the thick head of his cock and surges into me, sure and deep. I gasp at the sensation, clinging onto him for dear life, as he proceeds to pound into me. Guess we're both yet again working out some feelings. And what better way than through rough sex?

My spine feels like it's stuck to the wall, one of his hands on my ass and the other cupping the back of my head. Protecting me. A good thing one of us still has the capacity for thought. My skull has definitely already taken enough damage in this life. Again and again he drives the hard length of his dick into me. And we're more than a storm—we're a cyclone or a hurricane. Something wild, a bit scary, and out of control. But I trust him. How could I not? I love him.

Impossible to come again so soon. Yet he angles my hips and starts hitting the magic place inside of me. Harry Potter has nothing on this shit. Soon enough, my insides clutch at him, trying to hold him deep. A sweet shock travels through me, illuminating me from within. It honestly wouldn't surprise me if I glowed in the dark just then. What he does to me is staggering, the way his body works with mine. How good he makes me feel and how high he sends me flying. His flushed face presses into my neck, his hips surging and hands clutching me tight. Like they couldn't pry us apart. Eventually his body quiets, still buried in mine. The silence feels heavy, a weight I probably can't lift and lack the energy to even try.

Pretty sure sweat has glued me to the wall. Ed's suit will definitely need dry cleaning. All he did to achieve access was lower his zip. Men have it so easy.

"You okay?" he asks, voice rough.

"Yes."

Slowly, carefully, he lowers me to the floor. My legs are still trembling. Those poor innocent muscles. Forget the tender state of my vagina. Every atom in me feels shaken. We certainly don't tend to go easy on each other when it comes to sex. Especially on nights like this. Nights where it's easier to express things between us in a physical way as opposed to opening up about our emotions. Though of course that was my choice.

"Can we just sleep?" I ask, suddenly tired beyond my years.

He cups my face, gently kissing me on the lips. He tastes of me. "Sure, baby. But we're going to have to talk about it eventually. You know that, right?"

"I know. Tomorrow."

"All right," he agrees. "Tomorrow."

And I lie there. Then I lie there some more because my brain will not shut down. Pretty sure Ed isn't sleeping either, so this is working out just great. Seems orgasms can't fix shit. Not even temporarily. Also, I know deep down that I'm doing the wrong thing, cutting off all lines of communication between us. Even temporarily, it's wrong. It's what did us in last time. Uncomfortable and awkward or whatever, we need to talk it out.

"I'm scared," I say quietly.

His arms slide around me, his body pressing tight against mine. I'm cocooned in Ed. "What about, baby?"

"That I said the wrong thing. Or that I said the right thing too early. That maybe I shouldn't have said anything at all." I sigh. The heaviness of my heart and weight of my soul feel all too real tonight.

"I don't know about that," he says. "Our inability to effectively communicate with each other was what did us in last time. I think if you're feeling something you need to tell me about it so we can deal with things together. You just . . . you surprised me, is all."

"Well, what are you feeling?"

He exhales. "I'm scared too, you know. This has all happened fast, us getting back together. And I wouldn't change it for the world, but I do worry . . ."

"Hmm."

His arms tighten around me. "It's more than that, though, Clem. I'm fucking terrified about this idiot being out there gunning for you. What if I can't stop him? You don't want me treating you like glass and following you around all the time. But the thought that he could get to you when I'm not there . . . I can't lose you again. I won't."

"Yeah, it frightens me too. But we can't just stop living."

Lips brush against my shoulder, pressing a soft kiss.

"I just feel jittery all the damn time," I say. "On edge. It's driving me nuts."

"I'm so sorry, baby."

"It's not your fault. You're the one good thing that's come out of all of this."

"Sorry I wasn't ready to tell you I love you back yet." His voice is low and telling. Like he too has all these feelings going on that he doesn't know what to do with. Like there's a burden in his heart, the same as mine. Perhaps I shouldn't wish emotional turmoil on him, but it's good not to feel alone.

"Love is complicated. Well, whatever this is, is complicated."

"That it is," he whispers. "But I'm here, Clem. I'm not going anywhere, okay?"

"Okay." I relax against him, shutting my eyes to sleep. Honestly, it feels like a weight has lifted. Tonight, lying in Ed's arms, I don't think I'll need a pill. Maybe talking things out isn't so bad after all.

CHAPTER FIFTEEN

"You're a hard person to catch alone," the voice comes from out of the darkness.

It's some stupid hour of the morning. Two or so. And I'm standing out front of the apartment building beside the dogwood tree because Gordy needed to pee. Also, I did too, but I did my business in the bathroom as per human tradition.

I startle at the sound of the voice, keys already held in my fist with the ends pointing out between my fingers just in case. Eyes-throat-groin. Eyes-throat-groin. I almost blurt the words out, so strongly has Gavin welded them into my brain. "Who's there?"

A shadowy figure wanders up the footpath toward me. Better lighting in this area would be really fucking helpful right about now.

"Clementine," the voice drawls. Male.

I say nothing.

Finally, he's close enough for me to make out his face. It's Tim, the friendly neighborhood creeper. Great. His hands are in his pockets, a sly sort of smile on his face as he stands closer than necessary. "Out with the dog, huh?"

"Gordon. Yes."

Gordy raises his head and wags his tail once, before going back to sniffing along the fence line.

"Haven't had a chance to talk to you in ages. You're always with your boyfriend."

"Ed. Yes."

"Guy acts like he's your bodyguard or something." Tim chuckles. "Like you need protecting."

I can't step back on account of the tree so I step to the side, putting some distance between us. Tim steps toward me, getting back in my personal space. All the little hairs on the back of my neck stand on end, my shoulders tensing.

"Am I making you nervous?" he asks, still smiling.

"I don't know. Does my dog make you nervous?" I bump Gordy's butt with my knee, wishing he'd mount some kind of protective display. Growl even. But his tail just wags a little and he snuffles more deeply at the fence. Worst. Dog. Ever. "You're out late."

He just shrugs. Probably been out peeking through bedroom windows. Or riding public transport, standing too close to women so he can sniff their hair or something. Whiskey taints his breath. So not only is he gross in general, he's probably drunk too. My luck just can't get any better. And my fight or flight instinct is screaming at me to get away. Meanwhile, with me in only a small pair of sleep shorts and a tank top, the guy is eyeing my chest. Full on fucking ogling the outline of my breasts beneath the thin fabric. It's so gross, the way he's staring. I feel dirty, exposed, and I'm not doing a damn thing, but walking my dog. It's all him, this disgusting horrible person. Amazing what he can achieve by doing so little. Just a few looks and a couple of words really. Shit.

"Gordy," I say, voice trembling. Dammit. "Time to go in."

Unfortunately, whatever has caught his canine fascination is far more interesting than me. The good boy does not come. Should have put the leash on him after all. Ed would give me such a lecture for yet again not maintaining strict doggy protocol.

"Clem, c'mon," protests Tim. "I only just got here. Surely you can spare me a minute."

"Good night."

"Seriously?"

"You're acting like I owe you my time or attention or something. I don't. Goodbye."

He grabs at my elbow and I yank it back, dislodging his hold. "Hey—"

"Do not touch me!"

"Jesus." The face he makes, like I'm the one being unreasonable. He staggers a few steps away. Give me strength, the hurt expression he casts over his shoulder. "Fine. I was just trying to be friendly. There's no need to be such a cunt."

I stand there, blinking. My heart going approximately a zillion miles an hour. Even my hands are shaking as Tim makes his way up the stairs, dicks around drunkenly with his keys for a minute, before finally managing to get the door open. And all the while, I'm trying to remember my self-defense training. Trying to call up what Gavin would tell me to do at moments like this. But my brains are scrambled from the fear. My mind is a useless blank. Then Tim's gone, disappeared inside.

Oh thank fuck. Holy shit. I take a deep breath and let it out slow. Everything's okay.

"Gordy. Not cool, buddy. You need to come when I call you."

Gordon hangs his head.

"Come here." I hold out my hand until he's pressing his head against it, angling for an ear rub. If he wasn't so gorgeous I'd be seriously irritated. But how can anyone stay cranky in the face of such doggy perfection. "Are you finally finished screwing around out there? Does everything within a ten-mile radius now carry your scent, hmm?"

His butt wiggles, tail whipping back and forth. I crouch down to give him a cuddle. One of us needs the comfort. Let's not say who. "We need to keep a baseball bat by the door like Frances has, don't we? Or I should have brought my mace out with me. That would have been the smart thing to do."

Gordy gives me a nice sloppy kiss on the cheek.

"I love you too. Yes, I do."

In fact, I'm so busy focusing on the puppy love and catching my breath, I don't even hear the door reopen. Miss the light tread coming down the front steps.

"Hey, Clem."

I fall back on my ass, I'm so startled. "Shannon. Hey."

"You all right?"

"Yeah." I shake my head, trying to clear it. "Just got paid a visit by our neighbor, who was particularly rapey tonight."

"What?" Her brows rise. She wanders closer, hands behind her, tucked into her back jeans pocket or something. At least she had the sense to get dressed to come out here.

"Ugh. It's nothing. But if you ever meet a guy named Tim, avoid him."

"Will do."

"What are you doing awake?" I ask, continuing to give Gordy pats.

"I could ask you the same thing. Leif is out, but . . . I don't know . . . just couldn't sleep." She smiles. "Did you have a good time tonight? That was really great of Ed getting everyone together. Even Tessa seemed to be in a good mood."

"It was wonderful of him, and Tessa's not so bad. She's more bark than bite."

"Hmm." Shannon does not look convinced. "Well, I think it's very brave of you, not freaking out your boyfriend working with his ex in such close quarters. Not sure I'd be as understanding if it was Leif."

I pause.

"Can't be easy when the woman looks like a Victoria's Secret model. No one would blame you for having your doubts. Especially since her and Nevin seem to be having some issues lately." She tucks her hair behind an ear. "I shouldn't be saying anything, but—"

"No. I trust Ed."

For a moment, she just watches me, face blank. "You told me, last time."

"What?"

"About Ed and Tessa. How you knew. What you'd found."

What I'd found. With those three little words, my heart stops. And suddenly, everything feels wrong somehow. Me. Shannon. Gordy. The silent street. The laughably weak streetlight. Terribly, unutterably wrong. And the strangest certainty comes over me that Shannon didn't just wander out here on a whim. She pulled on those jeans, and laced up those boots, and came out here deliberately. To tell me this.

I rise to my feet, dusting off my behind, taking a step back. Trying to act calm and casual. "I told you?"

"I didn't want to say anything, seeing you seem so happy. But I figured you had a right to know."

"No."

"What?" She seems surprised at the firmness in my voice. Maybe I surprised myself.

"No, I don't want to know."

"How can you not want to know?" She frowns, her face shrouded in shadow. "You found Tessa's—"

"Because I trust him," I snap, refusing to hear her words. To fall into the trap of jealousy. "And because I'm not going to repeat the worst mistake of my life all over again. No way. No fucking way."

For a moment she studies my face. Then she nods slowly. "Okay. If that's your final decision."

"It is." Relief floods through me, and for a moment I'm glad that Shannon came out to speak to me at this ridiculous hour. Glad? Hell, I'm almost elated. Because I feel like I finally got the opportunity to put that past disaster to bed. To rise above it. "We, ah, we should get back inside. Ed will be wondering where I got to."

There's the sound of Gordon growling and that's it. She moves so fast. There's only pain. So much exquisite terrible pain. I gasp, grabbing hold of her arm for balance more than anything. Unable to withdraw the knife from my gut, she shoves me back instead. Now Gordon is snarling. Shannon kicks out at him, again and again. I guess one of her kicks land because he whines and retreats.

"Fucking mutt," she hisses, putting her hand to her foot. I guess Gordy got a bite in. What a good dog.

"You."

"Of course it's me." She rolls her eyes, actually looking to heaven. It's kind of insulting. Her pretty mouth is skewed in an ugly manner. "You're so fucking stupid. You could never deserve him."

It's about Ed. Of course it's about Ed. Jesus fucking Christ, my love life.

So I lie on the ground, just trying to breathe, to stay alive. All of my torso is warm and wet, blood soaking into my pajamas. My hands cover the knife's handle, too scared to move. Actually, I feel cold. Distinctly chilled. Maybe I'm going into shock. That would make sense. Wonder how much blood you have to lose before you pass out?

If Gordy was pissed before, now he's full on rampaging. Loud barking fills the air, echoing off the apartment buildings, reverberating down the street. The very good dog is outraged and in a frenzy.

Standing over me, Shannon glares at him. It's like she's a complete stranger with the manic light in her eyes and twisted expression. Above her the branches of the dogwood stretch out, covered in pretty blossoms. Then there's the dark night sky, the stars, and the moon. A car glides by, but we're in the shadows. Hidden in plain sight. In fact, there's a whole city, a whole universe all around us going about its business. And I have the worst feeling I'm going to die here.

"Give me that," she says, reaching for the knife.

"Don't you fucking touch my dog."

"Shut up, you useless bitch."

"No."

For all my bravado, there's only so much you can do with a knife sticking out of your belly. I kick at her, slap at her hands. All of the movement jostles the blade and pain shoots through me. Then her foot connects with my side again and again. Something cracks. A rib, maybe. Pretty sure she put on steel cap boots for the occasion. The woman plans ahead. The knife is ripped out with all the delicacy it was first inserted. So none. All the while, Gordy growls and barks.

I roll away from her, as best I can, not sure if her next move will be to finish off me or the dog. My hands cover the wound, blood seeping up and over my fingers. God, there's so much of it. And all the while, darkness edges in, taking my vision, my body, everything. No repeat this time. No second chances.

"Gordy," I say, voice weak. "Go. Run."

Then Gordy makes a noise I'd never hoped to hear. A whimpered sort of howl. But past this, there's suddenly yelling. Voices. I can't tell who. Someone is screaming. An enraged, demented, inhuman sort of sound.

Hands cover my own and he says, "Baby. Stay with me."

If this is the last thing, I ever hear, I'm stupidly okay with it. Love. It makes fools of us all.

Three days later . . .

I wake up slowly, the white ceiling swimming into focus. It's the smell, however, that clues me in as to where I am. The sharp, chemical, clinical smell and beeping of machines. Blergh. Back in the fucking hospital. Again. From top to toe, my body feels floaty, distant. Apart from the stretch and pull of the bandages and stitches on my stomach when I move. Not so great.

Then I remember. "Gordy!"

Shuffling noises off to the side as Ed bolts upright in his chair. Guess he too had been sleeping. Soon enough, he's leaning over me, brushing back my hair. "Hey, hey. Baby, it's okay. Calm down, everything's fine. Gordy's at home safe and well. He's just got a couple of stitches in his face, remember? I told you."

"You did?"

"Yeah, you've woken up a couple of times before, but you were pretty groggy then too." His smile is small and tired, but the relief in his eyes is real. "It's okay. You lost a lot of blood and they've got you on the good stuff so you don't feel any pain."

"Oh." God, my voice sounds so weak and pathetic. "I hate hospitals."

"I know. Here, have some water. Just sip it, not too much." He holds a cup of water with a bent straw up to my lips. My throat is grossly dry and scratchy. Meanwhile, Ed's clothes are rumpled, dark shadows linger beneath his eyes, and he's heading into beginner's beard territory. He looks worn out, like he's been sleeping here for days. "But the doctor said you're recovering really well. And look at all the flowers you got."

The man speaks the truth. Every available surface is covered in blooms. I must have a lot of friends these days, people who care about me. What a fuzzy nice warm feeling.

"Got to say, though, every time you wake up, you say Gordy's name first," he mutters. "Pretty sure you're just keeping me around because of my dog. You're not doing my confidence any good here, Clem."

I snort. Shit. It kind of hurts. "Don't make me laugh."

"Sorry." His gaze lightens. "Frances will be back later; she's just handling some work stuff. Leif and Tessa and Iris have all been in, though they're still limiting your visitors at the moment. Can you believe they tried to get me to leave the first day? I told them straight out that wasn't happening."

"Thank you. I'm so glad you're here."

He just smiles.

"They got Shannon?" It's all coming back now. The blood, the sheer fucking craziness. "I can't believe she stabbed me. What a psycho bitch."

His eyes go wide. "They got her all right. Well, Leif did."

"Leif?"

"My brother saved the day." Ed smiles. "When we got out the apartment doors, I went straight to you, didn't have eyes for anything else. But Leif saw someone running off onto the street. Well, limping quickly, 'cause Gordy got her good, even through her jeans. She made it about a hundred feet before he crash-tackled her to the ground. Fortunately, she'd already tossed the knife away into some bushes. So he was able to hold on to her until the cops showed up, with just a bunch of face-scratching to show for it."

"Wow." I couldn't get my head around it. All of it. "So Shannon's in jail? Arrested? Charged?"

"Aggravated assault, attempted murder, all sorts of things. Detective Chen said they're still settling on the exact list. But she isn't going to be seeing the outside of a cell for a very long time."

"Good."

"I'm sorry, baby. Never even fucking suspected it could have been someone that close to us."

"Not your fault. It never occurred to me either.

What's the damage to me?"

"One broken rib and one fractured from her kicking you, internal injuries from the stab wound which they operated on, and a cut on your hand from fighting off the knife."

"No wonder I feel vaguely all over like shit."

"You want me to call a nurse?"

"No, just stay with me." I shake my head ever so slightly. My poor body. Maybe never moving again would be best. It's weird; my head feels heavy and insubstantial at the same time. Like I might sleep for a hundred years. And as much as I like looking at Ed, my eyelids drift closed. "Is that okay?"

"I'm not going anywhere. I love you, baby," he says, pressing a kiss to my forehead. "I'll be here when you wake up again."

Three weeks later . . .

"Oh, I don't believe this shit."

"What?" he asks.

"What sort of monster would put *Caraval* in the adult fantasy section? It should be shelved in YA. It's clearly a coming of age story." I pass the book back to be added to the pile he's already carrying. And I'm holding it there for just about forever before he grabs it. "Ed, keep up."

"How about you slow down?"

"No, thanks."

"Seriously, Clem—"

"Just because some books have grit and sexy times people think they can't be YA. It's ridiculous. Such an old-fashioned, out-of-date point of view."

A heavy sigh from Iris over behind the counter.

"Thought you were happy to have me back," I say.

"Clementine, my darling, I was delighted until I realized how cranky convalescing has made you."

"Rest and recovery apparently doesn't come easy to some people." Ed follows along behind me, balancing a tower of books. "We're very grateful you let her return."

Iris snorts. "That's because she's been driving you crazy."

"That's true," the traitor answers in his beautiful deep voice.

Whatever.

Iris finishes tidying up the till, bundling up a bunch of twenty-dollar bills. "I suppose I'd be bored silly having to lie around all the time and do nothing."

"It's not like I didn't read the books you brought over. I read the whole *The Others Series* by Anne Bishop, and all the rest. But that much recuperating would drive anyone insane."

"Some clearly more than others."

"And I don't blame you for the state of the shop, Iris."

"What a relief," she says drily.

"It's whoever you let in here while I was away that needs a good kicking. No respect for our shelving system. And I'm not even going to mention what they did to the coffee mug display. How the whole lot hasn't fallen down yet and smashed is beyond me." I shuffle along carefully with a hand to my side. Sometimes I'm a bit sore, but no big deal. Broken ribs and stab wounds just take a while to heal. "*The Secret Garden* in gardening? Are you kidding me?"

Iris sniffs. "Antonio was just trying to help."

"The man should stick to gelato."

"Ed, please," she says. "Can't you give her a pill or something and make her go to sleep for a while?"

My boyfriend takes his turn at sighing.

"You know, you could go to the tattoo parlor," I say. "I'm perfectly fine here."

He stares down at me, nonplussed. Sadly, even this looks good on him. The sharp angles of his face and stern set of his mouth. "Within five minutes of me leaving you'd be doing something stupid like trying to climb a ladder."

"I like to think I'm past the jumping counters and tackling people stage of life," adds Iris. "Even if it's for their own good."

I open my mouth, but Ed gets there first. "Baby, don't tell me you wouldn't do it. I've seen you checking out those high shelves. If you need something from up there, I'll be getting it down."

"I'm a bit past climbing high ladders as well," says Iris.

Like she doesn't just want to check out his ass and gawk at the muscles in his arms as he reaches for stuff. The woman doesn't fool me at all. She's about as demure and frail as me. Which is not. Well, mostly. "You might as well put the books down on the couch, Ed. I'm going to need to sort them. By the way, I find it very hurtful that you don't trust me."

"I trust you just fine, but I also know you." He sets the books down, then puts his hands on my shoulders, rubbing gently. "And I love you, which is why I'm sticking to your ass until I know you're okay. Now, you've got another hour before I'm taking you home to rest. Okay?"

It isn't the first time he's said it . . . about loving me, not about only letting me work for a couple of hours a day. We actually fought quite heatedly regarding this matter. But it's still highly thrilling to hear his regular outpourings of affection. Turns out that watching someone almost die is wonderful for making people push past their concerns and confess their true feelings. Though I don't recommend stabbing yourself just to try and level up your relationship. For one, it hurts. And secondly, the medical bills are a bitch. The ones from the vet for treating the cut to Gordy's head weren't much better. Such a heroically good boy, helping to stop psycho Shannon. He'd even been allowed to hang out on the bed with me during the day once I got out of the hospital. Nurse Mike and Doctor Patel were less than delighted to have me back in with new injuries. But apparently such is life.

While Shannon didn't have time during the attack to pour out the intricacies of her plan to me, she had shared them in depth with Detective Chen. How she'd oh so cunningly fed me a torrent of lies regarding Ed and Tessa spending alone time together in the back room and after hours. Right up to her secreting a thong in a little used top pocket of his jacket. Of course, she'd told me she'd seen Tessa slip it in there herself while Ed had the coat on. Guess previous me packed her bags and left rather than confronting him with the evidence. Highly doubtful I'd have listened to anything he had to say in his defense at that point, anyway. Shannon completely messed with my head, and this was even before the bludgeoning with a bottle. It's amazing how insecurities can tear us apart.

Apparently Ed wasn't getting over the breakup and responding to her attempts at seduction as well as Shannon had hoped, and that's when she lost it and attacked me the first time. Just to make sure I was out of his life for good. Turns out she has a history of fixating and stalking we knew nothing about. Leif feels awful, for inviting her into our home, for sleeping with her. But I think she would have devised a means to be there one way or another.

She'd been hoping to blame my death in the front yard on my mysterious unknown attacker, obviously. What with the dark and lonely street, and Ed and Leif being fast asleep inside, it might have worked. But Gordy's barking put an end to that, bringing the brothers Larsen to the rescue. Hard not to believe DNA evidence or something wouldn't have given her away. But then, Shannon obviously has some issues with reality. Apparently after my untimely demise, Ed having seen what wonderful girlfriend material she made, care of her display with Leif, would have somehow fallen into her arms during his grief. Can't really imagine Ed taking up with his brother's ex, but whatever.

Gordy and his mighty bark saved the day. Or the

night, rather. Leaving me with another scar and another chance to get things right. A chance that I am not going to mess up. Love and life sure can be scary. But not living your best life, not loving as hard as you can . . . what a terrible waste that would be. And the man standing in front of me is the best of everything.

"What are you thinking?" he asks, gaze warm, loving.

I could soak it in forever. In fact, I think I will. "I have a question, but I'm not sure if you'll like it."

"When has that ever stopped you before?"

"Good point."

"Go on, Clem. Ask me anyway."

"All right then," I say, taking a breath. "Would you marry me?"

Over at the counter, Iris gasps.

But Ed opens his mouth and out comes nothing. Lots of lots of it. The hands on my shoulders falling perfectly still. Oh, fuck me. This isn't working. There is none of the expected or at least hoped for explosion of love, delight, or any other positive response sort of indicator crossing his face.

"You don't have to, of course. I mean . . . it was just a thought."

He licks his lips. "It was just a thought. So you didn't really mean it? Asking someone to marry you is a pretty serious business. You can't fool around with that sort of thing."

"I didn't say that."

"Well, what are you saying?"

"I'm saying, or asking rather, would you marry me?" I

explain, lungs tight and awful. More emotion than trauma. Or maybe a bit of both. "But then you didn't say anything and I got scared so it all kind of went sideways."

He just studies me.

"Maybe we should talk about the weather or something a bit safer than . . . you know . . . weddings."

Slowly but surely a smile spreads across his face. "Yes."

Shit. "You want to talk about the weather?"

"No." He laughs. "Clementine, I would like to marry you."

"You would?" I exhale, suddenly about a hundred times better than I had been a moment before. This is right. In fact, it's quite possible the rightest thing I've ever done, apart from searching him out in the first place. "Good. That's good. Phew. I love you, you know?"

"I know. I love you too, baby."

Perhaps not the most romantic of proposals, but given the state of my poor stomach, getting down on one knee just wasn't an option. And it worked okay in the end. Then Ed's mouth covers mine and it hardly even matters that Iris is sobbing loudly in the corner. Ed and I are getting married. This life is great.

Three months later . . .

"I'm not so sure about this." Hands out to either side, I stand oh so fucking precariously in the stiletto heels.

While they do look amazing with my sharp white pant-suit, balance is definitely eluding me. Big time. And my peony bouquet is no help at all.

On the plus side, my French nail polish looks awesome with the antique engagement ring Ed slid on my finger a few months back. Not landing on my ass in the cobblestone street, however, would be good. We'll obviously be getting no help from the driver since the car just took off. Never mind. It's just me and my unofficial bridesmaids. Since we decided on keeping things simple, there's no big wedding procession or anything. But Tessa and Frances have been at my side through all of the recuperating and planning. I'm lucky. This is a fact.

"I told you to practice walking in them," says Tessa. Pregnancy hasn't mellowed her much despite all of the glowing. But we've been having a huge amount of fun shopping for baby gear and maternity wear. "One of these days you're going to actually listen to what I say."

Frances just sighs. "Knew you'd regret the choice of footwear."

"But they look so fabulous," I groan. "Maybe I'll just take them off."

"No, wait. Knowing your luck, you'll step on a piece of glass or something. Just hold on a minute, I can fix this." Tessa strides across the cobble stones in her fancy wedges with nary any difficulty at all. At the restaurant door, she signals to someone inside. A moment later, Nevin comes out, followed by Ed, Leif, and Niels. All of them looking mighty damn fine in black suits. Like seriously, so much eye candy. If I wasn't head over heels in love with one of them, I wouldn't know where to look first.

Leif wolf whistles. Such a flirt. I carefully wave my bouquet in his direction. There's been kind of a cloud hanging over the man ever since the attack. Guess having your choice in bed partner turn out to be so disastrous would be hard to take. Not that I ever blamed him about Shannon. But I think he still blames himself.

Niels just nods. He's every bit as big, silent, and intimidating as his little brother made him out to be.

"Go rescue your bride, Ed," Tessa slips into Nevin's arms, being wary of her bump. They make such a great couple, and they're going to be awesome parents.

"He's not supposed to see you before the wedding!" Frances laughs, holding my hand, helping me stay upright. My big sister is the best. Also, we drank champagne in the car. We even had a glass each for Tessa since she's otherwise indisposed. These are the sort of hardcore sacrifices friends and family make for one another.

"You know, Mom would be appalled," Frances continues. "No froufrou wedding dress, Vito's cannoli instead of a cake, and now this. You were her one hope for a big wedding since I just took to off to Vegas for a weekend."

"Oh, well." I give her fingers an affectionate squeeze. "I'm wearing white at least."

Ed lopes over with his long-ass stride. "What's wrong?"

"My pretty shoes are impossible to walk in."

"Those are some sexy heels." His smile is slow and wide and everything I want in this world. With no effort, he lifts me up into his arms. Inside of me is all of the swoon in all of the world, solely for this man. "You look beautiful."

"So do you."

"What's on your mind, Clem?" he asks, lowering his voice, making it just between me and him. "Everyone's waiting inside. Are we doing this or what?"

"Rest assured, there's no way in hell I'm letting you get away from me this time."

He grins and the light in his eyes . . . oh my. "C'mon then, baby. Let's get married."

Purchase Kylie's Other Books

It Seemed Like a Good Idea at the Time
Trust

THE DIVE BAR SERIES
Dirty
Twist
Chaser

THE STAGE DIVE SERIES
Lick
Play
Lead
Deep
Strong: A Stage Dive Novella

THE FLESH SERIES
Flesh
Skin
Flesh Series: Shorts

NOVELLAS

Heart's a Mess
Colonist's Wife

Find Kylie at:

www.kyliescott.com

Facebook: www.facebook.com/kyliescottwriter

Twitter: twitter.com/KylieScottbooks

Instagram: www.instagram.com/kylie_scott_books

Pinterest: www.pinterest.com/kyliescottbooks

BookBub: www.bookbub.com/authors/kylie-scott

To learn about exclusive content, my upcoming releases and giveaways, join my newsletter:

https://kyliescott.com/subscribe

Keep reading for a free sample of

it seemed like a good idea at the time

NEW YORK *TIMES* BESTSELLING AUTHOR

KYLIE SCOTT

Chapter One

Wednesday

In a fair and just world, he'd have looked like shit. The years would have ground him down to all but a shell of his former glory. Of course, this hadn't happened. My luck just wasn't that good.

"You made it," he said, walking barefoot down his front steps.

"Don't sound so surprised. You taught me how to drive."

Pale blue eyes gazed at me flatly. No visible gray in his dark hair. Not yet, anyway.

"Hi, Pete," I said.

Nothing.

"I come in peace."

More of the same.

I climbed out of my car, muscles protesting the

movement. My sundress was a crumpled ruin. What had looked hopeful, happy, and bright in the wee hours of the morning didn't hold up so well under the late-afternoon light. A twelve-hour drive from Sydney to South East Queensland's north coast will do that to you. I pushed my sunglasses on top of my head, ready to face my inevitable doom. A light breeze smelled of lush foliage and flowers. And the heat and humidity beat down on me, even with the sun sinking over the hills. I'd forgotten what it was like being in the subtropics during summer. Should have worn more deodorant. Should have faked a communicable disease and stayed home.

"What's it been," he asked, "seven years?"

"About that."

"Thought you were bringing a boyfriend with you."

I paused. Dad must have given him that idea. God knows where Dad, however, had gotten it from. "No. No . . . he's ah, busy."

He looked me over; I guess we were both curious. Last time we'd been in the same room was for my eighteenth birthday party. My hair had been short and my skirt even shorter. What a spectacularly awful night that was. As if he too, remembered, he suddenly frowned, his high forehead filling with lines. Victory! The man definitely had more wrinkles. Unfortunately, they kind of suited him. Enhanced him, even. Bastard.

"Better come inside," he said.

"If you're still pissed at me, then why am I staying here?"

"I am not 'pissed at you.'" His tone was light and just

a bit haughty. A sure sign he was pissed. "I just was expecting your boyfriend too, that's all."

I crossed my arms.

"Look," he said, "you're staying here because we're both doing a favor to your dad. I know you haven't met her yet, but Shanti's a nice woman. She's good for him. They make a great couple and I want their wedding to be hassle free."

"I didn't come to cause trouble."

"But with you, from what I recall, it just seems to magically happen." Hands on slim hips, he gave me a grim smile. "It's just a few days, kid. Apparently, your old room is filled with bomboniere, whatever the fuck that is. So you're staying here with me."

I'd heard worse ideas in my life, but not many. Also they usually involved the risk of possible loss of limb, death, or incarceration. I'd tried to talk Dad into alternatives, but he'd stood firm, dammit. "That's kind of you, but not necessary. I'll go get a room at a hotel, this isn't—"

"They're probably booked," he said. "It's peak season so even if you could find somewhere, you'd pay through the roof. Anything nearby is going to already be busy with other wedding guests. Look, your dad wants you close so he can spend some time with you."

I said nothing.

"It's only five days," he repeated in the tone of voice he usually reserved for those dancing on his last damn nerve. "Let's just get through it."

Great. Awesome.

With a nod, I headed for the back of my car. All the

better to hide and take a second to pull myself together.

"Did you bring much stuff?" he asked, following.

"No. I've got it."

Except, of course, I didn't. As the hatch opened, he was there, reaching for my suitcase. Muscles flexed in his arms, slightly straining the sleeves of his white T-shirt. The man had always been strong, solid. Unfortunately, he hadn't shrunk any either. I was around average height, but he still had at least half a head on me. Just perfect for looking down and putting me in my place.

"Lock up your car." He headed for the house, tugging my wheeled suitcase behind him. "We might be in the country, but things still happen."

"Yeah, I know to lock up my car," I whisper bitched.

"I heard that."

"I don't give a shit."

He laughed grimly. "Oh, kid, this is going to be fun."

Out of options, I followed. Up the stone steps and into the house. Pete had never been much of a gardener, but someone had done a wonderful job with the grounds. Not that I was willing to say as much. We were apparently at war, and I couldn't even blame him since it was all my fault. God, I hated the old familiar feeling of guilt. Life would be so much easier if I could hate him, push some of the blame his way. But the truth was, he hadn't done a damn thing wrong. Not back then. Not even really now.

My pity party almost distracted me from the house.

"You did it," I breathed, wonder pushing the no-compliment rule straight out of my head. "It's beautiful."

He stopped, blinked. "Yeah."

"Last time I was here you were still living in the shed," I said. "It was just dirt with some pipes and things sticking out of the ground. Now it's finished."

"Parts of it are still a work in progress."

I spun in a slow circle, taking everything in, from the polished wood floors to the gray quartz kitchen located off to one side. A television about the size of a football field hung on one wall, with plush-looking navy couches gathered nearby. A large dining table was made out of a solid slab of wood, the natural edges still rough enough to be decorative. I'd already seen the beginning of that work of art, so I knew he'd made it himself. And the rounded center beam was huge, standing in the middle of the room, holding up the pitched ceiling.

"What is that, two stories high?" I asked, staring up.

"Two and a half."

"Wow. You really did it."

At that, he almost smiled. Almost.

Hallways ran off opposite sides of the great room and there was a wide verandah running the whole length of the building out back. There'd be a barbeque, another dining table and lots of chairs to laze in, and stairs leading down to the pool. I knew it without looking. Just like I knew there'd be the main bedroom with a bathroom and an office off to the right. Two guest bedrooms, a reading nook, and another bathroom off to the left. A long time ago, I'd helped him design this place. We'd worked on it together, a dream house.

"It's perfect," I said quietly.

For a moment, his gaze narrowed. But then his lips

returned to their former flat, unhappy state. "Glad you like it. You're in here."

I followed his back into the left wing. The house was amazing. Sadly, my gaze slipped from his wide shoulders, down the length of his spine, to find his gorgeous ass had also lost none of its impact. So unfair. But Pete in jeans always had been a sight to behold. God, his loose-limbed stride. A careless sort of confidence had always just seemed to ooze from the man.

Not that I was looking. Looking was bad.

"This okay?" he asked, throwing open a door.

"Fine. Thanks."

He tapped the top of my luggage. "Where do you want this?"

"I'll handle it."

A nod. "Your dad and Shanti will be over for dinner in a couple of hours."

"Is there anything I can do?"

"No, it's all taken care of." He scratched at his stubble. "Right. Make yourself at home. I'm going to get some work done. Be in the office if you need anything."

I nodded too. Nods were so great. Much better than words.

He stood in the hallway, staring at me for a moment. Not saying anything along the lines of how it was good to see me again. Because that would be a lie.

"Okay, Adele," he finally said, using my name, which was never a good sign. Honestly, I think I actually preferred "kid." Then, thank you baby Jesus, he left.

Carefully, I closed the bedroom door, slumping

against it because excessive drama. I'd known coming back was going to be a certain level of hell, but not one quite this deep.

One hundred and twenty hours and counting.

"You looked?" Hazel hissed into my ear. "I can't believe you looked."

I lay mostly dead on the bed, my cell jammed against my ear. "I didn't mean to—it just happened."

"Rule number one was don't look."

"Yeah . . ."

She sighed. "Okay, it's done now. We just have to move past it. But out of interest, how was the view?"

"Better than ever."

"Bastard. How did you look?"

"Sweaty and crumpled."

"I told you to fly."

"Yeah, I know," I groaned. "But then he would have insisted on picking me up from the airport, and being in a contained space for the car ride to his home would not have worked. I would have just wound up having to throw myself out of a moving vehicle, and I don't think that usually ends well."

Nothing from her.

"He still hates me."

"He doesn't hate you."

"No, he really does." I stared at the ceiling. "What's going on there?"

"Hmm? Everything's fine."

"What is that weirdness in your voice?"

"What?"

"Don't 'what' me. What is it?"

My best friend groaned. "I'm not sure you need this news right now, given everything already going on."

"Just tell me."

Some swearing. "Okay. But this is not my choice. Maddie and I went to dinner last night."

"Lovely. Where?"

"The Bombay Diner and it was lovely, but that's not the point," she said. "Listen, Deacon was at the restaurant with another woman and they were very much together. Heading into serious get-a-room territory."

I exhaled. "Oh, I see. Okay."

"Okay?"

"Well, it's not completely unexpected. We had a bit of an argument last week. I don't remember what it was about, but it seemed important at the time."

Silence.

"What?"

"One of these days, you're actually going to care about one of the people you date."

"I care."

"Beyond the normal non-sociopathic 'I hope he doesn't get hit by a car and killed in the street on his way home,'" said Hazel. "Think a more advanced level of caring than that."

"Well, it's fortunate I didn't, seeing as he's cheating on me."

"I knew you'd say that."

I didn't bother answering.

"Did it ever occur to you that he started seeing someone else because you don't care?" she asked.

"You think I wasn't meeting his emotional needs?"

"That's one of my theories about your dating issues."

"See, this is why I have a therapist for a best friend," I said. "You have all the answers."

She laughed. "Only I don't get paid to listen to you."

"Sorry about that."

"Luckily, you're normally pretty boring. So I don't mind this bit of drama."

"That is fortunate," I said. "Thing is, Deacon and I had only been out like four or five times. We hadn't even had sex yet. Can I really be expected to emotionally prop up men after such a small amount of dates?"

Hazel snorted. "You're willfully misunderstanding me. I give up."

"Good. How's Maddie?"

"She's fine. We're going to her parent's place for dinner soon," she said. "Are you going to survive where you are?"

"No. I'll probably just die in a really sad and pathetic manner, slowly becoming a smell in the hallway that he eventually can't ignore. Or not. I haven't decided." More sighing from me. "God, I feel so wound up, like there's something heavy sitting on my chest. Maybe I should just have a mild panic attack and get it over and done with. Tick that box, you know?"

"Panic attacks are nothing to make jokes about," she

chided. "Now go have a drink and calm down. Make peace with your situation . . . if you can't make peace with him."

"He won't make peace with *me*."

"Show him what a glorious, mature person you are these days."

"I'm a glorious, mature person?"

"Sure you are. Or at least you can pretend. Your acting skills are quite good. I believe in you." Hazel made kissing noises. "I have to go. Will you live?"

"Yeah, I'll be fine." I smiled. "Thanks for the pep talk. And the information. I promise to be a mess of tears next time a guy's cheating on me. Cross my heart. Have a nice night."

"I'll believe that when I see it. 'Bye."

I tossed my phone aside, surrendering to despair. Or just the oppressive heat and general tiredness. That's when the giant-ass spider ran up the wall directly above my head, long legs skittering as it navigated the edge of the ceiling.

"Jesus!" I scrambled off the bed, heart pounding. "Not cool."

Footsteps came running from the other end of the house, and Pete dashed into the room. "What's wrong?"

I just pointed at the wall.

His brows rose. "It's just a huntsman."

A huff of breath left his body, and with it all sense of urgency. Given my shriek, he'd probably been expecting a snake. While mostly the local populations were just harmless green tree snakes, occasionally an eastern brown would appear. Those things were aggressive and deadly poisonous.

"It's the size of my hand," I complained, trying not to sound defensive. "Ew."

"*Ew?* Seriously?" Yet again, he came dangerously close to smiling. Though this time it was more of a mockery-type thing. "You used to deal with these all the time."

"Yeah, well, I don't anymore. My spider-catching skills have lapsed," I said. "On the plus side, I've mastered Sydney's public transport system. Talk about intimidating."

He just looked at me.

"Can you please get it out of here?"

"Open the verandah door." With a heavy sigh, he disappeared back out into the hallway, reappearing shortly with a big plastic container and a piece of cardboard.

I stood by the open doorway, watching as he crept up on the ugly, hairy eight-legged monster. Realistically, I knew I'd probably scared it worse than it had me. Huntsmen weren't even very poisonous, their sting not much worse than a mosquito's. But creepy-crawlies really weren't my thing. Not anymore, at least.

Pete stepped up onto the bed, his bare feet spread wide apart as he positioned himself for the capture. The clear plastic container closed down on the creepy thing, as Pete tried for the slow and steady approach. At the last moment, its spider sense kicked in, and it leapt into a mad dash for freedom. I bit back a squeal of fright, but Pete's reflexes were up to the task. The container knocked against the bedroom wall, all eight legs and any other bits and pieces of the beast safely inside. I tried to avoid any feeling of grudging admiration. It took a fair bit of skill to nab a big, fast-moving one that smoothly.

Pete carefully slid the piece of cardboard between the wall and the container. Lots of spider jumping and scurrying ensued inside the plastic box. Continuing my display of extreme bravery, I stood back out of the way as he carried the thing outside and then took off the cardboard covering. He flicked the container so Mr. Spider went flying off into the garden, to live wild and free. Much better than copping a load of bug spray in the face.

"Happy?" he asked.

"Delirious. Thank you."

A grunt.

"Remember the first time you taught me to do that? I didn't get it right and the poor thing lost a leg under the edge of the container. Half of me was petrified, and the other half in tears." To be fair, huntsmen's legs were strangely brittle, and you had to be pretty agile to make sure they didn't lose a leg or two in the process.

Another grunt.

Great. Was this how it was going to be for my entire stay?

"Not that I don't adore the whole grouchy thing you've got going," I said. "But out of curiosity, should we just possibly talk about the issue and get it all out there? Deal with it, maybe?"

He frowned. "Hell, no."

"So we're never going to discuss it?"

"Got it in one."

I took a deep breath and gave him a thumbs-up.

"Okay. Great. Good talk, Pete. Thanks again for getting rid of the spider."

Another disgruntled look and he was gone, wandering back inside. Off to hide out in his office, no doubt.

Skittering spiders and taciturn men. What the hell had I gotten myself into?

To keep reading, purchase

IT SEEMED LIKE A GOOD IDEA AT THE TIME

from your favorite online retailer today!

CPSIA information can be obtained
at www.ICGtesting.com
Printed in the USA
LVHW032150031022
729850LV00004B/119

9 780648 457206